THROUGH
THE DEADFALL

THROUGH THE DEADFALL

BARRY KENNEDY

Doubleday Canada Limited

Canadian Cataloguing in Publication Data

Kennedy, Barry (Barry G. J.)
    Through the deadfall

ISBN 0-385-25605-1

I. Title.

PS8571.B62725T47 1997   C813'.54   C96 932254 2
PR9199.3.K46T47 1997

Cover photograph by Nicholas Pavloff/Photonica
Cover design by Tania Craan
Text design by Heidy Lawrance Associates
Printed and bound in Canada

Published in Canada by
Doubleday Canada Limited
105 Bond Street
Toronto, Ontario
M5B 1Y3

To my mother, the Mighty I.

PROLOGUE

The Island straddles the line on the compass rose that points true north. The upper end of the sliver stares off northwest to Alaska, the lower probes south of the 49th in search of Juan de Fuca oysters. There are elemental shards of magic about her, ingredients that bob and weave around the punches of primary industry. Her indigenous cultures are still trying to regain their feet after the traditional battle with invading Europeans, and if her early Spanish — and later English — investigators and conquerors did not manage to wreak devastation with the thoroughness they displayed farther south in the Americas, they at least would have provided Bernal Díaz del Castillo with material enough for a good-sized pamphlet.

Waters flushed from the Bering Sea chill her garments. Snow caps her spine. She sits above it all while her plates drunkenly argue tectonics.

She is my home. Or was, before I short-sheeted my future.

Vancouver Island is a beautiful, willful thing, so brazenly steeped in self-esteem it never quite manages to accomplish anything with the power of its assurance. Out for a stroll by day, smug in the knowledge of the hoard back home under the mattress; show a flash of calf but with modest hands hold down the skirt. A bunch of the boys were whooping it up ... then called cabs and went home.

Salish Spit is crowded between mountain and sea, glacier and spit on the east coast of the Island and comprises some fifteen hundred souls. The folks work or don't and play or not amid the healthy and deathly contradictions of their time and place. The accident of birth and my wish not to correct it has made them my people. My friends and enemies. I believe them to be a distinct, peculiar, special group. Most likely they are not.

The winters in Salish Spit are velvet tickles of orographic rainfall so, while depressing, they leave no more lasting effect than a mild inertial lethargy. This past one, though, was rough. I seemed to be coming out of it with a predatory anticipation of spring, eager for plunder. But maybe this is all histrionics. I hadn't been getting many breaks lately, so it could be I was just looking for attention.

O N E

"There you are again," my wife called from the front of the hardware store. "Always doing something."

Nothing upset Elizabeth so much as the fact that I did things. I could hear her banging around on the unvarnished hardwood floor, seeking me out.

"I'm sorting screws in the storeroom!" I yelled.

"There's no need to scream," she said. "And I'm not coming back there." She spit the statement out like a bad oyster. Her heels snapped along, and the old cash register chinged as its drawer popped out.

I tensed. Elizabeth was able to trigger this reaction merely by her presence. Aware that no one is saddled with that kind of power to the degree Elizabeth seemed to be, I had to admit my share of the guilt. Our whole marriage had me buffaloed, and I had taken to claiming victory in our minor battles even if all I did was run away. I had long ago stopped congratulating myself for this ability to withdraw and survive — a victory is dull indeed if the war was due to the hero's own shortcomings.

I could hear Elizabeth flipping the bill clips in the cash register and muttering. "Never content. Just have to be doing something. Sorting screws, of all things." Then, louder, "Screws should come already sorted. Don't they sort them when they put them in the boxes? What are you sorting screws for?"

I reached between my knees and dug in the Beatty washtub — an ancient galvanized tin thing — and let all but the drywall screws plop back in.

"Snuffy had an accident unloading them from the truck," I said. "The tailgate let go and a bunch of the boxes broke. He thought it would be more convenient for me if he emptied them all into one batch."

"That moron," Elizabeth said.

"Don't call him that!" I dropped the drywalls into a box on my right.

"He is one."

"That's my point. Vent your spleen on someone who can defend himself."

"I don't understand why you keep him on."

"I'm sure you don't."

The afternoon was ruined. Don't think sorting screws is my idea of a rapturous good time, but there's something about mindless occupation I find soothing. Alternating between a cigarette and a coffee mug with one hand while with the other tossing half-inch slot heads into a box carries with it the out-of-body quietude of staring into a fire. I rose and kicked the milking stool back against the wall and left the storeroom. I made my way through the shelf clutter, dimly aware of muffled hoots and clanks from outside; Snuffy was practising his horseshoes.

Elizabeth was still rooting through the cash register and looked up at the sound of my boot heels. "There's nothing in here," she said.

"Hardware store ain't a bank," I said. "An Iranian Christmas tree lot has more cash flow than this place."

She left the drawer open and poured a coffee from the filter job on the counter. I went to the window to watch Snuffy pitch his shoes. I still loved her. The twinge I felt when I saw her at the press conference seven years ago was there yet. The twinge was subdued — bile thinning the blood — but the emotion remained and it was recognizable. I turned as she tipped in the cream and smiled at her sharp, almost brittle profile. She was heavier now, but solid and sure, magnificent really, and I stirred.

That was before this hardware store caper. It had been boom time at the institute, back when oceanography in all its forms still had me on my knees with dedication, funding coming in great gobs from the government and private oil concerns, everyone hell-bent on turning the entire continental shelf from the Baja to Barrow into nesting grounds for offshore rigs and wells. It was an odd place, determined as it was to balance pure research with doing what was demanded of it in order to keep the chains off the doors.

I was smoothly sailing along with a grant, a salary and a will to tap oil reservoirs while maintaining my environmental morals. This last took no small lashing of rationalization. I was playing scrum-half for the Valley Rugby Club, working twelve hours a day, getting stinking drunk four or five or six nights a week, and sleeping with the director's daughter. Then came the day Elizabeth walked into the press conference with a vice president from South Central Oil.

Three months later we were married and my life was flung assovertit. Elizabeth didn't alter it, and the marriage can't be blamed. It was me. I had reached one of those periodic upheavals of the psyche and, in my usual drastic, self-serving way, pissed in the fruit jar.

Elizabeth stared at me over the top of her cup. "Is that all you've been doing since you left the house?"

"No," I said. "I went through a deck of smokes." Snuffy sailed a shoe eight feet over the post and I heard it *fwang* against the storage shed. "What have you been up to?"

"I went to lunch with Bernice," she said. "The new place. God, all I want is one decent meal before I die."

"Maybe you're aiming too high."

She snorted and slammed the cash register shut. "I don't see you aiming at anything."

"I'm happy," I said unconvincingly.

My breakfast of coffee and cigarettes collided briefly in my stomach. It was only recently this diet had been turning rabid on me, perhaps marshaling its strength all these years, now sensing my anxiety, my weakness, and attacking under a creeping barrage.

"I don't think you are," Elizabeth said. "You once had me convinced that the simple life was your lot, but you've developed an edge, Jack. You're a nasty man these days. Nasty, nasty."

I decided to backpaddle against the ebb tide and hug the shore. "That new restaurant no good?"

"More of the same — ribs and seafood."

"Cater to the majority," I said. I turned back to the window and Snuffy. "Loggers and fishermen."

"All of them out of work and roaming around town like a bunch of street people."

"They can't help that."

"Mankind's defender," she snorted. She was rummaging around the shelves behind me, lifting and replacing items, sorting things I didn't want sorted, stacking things I didn't want stacked. "A good vegetarian place," she said. "That's what I could go for. Is that too much to ask? I think that's why you're nasty, Jack. All that red meat. Blood pressure up, aggressive — red meat does that."

Elizabeth was a vegetarian. All it took was for her to see a woodcut of a Black Forest stag hunt on one of her flea market forays and out popped a theory on Prussian aggression.

"Myself," she announced, "I can't see how anyone could slaughter a defenseless animal for their own personal use."

"What are those shoes made out of?" I asked. "Green peppers?"

"Nasty."

"They're leather, Liz. They came off a cow's ass, and he didn't give them to you."

I was losing my elasticity. It was the strain, the daily sniping and carping and competition. All for no reason, all to no end. Nature avoids confrontation, erects warnings; even in mating season the weaker usually accepts the inevitable and flees from the stronger, making its point before hothoofing it away without serious damage. I could no longer do it, instinct losing out to anger, and I had the scars on my snout and soul by way of illustration. As much as I abhorred injustice, it was something I both suffered from and was guilty of.

I picked at the paint I had slopped over the edges of the window, thus sealing me off from the damp magic of the shoreline. I am accustomed to approaching everything with a scientific viewpoint, preferring reason to intuition, but lately I was allowing my prejudices to affect my analyses. That, of course, skews the results. So I was gaining none of the freshness and understanding I needed so badly. I suppose it comes down to the old conundrum of being unable to dissect a system from within the system, a sort of quantum inability to measure behavior without short-circuiting the works by the very act of observation.

Elizabeth. Her, though. I felt like crying. Crying or dragging her to the daybed in the storeroom and loving her roughly and gently, and doing anything in the world for her, abasing myself if she wanted, admitting to everything including assassination attempts, telling her she was my life and my love and my partner, then hurting her and myself and leaving for good, then coming back and starting again on another round of peace talks.

My eyes clouded with the confusion and the pain, and then Snuffy came flopping through the door, grinning and so happy with himself that I laughed and grabbed him by the shoulder, needing to touch someone whose love was unconditional.

"Hello, Snuffy, you old goat."

"Old goat, he says. You kill me, Jack."

Snuffy was around forty. A squat, funny type of guy with liquid features, a hogshead of hair growing out of his ears, and a learning disability that had never been properly diagnosed. He seemed to have no specific loves, just everyone and everything. He certainly had no hates. He hoisted a horseshoe up over his head like a fighter raising a championship belt. "Ringer!" he crowed.

"Hello, Snuffy," Elizabeth said, stepping out from the aisle.

Snuffy slowly lowered the shoe. He didn't know what to make of my wife. He guessed he liked her, but was tentative, scary-eyed in her presence, a similar state to the one I had worked myself into the past while. Snuffy gave her a half grin, his eyes checking with me for encouragement, then again said, "Ringer."

Elizabeth looked with mild amusement at the horseshoe. "Just one?" she said.

"Nope — four!"

"That is an accomplishment." She flashed him one of her knee-tremblers. Jesus, she was gorgeous.

"Four," Snuffy repeated.

What Elizabeth didn't know was that this was a cumulative total. When Snuffy wasn't helping me around the hardware store or oddjobbing for Don at the pub, he pitched horseshoes. Six years now he had been out of the home and four ringers represented his career total. He hustled behind the counter and chalked a vertical line on the blackboard I had nailed up to keep score of the Sunday dart matches. Snuffy had his own corner of it for ringers. He stepped back and eyed the four strokes and nearly pissed himself with pride.

"One more, Mrs. Thorpe," he said, "one more and I get to put a sideways line through them other ones and that makes five and a batch. Jack gets a whole batch in one game against Eagle sometimes, but he says he just does it so Eagle will get mad. I'm almost as good, Jack says, but usually only when it's me and him playing. Then I'm hot as anything. I got his number, is what Jack says." He wiped the chalk off his fingers onto his pants. "I love this game."

Snuffy got his nickname through an attempt to imitate Eagle, who dipped shredded tobacco as if it were an elixir. Snuffy would stare in rapture at the bulge in Eagle's lower lip, finally deciding one day at the pub to copy his friend's heroic habit. Snoose should come with directions. Snuffy downed two tins of Copenhagen wintergreen and washed it down with grape crush before his stomach heaved it back up all over my wife's purse. Perhaps this explains his timidity in her presence. Timidity was not one of his characteristics, but neither was confidence. Snuffy simply was. A man doing his best and suffering. I liked him.

"Anything I can help with, Jack?" he said.

"Naw." I dug in my shirt pocket for the deck of smokes. "Got to knock off early today. Meeting at the Square Rigger, remember?"

"Yeah. I already did most of the stuff you wanted. I ripped out all those weeds over by the storage shed. Trouble was they had oil all over them. There was oil on them, so when I pulled them out I got oil on my hands." He looked down, consternation twisting his features. "I must have wiped my hands on my pants. They got oil on them too. I think when I got oil on my hands from pulling on the weeds I must have wiped it on my pants. See — there's oil on them."

"That's okay."

"I left the clippers out there, too."

"Don't worry."

"They're in the grass."

"Get them later."

"But the weeds are gone. Well, they're not gone, but I put them in a pile. They're in a pile by the compost heap. I just have to put them on with the other stuff. Hey! I could put them on when I go out to get the clippers."

My thoughts were on the meeting, so I couldn't pay attention to Snuffy. The rush you get from having a mission was impossible to sustain these days, and if as the leader I couldn't energize myself then I had no hope of driving the rest of the crazy bastards forward.

You see, they wanted to build a bridge. Or a tunnel. A tunnel/bridge is what the witless pricks would settle on, I guess. Simply stated, the economy dictated a link to the mainland, and that was what we were fighting against. Oh, the idea had been beaten around for years, but the unholy tandem of government and industry looked serious this time. Febrile determination veiled with platitudes about social and economic advancement.

Paramount was the fact that no one knew exactly what the environmental consequences would be. Hell, they barely suspected. The interrelatedness of factors allowed no firm conclusions, and we were smack in the middle of an attitude shift: Did we back off from something with the potential to seriously harm our tiny corner of the world? Or did we hew to the tone best represented by Nebraska senator Kenneth Wherry's 1940 declaration, "With God's help, we will lift Shanghai up and up, ever up, until it is just like Kansas City."

It was time for a change, and this time around the Island's defenders were not exclusively from the ranks of the lunatic fringe. Our home, in concert with the sprinkling of Gulf Islands decorating the Straits, was mutating from a simple yet utilitarian beauty to a complicated stew going by the name of progress.

Elizabeth could see both sides of the issue and so far had done nothing to indicate she was taking sides. Overwhelming all sense of what she thought or believed was the irritation she felt for my involvement. To her, it was merely another example of my doing things.

I eased back into my surroundings to find Snuffy on the verge of tears.

"I mean, I could get the clippers now, and leave the weeds for later. Or I could do it all now. But then I wouldn't have time to change my pants before the meeting. I have to be at the meeting 'cause Don said he has lots for me to do. All the guys are going to be there."

"Leave the outside till later," I said. "Change your pants and I'll meet you over there."

"The committee." Snuffy was boggled by the mystery of the word. No freemason clammed up like Snuffy contemplating the cosmological implications of the committee. "I'll change my pants."

"Committee!" Elizabeth said. "Another pub meeting, nothing accomplished. All the boys trying to reach decisions on the welfare of the town while being totally out of touch with the real organization. Plans that will never be put into place. Notes taken and lost, then everyone switching the conversation to baseball. At two in the morning you'll invite them all back here to finalize the plan of attack on the mayor's office. Eagle will wreck his truck on the way and you'll spend the night passed out on the daybed in the storeroom."

I didn't say she was always wrong. I went to get the keys to lock up.

T w o

Usually the walk to the Square Rigger was cleansing, almost diuretic. For that matter any time spent afoot in this land tends to attach me more firmly to it, clasping it closely to my breast. But it was different on this day. It was all I could do to keep from running, sprinting away from my wife and my vocation and my involvement in the community.

All around me was a sense of physical imposition: The pavement looked alien the way it cut through the trees and rock; the pathetic drizzle was irritating as it leaked from the sky; the clouds themselves were wimpy things formed by breezes being forced aloft by the mountains, having none of the power of prairie clouds that are fashioned by heated parcels of air soaring aloft. That's how thunderclouds develop — big cumulonimbus anvils proud of their independence and ready to split your head to prove a point; these Island clouds were pitiful, working under too many constraints.

I endured the trip and entered the Square Rigger to hoots at my tardiness. I sat at the bar, and for the first fifteen minutes tried to disabuse Eagle of the notion that the best approach to our problem would be to kidnap the mayor and fire her house. Grudgingly he came around, but no idea even marginally appealing to his love of the decisive and the drastic ever completely left him once he wrapped his skull around it. No doubt it was collecting straw and shiny bits of trash with which to build a nest in his longterm memory.

"You're too easygoing, that's your problem," Eagle said from beside me at the bar. "If a rat shit in your chili you'd pretend it was a jalapeño."

"That's the difference between us," I said. "I'd pretend. You'd mistake it for one."

"Up yours, hot shot," he said. "I know a good load of stuff you don't."

Eagle wasn't angry. At times he was a raging abuse machine — beer, ego and unemployment fueling an output of invective. But he only rarely meant what he said. Not that he was always a teddy bear. He could be no more than a big bearded sonofabitch who took delight in terrorizing people.

Hey, I saw him take a logger apart one night in the pub, whaling away with his big ham fists, then dragging the man outside and finishing him off against the guy's own pickup. Doing a fair job on the pickup, too, bashing and smashing the thing all across the hood and busting a couple windows — but then clomping back in and laughing and draining his beer. Another beer and he drove the guy back to camp twelve miles into the bush. Two months later he was an usher at the logger's wedding.

Eagle belonged to the bush and the town and the Valley. Salish Spit: Island town. Pulp mill up the road a ways, shut down now with the decline in the forest industry, gone the choking but accustomed reek that gets right into the mucus membranes and the sinuses. The sweet smell of the sawmill toned down, what with the men on half-shifts. The shake yard hanging on, only occasionally spreading the healthy, fibrous scent of cedar over the land.

The Valley men were laid off or on strike or locked out. The lucky ones were working construction or deckhanding if they knew someone with a boat, though with the bad herring and salmon seasons of these times even the fishermen were moving to the mainland or fishing strictly west island and Queen Charlotte spots or even working in drugstores or selling clothing if the merchants weren't too patronizing. Trying to support families and pay mortgages by taking jobs for which they were physically and emotionally ill prepared, fucking government and easterners and real estate assholes and Jap cars anyway!

Eagle could only adumbrate his more complex feelings, as a result overemphasizing the raw emotions that scared the shit out of most people. But he was a warm, caring man. We had grown up together, playing and fighting and working in harness until I abandoned him — his term — for university and seven years of study toward a doctorate in oceanography. Formal study was not his way, yet my quitting the institute in the midst of my Ph.D. work to run a hardware store stood in his mind as a monumental disappointment. I once told him it was ridiculous to take it as a personal betrayal, and he reminded me of the frequent loans he had tendered during my school years, which made him an interested party, as if he had grubstaked me in a pool tournament that I maliciously tanked.

That one came close to blows until Eagle calmed himself by jacking a shell into his 12-gauge and blasting my picture off his kitchen wall. We spent the next two hours trying to decide whether it really was my picture or the one of Eagle in handcuffs he had proudly clipped from the front page of the *Salish Spit Examiner*.

Our man Eagle had done about a fistful of magic mushrooms on the way to a fastpitch softball game the night before, then sluiced down a dozen beers. So pleased with life in general was he that he unflinchingly took an eighty-knot fastball square in the beak. The boys said they'd never seen anything like it in their lives — Eagle tossing his bat to the batboy and blithely strolling toward first until crashing full length into the dirt and the lime.

"And one thing I know," Eagle continued, "is that we could sit here till roots grow out our asses and not get a free round off of Don."

The bartender grunted and looked away.

"How about you, Robert?" Eagle asked, pivoting on his stool.

Everyone laughed. Just wave a waiter's cheque in his direction and Robert did everything but scream aloud. I dug in my pocket and slapped a wad of crumpled twos and fives on the bar.

"Attaboy," Eagle said. "Gotta cure that old depression. I seen it in you when you walked in."

"Elizabeth," I mumbled.

"Don't see why you can't handle her," Eagle said. "Course, I wouldn't be able to neither."

"You tell her otherwise."

"Yeah, I know it. But I couldn't. I can't do nothing with women that gorgeous. You know, if you could talk to them straight up, like guys, it would be okay. But I always say something stupid. And they know you're scared and probably only want you to talk to them normal, but maybe 'cause they been shit on for so long something in them makes them shift a little so their tits jump out at you, or they cross their legs so you get half a eyeful of curly pie, then I gotta go back to my beer or play pool or something."

"Curly pie," Snuffy said. He had finally arrived and was wearing the same oily pants.

We all laughed.

"That's right, Snuffs," Eagle said. "That's right, you baboon."

"Baboon, he says! You kill me, Eagle."

"Anyhow, Thorpe," Eagle continued, "what I'm saying is that you should be able to handle her. Trouble is you pile a lot of crap on Elizabeth's shoulders that you should be hauling to the dump yourself."

"Profound," I said. "And coming from an expert on relationships, no less."

"I just can't figure how come you don't judge your friends when they fuck up but can't give your own wife the same break."

Automatically I started to defend myself but, as usual, Eagle had delivered his pronouncement then immediately removed himself from further debate. He turned away from me, dug in his shattered nose and flicked a gob of caked blood at the floor. It hung on too long and redirected its way to the glass-washing machine, sticking to the stainless steel.

"You're a pig!" Don screamed. "You know that? You're a pig!"

"Probably." Eagle winked and raised his fresh mug to me.

Don had his faults as owner of the Square Rigger. He was fussy and overly fastidious, tsking and fretting when we didn't use our coasters or threw butts in the urinals. He didn't drink, which made him suspect in Salish Spit but not reviled — it was such a grotesquerie people felt afraid to upbraid him for it. He never bought a customer a round, and for this he was reviled.

But he was an honest, hardworking man. He abstained from calling the cops or even bouncing patrons in a fistfight, letting them have it out and wreck his furniture, then presenting them with a bill which he never followed up on. Perhaps this was his concession to the regulars, atonement for being cheap when it came to free rounds.

Donna, his wife, was a lovely woman who towered over Don and loved him and toward whom everyone had a slavish regard. She seldom came in the bar, but when she did even Eagle cleaned up his act.

"Are we going to get on with this meeting, or what?" Robert asked. "You guys realize we only have three more weeks to forward our proposal to the mayor's office and convince the whole town? I used to be a lawyer, a good one, and I know."

Everyone looked my way. I stared down at my mug. It would come down to me at a time like this. I felt frail, as if I had the scuba gear on and was battling an undertow — nothing visible arresting my progress, but nonetheless an irresistible flow. I should have been planning and leading, accumulating facts, using my old powers of charm and persuasion, some bluff and bluster and all determination and righteous wrath. I had thought, I did care, I would try. But I felt feeble, any kind of useful focus eluding me.

"We're sort of stuck, guys," I said.

"Sort of stuck," Robert said. "What does that mean? You

run out of ideas? We've listened to you all along and now you say we're stuck."

"You knew right out of the gate that this would be tough. Everyone agreed to go our own way."

It was eighteen months ago that governmental pressure hit the critical point. Using data that was out of date, incomplete and astonishingly selective, they combined it with emotional appeals to push through their link proposal.

An environmental review panel came to the unsurprising conclusion that the government had done insufficient home-work, essentially coming up with an answer to an equation without showing their work. Personally, I didn't think it was an equation. It should have been an essay question to begin with.

Due to various factors — including a phobic reaction to joining any group — our ragged farrago decided to go it alone, declining to join forces with the main environmental coalition, which took to calling itself BAT GUANO — Bridge And Tunnel: Growth Underway Amid Noisy Opposition.

Our style had nothing to do with collecting independent data or amassing support or drafting petitions or parading in costumes festooned with imperiled sea life. (Although I for one would drop good coin to see Eagle on the six-o'clock news wearing a bedsheet poncho bedecked with starfish and clams — his first idea until I reminded him they would die. "Oh, yeah," he said. "And I guess I couldn't fuck one of them TV girls smelling like low tide.")

We were ruggedly independent and, not incidentally, a little selfish. The bridge would fetch up right here in Salish Spit. Right smack on top of my hardware store, to be precise.

But it was hard to find a totally selfish attitude in this town. The people were a reflection of their predecessors who had built a small town ten miles and a hike away from the outskirts of bugger-all. They still worked on the barter system. No one built a fence alone. No one got married or had a baby without a party being held to start them off with something in their kick. So the best way to summarize all this is to say we weren't very effective. We spent the preponderance of our time indulging speculation and fantasy and doing little of the hard work done by the very groups we disparaged.

Fortunately, the only faction that matched us in spastic uncoordination was the dopey bunch allied with the mayor. As in combat, a platoon is not fighting the whole enemy army, just those bastards right over there! Gleefully we took up the challenge. At least we were picking on someone our own size.

"They have help," I said.

"Who?" Eagle said. "That bitch mayor?"

"Yeah. Contractor's representative in from Vancouver."

"What can he do?" Don asked.

"Public opinion," I said. "That's what it all comes down to. The possibility of an economic resurgence, jobs, housing, tourism — the works."

Eagle slammed his mug down. "What the Jesus pissing fuck is a bridge and tunnel combo from the mainland going to do in the long run except turn us into a suburb of Vancouver?"

"I know the arguments," I said. "We all do. But we have to convince the town. Salish Spit is the key. We've become a pretty influential up-Island town. From here on in it's strictly a public relations battle."

"Don't take this the wrong way," Robert said, "but we've had almost a year and a half. This is all you can come up with? Three weeks to go and we're just now starting a PR campaign?"

"I haven't seen any of you guys busting your hump. I'm sorry — I suppose I've been hoping along with everyone it was all a case of empty political wrangling. I'm not used to dealing with things on this level."

"You'll lose the hardware store," Snuffy said.

"I know, I know. Not so much, really, compared to what other people stand to lose, even if they don't realize it yet."

"The mayor's tough," Robert said. "She's a popular public figure. Shrewd, intelligent. I was a lawyer, a good one, and I know politicians like her."

"She's a withered-up old broad," Eagle said. "I wouldn't stick it to her on a bet."

"Good point," I said. "Maybe we should circulate leaflets with that information."

"Many people hold her in contempt," Don offered.

"Many people should hold her in the salt chuck," Eagle said.

"Slow down," I said. "This is a long shot at best. The mayor may not have the best and the brightest in her camp, but she does play things cool. We'll never win this fight by declaring *jihad*."

"Or by speaking French," Eagle said.

Don was deeply disturbed. He was a passionate believer in the Valley, the environment and the way of life we enjoyed on the Big Bump. So disturbed was he that he drew fresh beers and neglected to collect for them. Eagle and Robert almost choked getting them down before he snapped to. I toyed with mine.

"We need more help," Don said. "We started off with what, fifteen, twenty people? We're down to my wife and the four of us — sorry, Snuffy, five of us. Elizabeth still aboard, Jack?"

"She's with us but not me."

"Can we count on her, I mean?"

"She hasn't really taken a stand yet, but yeah … yeah, we can."

"Seven people." He mopped the bar.

"They only had seven people when they stormed the Bastille," Eagle said.

This bit of nonsense drove me to the can. When I got back I said, "I'm going to be gone for a few days."

"Hell of a time to leave," Robert said.

"I know someone who might be of help."

"Who?" Eagle asked. "The Queen?"

I scratched my head. "Sedro Tuckett."

"Whoa, now," Eagle said.

The others bared their eyeballs. Sedro Tuckett used to run this town. Founding father, mayor, fire chief and one-man-band beating his drum at every meeting, hearing, session or debate that remotely smelled as if it could affect Salish Spit. He had named the town, for chrissake. It had been his extended family, and it in turn vicariously lived and breathed through him as he stumped his way around the Island and through the provincial legislature. Legion were the times he was on the front page of regional or national newspapers, or staring out from the TV or proclaiming from the radio.

And never more memorably than fifteen years ago, before he left Salish Spit, when he was on trial for the murder of my father.

They all stared at me. I should have crept up to the subject instead of dropping it on their heads. I knew I was adding to our concerns by introducing my personal bugbear, but I could have been right. Maybe Sedro Tuckett could help. And so powerfully does the mind bulwark a predetermined position that I was already defensive about what the others had not said and may not even be thinking. It's hard to apply logic to something this close to home.

But like it or not, the decision had been made. I was going to load our hopes on Sedro Tuckett's back and see if we could hang on for the ride.

T H R E E

In honor of Elizabeth's prediction we switched to baseball, then I wandered over to the dart board and lazily tossed awhile. When only reluctantly dealing with a subject, years can go by without any need for action, but now Sedro had jammed his way back into my head. Something had to be done to relieve the pressure. As in genes directing an organism, the timing of growth patterns is as important as the degree of influence. Whatever I needed to do had to be done now. Trouble was, I had always reacted to Sedro, had never initiated anything, and I was feeling no more powerful in that regard than I had in those long gone days of crisis and catastrophe.

"No necessity exists for becoming excited," Sedro had said.

He had turned his gaunt, hollow-cheeked face up to me from his perusal of the tide pool. He straightened and his knees cracked. We both had on big black gumboots, but at sixteen I still hadn't grown much and mine came up over my knees. The tide was on flood, pushing us back from the mouth of the bay toward Sedro's cottage on the shore. The mayor had been nipping from his wineskin most of the day. He was happy and avuncular.

"Calvin Coolidge said that," he pronounced. He kicked at the pool and a saddleback sculpin darted for cover. "And if he wasn't already dead I'd soon settle his hash."

He spun, absently starting for another pool. We saw the squirt of water at the same time but he beat me to it. With three probes of the spade he had another big butter clam.

"That's twenty to nine in my favor," he crowed. He shook his pail in my face. "You'll never catch me now. You're on the run."

We picked our way around an extensive bed of sand dollars. I could tell by Sedro's walk we were done for the day and I dutifully followed his steps back to the beach. I walked with my head down, scanning and searching for something unusual. Anything found along the shore or on the tidal flats charged me with vitality for days. The peculiar tingle of finding money on the street never affected me like stumbling on a crab or a bed of sand dollars or a mess of polychaete worm holes. It is something I hope I never grow out of.

Of course those were the days when rookie baseball cards were only good for the spokes of your bike.

The dark volcanic sand grew firmer as we moved toward the shore. The gumboots allowed me to clump through the band of rocks and hit the beach. Inside five minutes we were sitting on the porch, Sedro in his rocker, me on the steps pulling off the giant gumboots. The clams were soon in a bucket of water, shells open, necks reaching for the oatmeal sprinkled on the surface. We'd let them clean themselves out then steam them at our leisure.

"Imagine," Sedro said. "Not becoming excited."

"We're pretty calm right now," I offered.

"But adopting that as a life pattern?"

"Dad hates it when I get excited over stuff. Mum, too. She says I'm always doing something."

"You keep right on doing things," he said. "What seems trivial is only mildly so compared to everything else our species does. We have no external reference point, so momentous issues are not perceived as being kindred to the mundane. Doubtless if there is an ancient extraterrestrial intelligence pontificating on our race, he would not consider Einstein's discovering general relativity to be of a different order of magnitude than the old genius picking his ear with a car key."

"My dad kicks my ass when I do things," I mumbled. I rubbed the hotspots the boots had left on my heels.

Sedro looked me over. "Not for much longer, I don't suspect. You're due to shoot up anytime."

"I hope so," I said. "I hate being short. I'm sick of sitting on the bench."

"You're a starter," he said.

"Baseball, yes. Not in basketball."

"Baseball, basketball ... " Sedro hadn't much time for organized sports.

Sedro had always looked old to me. The caverns and fissures of his face couldn't mask the craftiness, but everything about him seemed of a generation long gone on this earth. He wasn't much older than my mum and dad, but the clay of the world stuck to him, particulate wisdom and energy and emotion caking him and hardening into a crust of authority. His skinny arms and legs were as hard as rebar, and their vascular system stood out in glaring relief. Nobody could ever remember what he wore. Civic function or slopping through the tide pools, his clothes were not meant to impress, to convey an attitude or a style. They barely could be called utilitarian — just stuff thrown on to hold everything in place and keep the salt off his bony carcass.

It was marvelous how he could be everyman to all people while simultaneously driving half the town crazy. The invisibility of youth had allowed me many opportunities to measure people's reactions: Stage 1 began before his arrival and consisted of subtle feelers and innuendo designed to see what the others were thinking; Stage 2, when everyone had established the solidarity of their opposition, was a gutless dissection of everything Sedro stood for; when the man himself arrived

Stage 3 commenced, a hilarious bout of obsequiousness. When Sedro tired of the lack of input, he would sail off through a flurry of handshakes and backslaps, leaving everyone to return to Stage 2 with fresh ammunition, as if wondering why he had deliberately come by to fart at a funeral.

I loved the old man, and it was his love for me that kept me going through the harrowing pubescent growth period and the shambles of my home life.

I looked at my watch. Eagle would be along soon and that would be the end of my day with Sedro. I was selfish about my time alone with him.

"Look at that glacier, young Jack."

I couldn't miss it, and said so. It was the dominant feature of the Valley, hanging up there between peaks like a torpid river. It was a six-hour hike when I first started climbing to it. I had it down to four, doing it three times a week and recording the times in an old pilot's log book.

"Sitting up there, part of the landscape," I said.

"But what a beautiful economy of wastage and resupply. An open system. Snow converted to ice upstream, pressed down, borne along, then percolating back up downstream to be lost to melting and evaporation. The moraines, the outwash sediments, the scoured sides of its valley — you can read its whole life in its face."

"Eagle says the same about your face."

Sedro laughed. I had always been able to talk to him on an equal footing. I adored the man, marveled at his joy and knowledge. And he never allowed it to be a love based on wide-eyed innocence. He was startlingly open with self-analysis, at least when sitting with just me or a coterie of friends. He would offer himself up for criticism, talk about his faults and mistakes, errors in judgment. His ego, he claimed, was the best and worst of him, allowing him early successes while unfortunately driving him in directions he would rather not go.

Salish Spit: He founded it and ran it, bullying and cajoling, after naming it for its geography and the dominant aboriginal presence. His dog was named Nootka, after the west island tribes, his cat Kwakiutl, after the northern bands.

"My dad's getting worse," I said.

He rapidly looked me over. "Don't see any marks."

"He's learning. I'm more afraid for my mum, anyhow."

Sedro brooded. I kept a lot of things from him, at least I thought I did. He always seemed to know. I filled him in on minor things about my parents. If I was looking for aid or advice I could chat away about anyone, but if I was merely looking for corroboration or, worse, whining out idle gossip, I was bid to shut my sinkhole, in his words.

"You know enough, you're strong enough, to leave home soon," he said. "Some can do it young. You're one. Your father has an inner core of hostility he will never expunge. I do not believe that man should have been brought forth into this world, and clearly not loosed upon it. Your mother's just weak, young Jack. Frustration extended indefinitely becomes bitterness."

"Maybe when I go off to college," I said.

"Still going to be a scientist?"

"Oh, yeah. I couldn't learn all the stuff you know without making it a career."

"We're not so different," he said, and I felt proud.

"Besides, I'll need a job. What would I do, be your deputy fire chief and spend all my time collecting leaves and marine life?" I pulled up short and muttered an apology.

"No need to be sorry. I am quite aware that most people consider my pastimes childish."

"I don't."

"No, you don't."

Off inside, he stuck a couple of hunks of driftwood in the fireplace. He banged around the kitchen a bit and emerged with a bottle of Plainsman Rye. He poured some in a glass, tipped in a lot of water from his canteen and handed it to me.

"Oceanography, still?"

"Yeah," I said. "Or geology. But I've been thinking about anthropology more and more. Those Indian stories of yours get me."

"I met a man in Vancouver last trip, a young writer. Those were Indian stories. I don't have all that much to tell."

I didn't know how young this writer might be. Sedro was fifty-five that spring, and he referred to everyone as young this or that. He said it lent weight to his authority, like a Mountie stopping you on the highway and doing the opposite, calling you Sir with that tone they have, and the cop so young he looks surprised at his ability to stand on his piss-soaked hind legs, in Sedro's words. Sedro didn't much like cops.

"Or I might become a writer," I said, the rye expanding my ambitions.

"Ha! You'd give a priest's ass heartburn."

I had no idea what that meant, but Sedro had a lot of enigmatic sayings, so I took it as a compliment.

It was great, skipping school like this and tromping around the tidal flats and drinking Plainsman Rye with the mayor. I thought I was pretty cool. Then Eagle came by. He was my best friend, but he ruined the mood.

"Hey, Jack!" he called, striding up from the water's edge. The tide was in and Eagle had followed the beach along from the tiny parking lot at the bottom of the hill that backed the bay. He had just reached legal driving age and regularly stole his dad's 1960 Ford.

"Hey, Mr. Da Vinci," he said to Sedro.

"Hello, young Eagle."

"Saw seventeen whales beached the other side of the spit," Eagle said. "Thought maybe you guys would want to collect them up. They were fighting with giant squids so I couldn't get too close. Had some interesting leaves stuck on them too, Mr. Da Vinci."

"Probably greys," Sedro deadpanned.

"Huh?"

"Grey whales. Springtime they migrate from the Baja up the coast to Alaska, reversing the trip come fall. The ones you saw probably split from the pod and lost themselves in the Straits. The squids are hard to figure, though."

Eagle stared and jammed his hands in his corduroys. "You have been collecting, ain't you?" he said to me.

"Just for food," I said, sloshing my drink in the direction of the clams. "Though we did see some *Oligocottus snyderi*." I winked at Sedro.

"Yeah," Eagle said. "My dad says I'll get that if I don't stop fucking Mrs. Fairbanks."

Sedro laughed but it just made me mad. Eagle was some piece of work. He was shaving at fifteen and towering over his contemporaries. The surprising coordination and grace that would characterize the adult had yet to surface in the teenager, but whatever he had was more than enough for me, and his awkward thrashings actually had a beauty of their own.

His mother had left home years ago, but his father raised him perfectly, which to both of us at sixteen consisted of being left to do pretty much whatever the hell you wanted. As much as they were required, guidance and direction were curse words at that age, and Eagle's attitude ensured a surface too slick for their purchase in any case — his father's laissez-faire approach to parenting merely diverted the clashes of adolescence from the home to the school, the workplace and the courts.

Eagle always appears in my mind as a working man. At nine years of age he was selling his art class projects to people at the park; at ten he ran errands for Crazy Stan the Grocery Man; at eleven he was painting fences; twelve saw him stacking shakes down at the splitting yard; at thirteen he stole; the golf course in Nanaimo claimed him at fourteen, Eagle hitching down-island to caddy and clean clubs and shoes in the pro shop; last year he was the assistant groundskeeper for the playing fields by the bridge (until he accidentally set the tiny pressbox on fire); and now he was working in the steel yard for One-Nut Humphries of Humphries Fabrication and, between weekly sackings when Humphries took exception to his mouth and his attitude, learning to weld while he was at it.

Consequently, he always had money, which even at that age he flung around with an abandon that gained him a host of followers. That's how I see him as an adult: the Man From Eldorado in town for a spree, paying with gold and curse you for not partaking when by God there's enough for all, never too much of anything, more please and one for yourself and one for that sorry bastard over there — there! the one I might drag outside if my money's not good enough for him. Shit and corruption, all gone is it? Time to head back to the gold creek.

All around, the ineffable attraction to the rogue. Admiration for someone living life on his own terms. And he was genuine, you have to give him that — we all know the difference between posturing and generosity, between the troublemaker and the roisterer, between Phil the Drunk Uncle and the real article.

But it wasn't a good time to bring up the plundering of Mrs. Fairbanks's affections. I envied almost all the guys at school for what they claimed to be their sexual experience. Eagle wasn't like the others, wasn't all brag. Every month or so he'd arrange to get caught in the act with someone somewhere, after which a knowing glance in my direction would serve to deepen my sense of inadequacy. When he described his encounters I'd have to rush off and jerk myself furiously.

"Know them oysters from the spit?" he said on a day when he was feeling particularly superior. "It's just like them. Soft and sort of flabby but with muscle holding it all together. You know Gloria?"

"Not her, Eagle!" Know her? I loved her. I knew it. I'd smell her as we passed in the hallway at school and sidle up to her in lines or by her locker. Pitiful, really.

"Yup," Eagle said. "Only she don't like birth control."

"Then you're stupid." If I was inexperienced then I was at least attentive in class.

"So she takes it in her mouth."

"Get away. Take the fucking road, Eagle. Gloria? In her mouth? Gimme a break. Not your dirty old thing, after it's been in those fucking corduroys you never change and you don't wear any underwear? Gimme a break, you lying sack of shit!"

"So you can just hump one of your sea animals, scientist."

I rushed off to the washroom and jumped into a stall. I was getting a bit mixed up, thinking of Gloria while trying to force the image of an oyster from my mind, when I looked up and there was Eagle, his big ugly face staring down at me from over the wall of the adjoining stall. I hollered and dove under the partition and tipped him off the toilet seat and then I was pounding away with Eagle laughing and screaming, "Pervert!" and pointing at me still sticking up. Then the both of us laughing until we were nearly sick.

I did myself up and Eagle laughed again and we walked out and down the hallway. I didn't even see Gloria till we were opposite her locker and Eagle shoved me hard into her and we both went down in a heap.

"You should see the cock on this guy, Gloria!" Eagle screamed, then was off running.

He had trouble making the turn at the end of the hallway, so when I tackled him we went crashing through the glass door of the office. After that it was him and me sitting in the principal's office listening to another "It's always you two" lecture while the school nurse swabbed blood off Eagle's ugly face. We were kicked out for a week that time and spent every day hiking to the glacier and drinking lemon gin Eagle stole off his dad.

"Hey, Mr. Da Vinci," Eagle said. "You gonna hog all that rye?"

Sedro chuckled and motioned into the cottage.

Mr. Da Vinci. We had recently studied Leonardo in school. Eagle had no time for formal learning, but anything that could be used as a weapon he eagerly snatched up and pressed into service. The slightest convergence on a historical figure indelibly labeled his target. Most parallels were not so flattering. Years ago the town council's treasurer backed his car into a shopping cart holding a small child, harmlessly nudging the thing three feet, and to this day Eagle calls him Vlad the Impaler.

But only in public.

With Eagle barging around the kitchen, committing unknown damage and certainly pilfering food, I shook my head at Sedro.

"It's not such a comfort hanging around with him," I said.

"That's the way it should be," he said. "A man who gets too accustomed to comfort falls apart when life gets dirty. And it always gets dirty. Get used to the dirt and comfort's a paid vacation."

Sedro had a meeting to attend, so he took off. Eagle and I played some records — Sedro had a wild collection of Mozart, Keith Jarrett and Haggard — and Eagle gave me the update on Mrs. Fairbanks. We wandered out around eight and built a big bonfire on the beach and worked through the rest of the bottle of Plainsman Rye and threw it into the broom bushes and started on another.

When Sedro came back around eleven I was passed out on the couch and Eagle was naked on Da Vinci's bed. One of us had been sick in the kitchen and we had a brief inarticulate fight over which one, but both of us were filthy and smelled like hell, so the argument died.

Sedro drove us home and my place had the picture window bust out so my dad had been at it again. I was sick but happy so I didn't think much about it.

Three weeks later Sedro shot my father and life got dirty.

F O U R

I left the Square Rigger ahead of the others, hoping the walk back to the store would be more restorative than the ugly journey of seven hours before. It also would give Don time to cash out and lock up before he dragged the others along.

Don was in a despondent mood and nobody else had helped. Robert was lost in his own concerns. Snuffy's good spirits could usually get us laughing, but after I had outlined my plan to get Sedro on our side his gaiety only served to irritate. And Eagle was on full scholarship at the nut house with a guarantee of making the varsity.

The Island was working its magic. A springtime hiss of water — not from the sky, but dropping from leaf and branch in the forest, the palisade of trees concealing creatures on the hunt. A time when it is hard to accept it all was not created for our benefit, for contemplation, and impossible not to feel in intimate alliance with the whole grab bag. It was beautiful and quiet and precious, and when I reached the store I didn't want to ruin it so I sat on the steps and smoked a cigarette before I went inside.

I turned on the lights over the counter and went to the storeroom. I stretched out on the daybed, pulling the patchwork quilt up to my chin so my boots stuck out the bottom, and wished like hell I was starting everything over.

I couldn't have been sleeping long.

"Of course I didn't bring my truck from the pub," Eagle said. "I'm too drunk."

"Good," Don said.

"I ordered up a taxi."

"You're getting smarter."

"Then when the driver come inside to look for me I drove his cab over."

Struggling out of a poorly formed dream, I tossed off the quilt and went out to join them. Don was at the long counter mixing drinks, taking his job on the road. The fixings were lined up beside the old cash register. I waved and went over to the window, shedding fatigue by the minute.

I could see the cab sitting under the ghostly pale post light we used for night horseshoe games and barbecues. Snuffy was out there pitching. Eagle was draped all over a caneback chair. Robert was thrashing around the shelves. He never bought anything by the light of day, hoping for a deal if he turned up something he needed after hours.

I would lose the hardware store if the bridge came in but it would be no debilitating loss. The warped hardwood floor supported rows of shelving crammed with a tinker's wagon collection of odds and ends. The windows were caked with dust and grime, reminiscent of the greased paper used on the frontier before glass was available. The counter was crowned with an old enameled set of weigh scales, providing symmetry down the end from the cash register. My room, the storeroom, was in the back, your basic male sanctuary, a confined space for concentration, energy, focus. It held a daybed, a TV, many of my reference books, and any supplies that wouldn't fit on the shelves or stack on the floor or hang from the ceiling. I was half sick of the store these days, but to our friends it was a clubhouse.

It was called the Store, just as everything in a small town loses its name: the Apple Stand, the River, the Park, the Pub.

"Do we really have a chance?" Robert asked.

He dropped an armload of stuff on the floor, items he would leave there when I refused to knock a few cents off. I would restack it all in the morning.

"Who knows?" Don said.

"I mean, I was a lawyer, a good one, for a long time and I know people don't think in the long term. Grab and run. Insurance, personal lawsuits, anything."

"It's not right," Don said. "I have spent forty-one years living right in the Valley and I tell you it will be ruined if that bridge comes in."

"I'll move," Eagle said.

He dug in the sack of burgers and fries he had picked up on the way then kicked the bag in my direction. He bit off half a burger in one pass. Mustard and relish cascaded onto his shirt front.

"Maybe look up Jean in Toronto. She must miss me by now, if she ain't shacked up with some bastard wears a tie to work."

"Toronto," Robert said. "What would you do back there?"

"Maybe bring the chainsaw, put on the spurs and top the CN Tower. See the looks on their faces, ninety foot of concrete dropping into the SkyDome, letting fly a bladder of piss on anyone tries to come up after me."

He mashed the rest of the burger in his fist and popped it in his mouth. Robert snorted in disgust and turned away. Eagle wiped his hand on the tail of Robert's sports jacket.

"I have to bring it up again," I said.

"He'd do more harm than good," Don said quietly. There was a moment of silence.

"He shot your father," Robert said. "Jesus, Jack."

"You didn't know his father," Eagle said.

"He was acquitted," I added. "Accidental homicide."

"Even if Da Vinci stalked your old man and drilled him like a rabid dog, I don't lay any blame," Eagle said. "But you're too stuck on Sedro. He himself didn't explain nothing to you and he sure didn't say sorry. He took off after the trial like nobody's business — left his office, his house, the works. He ain't been back and he ain't coming back. You think after fifteen years he'll return to the scene of the crime to help us keep from getting a tunnel and bridge built? Shake your head — there's something loose up there."

I sought refuge in looking out the window, watching Snuffy disappear from the light as he went to retrieve a wayward shoe.

"Forget everything that happened," I said. "Forget it and consider this —"

"Can't," Eagle said.

"Just for the moment —"

"Can't."

"For argument's sake —"

"Can't."

"Shut the fuck up, Eagle. Shut up and consider if his coming back will work. Sedro is a legend in Salish Spit. It was his town. Will his weight — to say nothing of his pure ability — help defeat the proposal?"

"I don't know what'll work," Eagle said. "I don't know nothing these days. Things're all screwy."

Don came around to the front of the counter and handed out the drinks. He leaned back on the wood, a Coke in his hand. "Everything changes," he said glumly. "I'm so tired of it all."

"If they'd give me back my license to practice …," Robert said.

"They give your license back," Eagle said, "and I'll fuck a pumpkin."

Robert was born in the Valley and went off to UBC when he was eighteen. Subsequent years were muffled in mystery until he moved back ten years ago, an unspecified misdemeanor having cast him loose from the bar, though how he passed the exams in the first place was knowledge locked in the same footlocker of selective memory that frequently made him such a pain. He ran the small in-house brewery out back of the Square Rigger and raised quarter horses, which is about what anyone would offer for any of the sorry beasts. Thin and dapper, he wore tweeds and a hunted look.

I needed some air. I stepped outside and closed the door behind me. Snuffy was darting back and forth between the pits and roaming around for stray shoes, vanishing from the light behind broom bushes and scrub pines.

Economic resurgence was not the *sine qua non* of continued existence here.

Some residents were secure by virtue of ancestors who made money in the early days of the Island colony, in transportation or coaling ventures in Nanaimo or Comox, and who were now content to live like colonial Kenyan landowners, above it all.

Others were comfortable with the boom-to-bust cycle of affairs that has defined the place since its founding, back in the time when it won the fight to have Victoria as the provincial capital and lost the one for Esquimalt to be home to the great Pacific railway terminus — lumbering, salmon canneries, flour mills, mines, each in its turn making the residents giddy then despondent.

Besides, we were building on the grand tradition of Vancouver Island: Under all circumstances be against the policies of mainland B.C. until an agreement has to be reached to band with them against the policies of the rest of the country. In turn, cleave to Ottawa only to fight the Americans, and jump in bed with the gringos in the event a continental stance is imperative. Work from the inside out.

A third grouping, of course, comprised those who wanted nothing whatever to do with nothing whatever. I respected this stance, as there are not many places left these days to practice benign isolation.

But all that this evaluates is the extremities of the bell curve. The majority of the people were hands-on folks who simply needed a job to raise a family, and who were not so disposed as Eagle to endure poverty for independence. Pride can only carry you so far.

Could Sedro Tuckett help? Possible, not probable. But I was incomplete without him, or without his final say on the incident, if that's not too mild a word. He left immediately after the trial in Victoria. In the intervening years, even when I finally tracked him down, he rebuffed any attempt to meet. My letters were returned unopened and his phone was never listed. I craved his presence in my life. I needed contact. Ignorance is bliss only if the ignorance is all-encompassing.

And yes, I needed an explanation. Any old one would do. His eremitic existence hurt me more than anything had in my life, topping even the incomprehension at the news of my father's taking a .303 slug between the running lights.

I looked up and picked out Orion and the old hunter nodded. Snuffy whanged a shoe off the shed.

And as egocentric as I was feeling, I was concerned for Sedro. I had thought of him my last trip down the coast to San Francisco. I was climbing the hill up Powell Street when an old bum stuck out his hand. I dug in my pocket and plunked in his hand a bunch of American and Canadian coins. I made to continue on my way, but felt his hand on my arm.

"Take this," he said. He was awash in snot and rum. I looked at the dime he held between filthy thumb and forefinger and waved it away. "No, no," he insisted. "I pay my way."

"You're buying spare change with a dime?" I said.

"Holding out for more, are you? A bargainer, are you?"

I took the dime and smiled.

The next day I saw him down on the wharf and followed

him awhile till he vanished into the courtyard of the Cannery. Rounding the corner, I almost bumped into him.

"You're the guy I bought eighty-five cents off yesterday," he said after a second's deliberation.

"That's right," I said.

He looked me over and tossed off a weak grin. "I remember the day when a dime would buy a dollar."

The day after I set out to find him, for no firm reason, no agenda. About three in the afternoon, after questioning several street people, I ran into him on Broadway, pestering a strip-club barker. He saw me coming and I lost him up an alley, still not having a clue what I was doing. I left off the chase.

One in the morning I was making my way back to the hotel and cut up through a lane not far from the Irish pub I had been in. There he was. I was almost past what looked like a lump of sacking when I realized it was him, all twisted and skinny and bunched up and dead. I stared at him a long time and stuffed ten dollars in the middle of the sacking, knowing some other bum would find it, or not, but not caring either way.

I felt an urge to kick him, I was so mad, and did, then felt all shaky and walked the whole way back to the hotel praying someone on the street would say something smart to me so I could assuage my guilt and my sadness by taking a round out of him. I thought hard on Sedro then, and jumped on my motor-cycle and started back home the same night.

Two days later I was home and Elizabeth got on the war paint and argued at me, not with me, because I wouldn't fight back and didn't for three weeks.

I don't know what prompted the equation between the dead man and Sedro, who was more alive than anyone I knew.

I went back into the store and was followed by a set of probing headlights. A minute later Elizabeth walked in and I knew why I loved her.

"Hello, Jack," she said and gave me a warm kiss. She went to the counter and helped herself to a drink. "How did the meeting go?"

"I guess we're pretty much at loose ends," I admitted.

"What's the problem?" she asked. "There's a general meeting in three weeks to decide. All you can do is try. You're all well-respected members of the community. Give them your best arguments which, though half-formed, express the way a lot of people feel. Don, I couldn't begin to list your contributions to Salish Spit. You support every charity, sponsor six sports teams and run that little nerve center of a pub. Robert, you've a background in law and your relatives are charter members of the Valley. Eagle, you've worked for everyone in town at one time or another. You know the people inside out and you're the most well known athlete to come from the area. Jack, you're stubborn and that may count the most.

"Be honest and do your best." She poured more mix into

her drink. "Snuffy's getting better with those horseshoes all the time, isn't he?"

My first thought was that it was a ploy. Maybe Elizabeth was just fishing, trolling mildly along till I bit, then yarding me over the gunwale with hardly a fight or a jump. And then I felt unworthy for how quickly I questioned her motives.

While I pondered what the hell was happening to the two of us, Snuffy, perhaps still blinded by the headlights, fired a shoe through the window and caught me dead center in the back.

"Sorry, Jack." Snuffy barged through the door. "I'm so sorry. You okay?"

"Don't worry about it." I could feel the welt through my shirt.

"Get that man a grape crush!" Eagle yelled. "Best shot I've seen in years. Hey, I know! We'll make Snuffs our personal storm trooper. Get the bugger a couple hundred horseshoes, storm the mayor's office, whing, whang, cutting a path through them contractors and suits and government shitasses."

He plunged off into the aisles, heading for the outdoor wear. We couldn't help but hear him thrashing around back there.

"Get you a uniform, that's what you need. Snuffy the goddamned general. I don't doubt we'll have volunteers springing up from everywhere. Get them wearing sunglasses and them little radios in their ears like Secret Service guys and Mounties. No, like the Brownshirts, our own gang. Need some of these ..."

Elizabeth helped me clean up the glass. With a clatter of coat hangers Eagle returned, his huge arms hugging a bushel of clothes. Rubbers, suspenders, pants, slickers and shirts tumbled to the floor. A fishing rod, hooked by its tip to a jacket, joined the heap, along with a few cabinet hinges and a Coleman stove.

"The Plaidshirts," Eagle said. He rubbed his chest in manly appreciation of the idea, smearing the mustard and relish. "The fucking Plaidshirts."

Snuffy squealed and eagerly joined the game. The two of them were immediately entangled in paraphernalia, outfitting Snuffy for his new role. The rest of us sat it out at the counter, pulling up stools Eagle had swiped the year before from the Leeward Pub up in Comox.

Elizabeth topped up her drink. I didn't like the look on her face. There was something up her sleeve.

"Donna and I had a productive chat this evening," she said.

Don nodded. I braced, anticipating the worst, and pissed off at Don's concealing whatever secret we were about to be let in on.

"We have at least thirty people ready to come aboard," she said. "They're willing to do whatever is required to help stop this thing."

"What?" I said. "Where were they when I was canvassing? And what can they do that we aren't already doing? And who asked you to go behind my back?"

"Come on, Jack," Robert said. "Let her speak."

"You're in on this, too?"

"I was a lawyer, a good one, and at times focusing on one issue works, at others it's best to fire a broadside. Don't look at me like that. We're not your enemies here."

"Let me finish," Elizabeth said. "I want to make this clear."

Robert and Don were only too happy to let her continue.

"I'll start at your last question and work to the front. First, I'm not going behind your back, that's why I'm telling you. You don't have a monopoly on concern. No one elected you as the sole voice. You're following form by assuming — assuming — that you're the natural leader and everyone who doesn't line up behind you is out of line for good. There is an enormous number of people who want what you want but for different reasons, and none of them feel they are being properly represented, or can even say anything, with you in charge.

"Second — don't interrupt me — second, what can they do that you aren't already doing? Anything, Jack. You've been sitting on your ass for a year and a half. Your initial enthusiasm for going about this properly has disappeared, and there will be no heroic rescue in this battle. *Anything* is better than what you're doing."

"Hold on," I said.

"Wait, yourself," Robert said.

"Come on, Jack." Don was uncomfortable but clearly committed to the necktie party. To occupy his hands, he freshened our drinks.

"Third," Elizabeth said. "I'm not alone in these feelings. That is why there wasn't a rush to come forward when you were canvassing opinion, and why so many dropped out along the way. You're not so easy to disagree with. Once in charge you demand deference."

Rare is the person able to digest a meal at the table. I'd have to lie on the couch awhile with this one. Fortunately, dinner was interrupted.

"Salute, you peasants!" Eagle bellowed.

Snuffy had on a plaid shirt that was tucked into a set of chest waders up to his armpits. A double row of fishing lures stood in as medals — the Victoria Wiggler, the Iron Spoon, the Order of the Pickerel Rig. A hardhat surmounting a toque protected him from shrapnel, and safety goggles sheltered his eyes from desert winds. He was armed with a horseshoe and had three more as spare cartridges tucked into the back of the waders.

"We'll drive them off the Island," Eagle said.

"Off the Island," Snuffy said. He flung up his hands and the shoe flopped endoverend the length of the store, slamming to a stop securely around the leg of an Evinrude trolling motor.

"Ringer!" he screamed, and clattered behind the counter to chalk a sideways slash through his four marks on the board.

Five and a batch. He looked at it awhile then erased the line — he would play the game by the book.

Eagle sloshed rye into a tin camping cup he had been unable to attach to Snuffy. "This protesting shit is easy."

The break had allowed me to dodge the mutiny, but the ringleaders still had their cutlasses. To keep their attention diverted I pulled my old Martin off the wall and began to improvise a song about Snuffy the Famous General.

I had figured Elizabeth to be in a feral mood, but to be fair, her appraisal was so close to the mark it left her calm and confident of her position. Furthermore, she knew full well I had got the message, so felt her high spirits to be justified. She stayed with us, captivating her audience, charming and beautiful and altogether delightful.

The guys finally left around four and I made a grab at my wife and we made love on the counter, Elizabeth's arms up over her head, clasping the cash register while her legs squeezed my hips and my heart. Neither of us lasted long, and the aftermath left me feeling guilty at wanting to be gone while the mood lasted, before I got or gave another scar on the snout. I seemed always to be running away from her these days, even when we were running together.

F I V E

When we hit the house Elizabeth went straight to bed while I sat on the dog run with a beer. A postcoital glow was still in the air and I wanted to prolong it. Considering the way my mind was flinging itself around and ricocheting off the inside of my skull, my being in close proximity to my wife could have us at each other like junkyard dogs.

I considered the possibility that Elizabeth and I had more in common than was healthy — our shortcomings clashed as much as our strengths combined. The seven years we had been together seemed longer than that, probably because her arrival in my life had coincided with a period of general upheaval. When she showed up I was suffering both from a falling off of scientific fervor and a dissatisfaction with my day-to-day affairs. And now the confusion was back.

Trouble is, I have a contradictory line of attack. I like to analyze things but I act on instinct; I can recognize the workings while ignoring their importance; I am able to maintain a show of confidence while assailed by doubt. By very nature an investigator, I am beset by a terrific panic when my brain and my gut start pulling in opposite directions. It is a common result of skepticism.

After high school a lot of my friends hit the road to self-discovery by taking some time off to work or play or backpack around Europe before plunging back into formal education. I was so certain I knew where I was that there was no need to find myself. Besides, the whole process sounded too much like a cliché, so with a loan from Sedro Tuckett I jumped right into university — not without a little smugness, I might add. It wasn't till some time had passed at the institute that I began asking all the questions for which many people already had answers.

I did like the joint, though, and the beauty of science at least allowed me a ration of strength amid the general idiocy of my behavior.

And then I met Elizabeth.

"Why didn't you come right out and tell me I had food stuck to my face?" I asked.

We were in the second-floor hospitality suite. The press conference had ended ten minutes ago. I looked at the gob of guacamole on the napkin and tossed it behind the snack table.

She shrugged. "I didn't want to embarrass you."

"And it's not embarrassing walking around with a Mexican lunch on my face?" I said. "I'm going to get laid quick looking like that."

She laughed. She came from Houston, though she was born and raised in Toronto. She didn't have much of an accent, the Texas twang that manages to be so attractive while faintly moronic.

Her escort, or date, a vice president of South Central Oil, was polishing his boots on the back of his legs not five feet behind me. Ronny Digs, director of the institute, was heaping shrimp crackers onto the man's outstretched hands, forcing drinks on him and generally keeping him occupied. Good guy, Ronny.

The press conference had been called to announce closer cross-border ties between SCO and our research group, which did everything from seismic and geomorphological mapping of the continental shelf to the study of various effects on estuarine productivity and offshore marine life, my specialty. SCO was building a research platform in the Gulf of Mexico, not far from Stage 2 of the U.S. Navy Mine Defense Laboratory out of Panama City, Florida. We would provide the expertise for what ostensibly was to be a research project, though what SCO wanted with data on surface and internal waves, acoustic transmission and scattering, and the distribution of dinoflagellates in the Gulf was obvious to anyone prepared to investigate: A polite tip of the hat to the U.S. Environmental Protection Agency. The proposed platform was large and bore design features that made the withdrawing of sensing probes and the inserting of drill pipe an exercise of a few days' duration.

It was one of the few things over which Ronny Digs and I disagreed.

"I know we're committing to a capitalist venture," he said minutes before the conference. "A scientific guise is nothing new. Governments do it all the time."

"We're funded by the government, not run by it."

"We're also funded by private groups."

"SCO is not what I'd call private. That word implies a little mom and pop enterprise."

"You know what I mean. And why not look at it as a way to acquire money to pursue pure research?"

"Start with a lie and you end up with one. Righteous posturing is a flimsy pedestal, not a solid platform."

"We can't get by on government grants," he said.

"Why can't we work above board with these people? There is nothing inherently wrong in drilling for oil as long as environmental concerns are satisfied. I'm not an anti-mechanical lunatic. I can live with oil wells and logging and mines if it's all done properly and under control."

"There are people who won't let us," Ronny said. "They don't want their tax dollars going to a research institute that appears to be out grubbing in the ground alongside Gulf and Texaco and SCO."

"That's it, isn't it — appearances."

"The people —"

"I'd like to bend the people over a sawhorse and drill them in the ass."

"You sweetie," Ronny said. "Come on, we're starting in five minutes."

I didn't much feel like socializing. After all my protests I stood there with Ronny Digs on the dais and said the right things, cloaking the lies in rhetoric and jargon.

But I had seen Elizabeth and sought her out immediately after the announcements were over. I was talking to her now, and right from the start she had the ability to make me concentrate on her alone. Her mouth was in a slight pout, a look she took pains to accentuate. She was muscular for a woman and healthy and sure of herself.

"I like this place," she said. "A hospitality suite in a research institute — there's something human about that."

I howled. The public has the impression that scientists are a stodgy bunch smelling of formaldehyde, bespectacled and grumpy, eccentric and absent-minded. Mostly they are right. But science is a human invention and scientists are human. As much as we embrace the method of presenting a theory then trying to disprove it, or of objectively amassing data hoping to reveal a trend or a truth, all the human subtleties and frailties pervert our profession.

Science is a blend of induction and deduction and is wide open to inconsistencies and cultural biases and outright hoaxes. It is paired in single combat with religion, yet hope and desire taint it all the same, and the annals of science are replete with results that come from matching fact to expectation. But at least science has a built-in capacity for self-correction, though never without a few bloody noses, and in that I find its beauty.

"We have our fun," I said.

"Did you always want to be a scientist?"

"Yes. It's the best occupation in which to satisfy your curiosity. Want another drink?"

"Do you always do that?"

"What?"

"Tie two thoughts together in one breath?"

"Sometimes my mind works that way."

"I think I make you nervous."

"You do. If I'm off balance, might just as well keep everyone teetering."

"What happened to your hand?"

"Dislocated a finger playing rugby," I said. "It's taped to the other one for support."

"I see."

"Why do you ask? Want anything to eat?"

"No, just a gin."

I went to the folding table that was acting as the bar and poured the drinks. Ronny saw me and came over with the guy from SCO. The VP was tall and angular and shook my hand heartily till he felt the tape and eased off.

"Sorry," he said. "What happened?"

"Great white attack."

"Didn't know you got those sharks this far north."

"This one heard about the free food at the press conference."

I drained my drink and poured another. The rye tasted bad but I wasn't giving ground; I needed one victory today.

"Yes," he said. "Yes, Ronald mentioned you were a trifle intransigent about our partnership." He didn't sound like a Texan.

"None of my say, really."

"You scientists," he said.

I glanced at Ronny and he gave me one of his looks, the ones he dished out when someone broke a piece of equipment or punctured the inflatable boat on the rocks — or when his daughter had said she wanted to be a model.

"Maybe I should go back to ranching," I said.

"You used to ranch?" the VP asked with sudden interest.

"Oh, yeah," I said. "Chicken ranch. Just loved to watch those little buggers run around when their heads were cut off. Me and cousin Elmer used to set up wire obstacle courses for them, see how far they'd make it with no noggins." I got another look from Ronny. "And they call chickens stupid! One of them made it forty feet and three corners one time. We tried it on my uncle Mac and he didn't make it to the first bend."

The man shook his dumb fucking head and said, "You scientists."

"Can't you take anything seriously, Jack?" Ronny said.

I felt and smelled Elizabeth move in behind me, and I shifted so she could join the group.

"Here's my little darlin'," the VP said. He might not be from Texas but he was trying. "You've met Jack."

I passed the drink and smiled.

"We're anxious to get under way on this project," Ronny said. "I'm glad you agreed to come up and help us with the promotion."

Ronny was fifty-something back then. He looked like a hir-sute Greek chef and was one of the most dedicated researchers imaginable. He was ill at ease in social situations, for his work was his life, and his zealous fascination with it usually made him unintelligible in normal conversation — jargon and statis-tics flew from him as if propelled by a giant sneeze.

Ronny sensed the attraction between Elizabeth and me and was openly trembling at the thought it might queer the works. I was seeing his daughter Camilla on a casual basis but that part of it held no concern for him. I could have laid Liz on the buf-fet table if it didn't rupture relations with SCO. He was coolly disinterested in his daughter. Not uninterested, mind you, merely appreciative of her in a scientific way — a pleasant, large-breasted specimen made noteworthy by his having sired her. I asked him once if he loved Camilla and he said, "Oh, sure," and went back to the computer.

The VP was talking again and trying not to drop the shrimp off his Wheat Thin. "You have to be realistic, Jack," he said.

"Fantasy intrigues me."

He paused. If he said "You scientists" again I was going to pop him. "Do you want to spend the rest of your career digging around pilings?" he asked. "Trying to figure out if a new pier is going to mess up the flora and fauna?"

"Sounds pretty good."

"There's no arguing with you," Ronny said.

"I didn't know this was an argument."

How much of this was for effect? Around women I usually adjust my views to the left. Liberal Thorpe takes over from Colonel Thorpe. Elizabeth wasn't leaning either way and I caught myself wishing she would so I could cheat in her direction. I also caught myself wishing Eagle were there. He'd put an end to this nonsense in spectacular fashion.

The free food was almost gone and the liquor supply was dwindling, so the media began to lose interest in us. I was trying to get Elizabeth alone so we could put her time up here to good use.

The institute had laid on a fishing trip and a night on the town in Port Alberni for the next day, and I had to find a way to circumvent the crap and show Elizabeth my little piece of life up the highway. I pulled Ronny aside, ostensibly to run over some technical information.

"You're going to kill me, Thorpe," he said.

"I'm not homicidal."

"You're suicidal. Believe me, lay one hand on that woman, do one thing that little pissant from SCO doesn't like, and I'll lock you in a room with a gun and tell you to do the honorable thing."

"Look at her, Ronny."

"Stay away from her."

"I could take her to the aquarium room and show her the moray."

"You're a slob and you're not funny."

"I'm in love."

"There's something between those two," he said. "You're treading on dangerous ground."

"It's very simple, Ronny, my man. Let me find out."

"You'll find yourself at the bottom of the chuck."

"If there's something between them then she isn't the woman I think she is, and I walk."

"The woman you think she is. Listen to yourself."

"If there isn't, then no harm in a little socializing."

"At least wait till tomorrow night," he said

"You'll pick some goddamn restaurant where the staff sings 'Happy Birthday' to you."

"It's not your birthday."

"I can't do that to her on our first date."

"First date."

"She probably doesn't like fishing. I'll show her around Salish Spit. It's great up there."

"And introduce her to that friend of yours, I suppose. The one who stole my jeep and drove it into the front of the laundromat."

"I won't let Eagle near her. Believe me, it's in my best interest, too."

"You're bad enough."

"Then let me stay at your place tonight. I'll take her to Alberni. Tell the VP we're checking out a place for dinner tomorrow night."

"I'm telling him nothing. There's too much at stake."

"Take him home with you and cook up some of those baloney steaks you're so good with."

"There! It's out of your hands."

I turned, and there was Camilla coming through the door and heading straight for us.

"Ronny, help me on this one."

"Are you trifling with my daughter's affections?"

"Don't pull that on me now."

"I'll pull anything on you. I might pull something off of you."

I truly liked Camilla but was not in love. I had run through a succession of girls my own age or younger before meeting her at Ronny's house one night. She was six years older than me and was just back from Tanzania. She seemed worldly and fascinating and I made the common flub of mistaking experience for wisdom. She had been many places and seen many things and read many books, but over the past year I had come to realize that she was not a person who learned. She was not stupid, but somehow she didn't listen, didn't retain, or was a poor observer.

But I'm being overly critical. She was much like her father: Easygoing and friendly and funny. She was nice, with all the capabilities and disabilities the word implies. I had felt the end coming for some time. I didn't want to hurt her but knew it was inevitable to avoid hurting myself.

I stared at her and wished her away, but she plowed through the crowd and kept coming. I tried not to look wistfully at Elizabeth but I'm sure I did. I pushed roughly by the VP after letting a bungled excuse fall out of my mouth at Camilla's feet, then was off and away, on my bike, the engine noise buzzing in my helmet, banking and accelerating along the twisting highway forty miles back to my house in the Spit.

So you see how it was with Elizabeth. We had just met, yet with her I didn't even want to be around other women.

The next night Ronny Digs phoned at three in the morning and gave me holy hell for missing the fishing trip and the dinner.

"I gave your number to the SCO guy," he said.

"Wonderful."

"He thinks you might have taken offense to something he said."

"He's not all stupid."

"You missed a good day."

"Really."

"No."

"Good."

"How old are you?"

"Things are just building up, Ronny."

"Yeah, well. I gave your number to that woman, too."

"Elizabeth?"

"I think that's her name."

"Did she ask for it, or did you offer?"

"Find out yourself. I didn't get a Ph.D. to be a pimp."

"I love you, Ronny, I mean it. Honest to God, I'd fuck you if I wasn't afraid of getting my fingers tangled in the hair on your back."

"Laugh now while you can. She's taking some time off to visit Vancouver while she's up here, then heading back south."

"She'll never see Vancouver. I guarantee you she won't even get her hands on a postcard."

"Camilla's ready to bite the head off a cat."

I spent the next day mucking around the small lab I had attached to the back of the house, smoking cigarettes and dropping things whenever the phone rang. I finally called Camilla and did a pisspoor job of ending our relationship, filled with self-loathing at performing surgery over the phone. I hung up, and by the time Elizabeth called I was drunker than a vintner's dog.

But everything worked out.

Three months later I quit the institute and Elizabeth and I were married. Eagle was my best man, but he was too interested in the tiny bar in back of the limousine to drive, so I took over at the wheel and Elizabeth climbed in beside me. Eagle sprawled out on the back seat and spent the trip trying to tune in the little TV.

The hardware store came later, when I discovered an amateur scientist can't put food in the fridge, though myself I can live on submarine sandwiches or the open-face Denvers they serve at the Square Rigger.

What brought Elizabeth and me together was the unshakable conviction with which I approach all new things. Now I was suffering because of it. So was Elizabeth, and that hurt. I still loved her.

S I X

So long and so deeply did I sleep that when I awoke I checked
to see if I had a full beard. Elizabeth was gone and her side
of the bed had been made. Naked, I padded across the dog run
to the main part of the house and put on the coffee.

A cloudless day, but with haze in the air reflecting and dif-
fracting sunlight to form a blinding sheen in the sky, the eyes
unable to avoid it, to select a resting place and focus in for
stability.

I stood on the dog run with a coffee. Across the scrub and
the road and the rocks, on the edge of the shore, two women
stared up at me, probably wondering if they were seeing right,
but then wandered off along the waterline with the head-down
posture of visitors to the beach.

I showered and dressed in stages, each article of clothing
marking the completion of a task, so by the time I had on

my underwear, jeans, socks, boots, shirt, vest, jacket and mangled cowboy hat I had shaved, done the dishes, swept the dog run, had another coffee, read the note from Liz, played "Margaritaville" on the guitar, made and eaten a fried-egg sandwich, and thrown the committee notes onto the grate in the dead fireplace.

It took a bit of reefing to open the door of my old '66 Mercury halfton, but it finally shrieked loose and I set out in a spray of sand to the mayor's office.

The breeze through the window was restorative, and by the time I hit the town hall — a stucco affair with cross-hatched, vaguely Tudor lathing — I was feeling pretty good about myself. With a ticket for no destination you'd best be able to enjoy the trip.

The haze had burned off and the town looked clean and new.

"Come in," she called as I knocked.

"Get out," she said as I entered.

I glanced around the mayor's office, a likable enough place. Grays and greens and browns, an admixture of leather and wood graced with feminine touches: the Navajo rug on the couch, dresses and blouses on a makeshift clotheshorse in the near corner, the place feeling more like a live-in closet than an office. Behind the mayor was a large bay window through which I could see the river of history. By now the day was so spectacularly clear the glacier seemed about to slip its moorings and fetch up on her desk. It was a large partner desk, but I ignored the second cubbyhole and flopped on the Navajo couch. The mayor had to pivot to look at me.

"Get out," she said.

On the wall across from me was her framed law degree from the University of Victoria and a large abstract painting. I lit a cigarette and dropped the match in a bulky nephrite ashtray on a table by my elbow.

"Get out," she said.

"I heard you the first time, Audrey," I said.

She stuck her pen in a bud vase and pushed back from the desk. I like her looks — untouched gray hair, strong face and hands. "I'm too busy to go through this again," she said.

"You can't be selective about an open-door policy," I said.

"If you have anything new to discuss I'll be glad to entertain it. Otherwise, get out."

"Rehash something long enough and you may stumble on a fresh point."

"Not in this case," she said. "They're going to dig that tunnel under the Straits, hook up to one of the Gulf Islands and run a bridge to Salish Spit. Period. Done. I said exactly the same thing to Elizabeth and Donna an hour ago."

"They don't waste any time."

"You say that as if it's a bad thing."

"Committees should work like new sports franchises —

move in too close to an established market and you owe them compensation."

"Don't be ridiculous."

"Speaking about allies, has BAT GUANO contacted you lately?"

"They're fragmenting," she said. "As I thought they would. Yesterday a group of them dressed up in a sixty-foot orca costume and paraded in Victoria. By all accounts the head section slipped down, blinding the leader, and they ran in front of a sightseeing bus."

"Ha! Any injuries?"

"The man in the rib section, I think." She was laughing. She was the enemy, but it didn't preclude an appreciation of the finer points of silliness.

"The bus line could start up a dryland whale-watching business," I said.

"They actually had someone shake a champagne bottle and fire the spray through a blowhole."

"They get the whole thing on film?"

"Uh-uh. The cameraman got tangled up with the rest of the group — the pod, they called themselves — along Government Street somewhere. But listen to this ..."

I sat upright and craned forward.

"The only arrest was of a protestor who used his sign to beat the hell out of a CHEK TV reporter."

"No."

"The sign read 'U.S. Out of El Salvador!'"

I screamed. "Where do they get these guys? There has to be a clearing house for assholes, a big warehouse where they pool whatever signs they have from the old days and unemployed protestors hang around like movie extras till someone calls looking for warm bodies."

"See who you're working with?" she said.

"Gimme a break, Audrey. I'm not in their bed or even their camp."

"Good luck."

It had been a while since I had talked to Audrey like this. She drove me crazy but was always fun. "Okay, what did Elizabeth have to say?"

"Honestly?"

"No, string me on."

"She said no one but your drinking buddies trusts you to lead them."

"I know, we went through that," I said. "What are her alternatives? I'm not as driven to lead the posse as people think, but I'm not going to throw in with another bunch that wants to dress up in whale suits. My luck, I'd end up being the cloaca."

"If I were totally neutral — which of course I am not — I would still say there is no hope. Elizabeth and Donna are well intentioned, but they have no more clue about what to do than you. It's all uphill for you, Jack. I advise you to hook your store up to a truck and drag it out of the way."

I rose and poured a rye and seven from the sideboard under her law degree.

"Isn't it a little early?" she asked. "If I have to sit here and listen to your rhetoric I'd prefer you to be sober. I know you when you drink."

"No, you don't," I said. "You don't know as much about me as you think."

"Don't be too sure."

Time was I was unflappable in any circumstance, but age and the concomitant fatigue allowed it only now and again these days. But you know what it's like, those mornings when your feet hit the floor and you wag your tail. The fire starts at a glance, the eggs aren't runny, the bacon crisp. Your good mood has carried right through from your orgasm eight hours ago, and it isn't raining and no clouds obscure the glacier and the broom bushes haven't yet lost their blossoms. Nothing could rattle me, certainly not Audrey Weeks.

"You had another committee meeting last night," she said.

"That's right."

"Your presence tells me as much," she said. "But so do the police. They found a stolen taxi parked outside your store early this morning."

"Funny," I said.

"Funny."

"It was none of us. Probably tourists coming to check on the bridge site."

"I'm glad you've accepted the inevitable," she said.

"I haven't." I walked round behind her and looked out the bay window. She kept her back to me. "I haven't accepted the bridge or the tunnel or your arguments."

"Not mine. The pro-bridge group has extended a sensible, cogent argument. I'm only the mayor. I must act according to the wishes of the majority."

"That collection of weasels represents the majority?" I said. "They work for you."

"They're members of the town council."

"Your ministers," I said. "If you refuse to judge them I can only assume you're in cahoots with them."

"And if you refuse to run for town council I can only assume your concern is superficial."

I came around for another drink. There was no more rye so I filled the glass with ice and splashed in scotch.

"I like you, Jack," she said. "But my duty —"

"Please," I said. "Please don't act like an insurance salesman. We're friends — fine. But in official capacities we tolerate each other because it's the civilized way to behave. I think you're a poseur who considers the office more important than the job. You think I'm an anarchist who wants to tear down the courthouse."

"Aren't you? You're against everything."

"I'm *for* everything. Everything important, at any rate."

"You're just like your precious sea animals," she said. "Feed and mate and ignore progress."

"Don't attribute moral traits to animals. They are constitutionally unable to ignore anything. Besides, I'm a scientist, or was. But I'm not designing nuclear weapons. I work for progress and embrace it when it comes, but only as it applies to the individual or the species. So many people here have progressed to the point where house, hearth, family, friendship and food on the table are everything. That's progress, a way of life, an uncomplicated sense of themselves and their corner of the world. It is that uncomplicated life that is threatened by the link to the mainland."

"There!" she crowed. "You said it yourself. House, hearth, family and food. Right now, as you and I speak, a large portion of Salish Spit cannot manage even that much. I heard you won your rugby game by default last Sunday."

"So?"

"Because the Port could only field two players. Two players, Jack. There's nobody left in their town. So dramatically has the forest industry declined that people are literally walking away from their houses, leaving a pitiful realty sign on the lawn. That could happen here. Get your head out of the tide pools and look around you."

I went to the sideboard and poured another drink. Audrey was right.

"The general meeting is next week," she said. "Thursday night."

I whirled. "It was supposed to be three weeks from now."

"The official proposal has to be tendered by then," she said. "So I moved the meeting up."

"Jesus."

"Come on. Does it matter? You've had over a year to politic."

"So I'm not a pro at campaigning."

"Right. You're a scientist. Or a hardware store owner. Or a rugby player. Or a good old boy at the bar. Salish Spit is growing up and you'll be dragged along with it or left to cry in your beer."

The door opened and someone came in but I ignored the sound and tried to retain my line of thought, calm sifting through my fingers. I spilled some scotch on my shirt as I fumbled for another cigarette.

"You were raised here," I said. "You should be afraid of what will become of the town. Progress feeds on itself. They're talking about building townhouses when the bridge comes in. Townhouses, for chrissake. In a valley where people build their own homes or have them built by someone they've known since childhood."

"I used to live in a townhouse," a voice said from the doorway.

Emotion as well as progress feeds on itself. I stood staring at the tall, tanned woman, and I do believe my heart went into fibrillation on the spot.

"Take a hike," I said. "The mayor and I are in conference."

Audrey scarcely blinked and I don't know how the woman behind me reacted.

"This is my assistant," Audrey said. "And she stays."

"It's all right," the voice said from the door. "This is hardly an auspicious beginning. I'll wait out in the hall."

"You will not," Audrey said. "This is Jack Thorpe."

"Oh," the woman said. "Oh."

"Howdy," I said. She was beautiful. Oh, yes.

"This is Patsy Jillian," Audrey said. "She'll be helping coordinate and draft the final bridge proposal. She works for the government — don't grimace — and will be operating out of my office until the ratification. I assume you're about to apologize. Patsy's my daughter."

"Nice to know you," I said. Cool in her appraisal of me. "Nice tan," I added.

"Thank you," she said wryly, and took a seat at the desk.

"Patsy's just back from Florida," Audrey said.

"Should you be offering information to the enemy?" Patsy asked.

"If Audrey filled you in on me, you know by now I'd torture the information out of you in my storeroom. Matter of fact I have six people in there I'm working over as we speak."

"Christ," Audrey said.

"I don't see much family resemblance," I said. "Are you adopted?"

"I said I know what you're like when you drink."

"Harmless fun," I said and dove at the sideboard. There was still plenty of ice in my glass so it was a short dive.

"I'll be working with Audrey," Patsy said. "But I want you to know I haven't taken a personal interest in the case."

"I don't believe you," I said. "But if you haven't I wish you would. People without an opinion scare the hell out of me."

"You'd rather have an enemy than a disinterested party?"

"Yup." I sat on the couch and waited for one of them to continue, but neither did. Obviously I was the most uncomfortable one there, and displayed it by breaking the silence. "Sorry about the adopted crack," I said. "Audrey, I never knew you had a daughter, or even that you had been married."

"I never was married."

"That right."

"I'll be honest with you."

"The honesty again."

"Patsy's here for a reason."

"Figured."

"I don't altogether trust you — Let me finish! This is a big one, Jack. I don't need my past thrown around."

"Beautiful," I said. It was hard to keep from staring at Patsy

Jillian. "You think having an illegitimate daughter will hurt your cause. What decade do you think we're in?" Adopting my most tendentious tone, I continued. "There are conclusions to be drawn from this."

I held up a forefinger. "Overestimation of importance. If my little band can't sway opinion, then yours can't either. None of us is all that important to these people. If they don't build the bridge here, then they connect somewhere else. You're down on the food chain with me, Audrey."

Another finger went up. "Underestimation of the enemy. They are your enemies, and they don't care about you. They are stronger and better equipped than any of us. Do you think for a minute that once the connection to the mainland is complete they will happily leave the town to its own devices? They are out to make money. Money, money, money. Hell, you might even be out of a job. Add a few hundred people who settle here because of easy access, and if they vote their own way you could be down with Shaky Shelby bumming quarters in the bus station shitter."

A third finger joined its buddies. "Argument from afflatus —"

"You're insane," Audrey said. "Quit with the speech."

"I'm winding down."

"Make it quick."

"Argument from afflatus. You are not head of the Security Council at the UN. Who could care less if the mayor of a dopey town like this got left with a bundle? That kind of thing is pandemic in small towns."

"But the town —"

"An illegitimate daughter won't swing the town against you."

"In the right hands ... "

"Whose hands?" I said. "Not mine. And I doubt the government and the contractors are about to hire a gumshoe to probe your background."

"They have."

"Eh?"

"They have."

I checked with Patsy and got a pair of raised eyebrows and a nod. "Get outta here," I said.

"Three months ago," Patsy said. "And it was suggested in strong terms that I lay low."

"See? See the kind of motherfuckers we're dealing with?"

Nothing could have been designed to stir me up like this. It made it nearly impossible to think of Audrey as the opposition. She was family, of a type, and whether through loyalty or some cleaving to the hive, I felt the common good must be advanced. "Did they actually threaten you?" I asked.

Patsy was quiet awhile, then hesitantly said, "Not threaten actually. But I felt threatened. Do you know what I mean?"

I nodded and got up and banged another scotch in my glass. The sound of my drink going down was unnaturally loud.

"I want you to know it all," Audrey said.

"I told you I don't care."

"Sedro's her father."

I started laughing. Laughing and hooting and slowly parading around the room, touching the walls and lifting objects.

"That's the limit," I said. "Audrey, you got me on that one. I didn't think anything could surprise me, but that just did it with earflaps."

"What do you think now?"

"I really don't know what to think."

"You don't seem too upset."

I stopped and stared at her then at Patsy and back to Audrey.

"You never really approved of me," Audrey said.

"Look at you," I said. "Sitting there all shy and troubled and scared. You just made me like you a little more."

She looked at me as if I were on the verge of a fit.

"Approval!" I snorted. "What does that mean? I never got it growing up, you never got it from me, you never gave it to Sedro from what I remember. He left fifteen years ago — what did I know at sixteen? No, I didn't approve of you, but how much of that was a kid's hurt feelings? I guess I felt you were usurping my time with him."

"You haven't had much to do with me since."

"We travel in different circles. I don't like a lot of your ideas and we compete and you bug my ass most days. We've never gone much beyond that. You and Sedro, eh? Too much."

"Here I am," Patsy said. "Stuck in the middle."

"Not stuck anywhere," I said. "Want a drink?"

"Pour us all one," Audrey said, and she looked so relieved and suddenly so young I started laughing again. I poured the drinks and lit a cigarette and felt good.

"Do you know what a *cucumaria miniata* is?" I asked Patsy.

"Sorry."

"Species of sea cucumber found on the open coast of the Island, and you can find them at low tide in Puget Sound."

"Yes?"

"Nothing," I said. "Just that Sedro knew. He knew everything."

"Unimportant things," Audrey said. She no longer looked young or relieved.

"Important to him," I countered.

"Where were his human concerns?" Her face had fallen. "Look at us — his detritus. He discarded the three most important people in his life. So I don't care how much he knows about cucumparists or whatever. He was wrong. He lied and he left and he lied to himself by never coming back."

"I have to forgive him," I said. "I don't know his reasons, but until I know for sure that I won't ever do what he did I have to forgive him. And I'll never reach that level of certainty. It can't be done."

"You said you *have* to forgive him," Audrey said. "You didn't say whether you *do* forgive him."

"Same thing," I said.

"It certainly is not."

"In any event," I said. "We may get to hash it out at close quarters. I'm leaving in a couple days to go get him." Shocked reactions tickle me no end.

"You're not," Audrey said.

"Patsy's here to help you," I said. "I see some kind of warped ironic justice about the whole thing."

"He won't come," Audrey said.

"He will. I feel it."

"If he does it will only help our cause. The town won't forgive him for running out even if you do."

"And they won't forget that you rode into the mayor's job on his coattails."

"I've had this office since he left," she said. "I earned the position."

"Yeah," I said. "Like Eva fucking Peron."

"And I thought you were softening."

"I know," I said. "My wife tells me I'm getting nasty. Probably all the red meat.

S E V E N

As I trundled through the town, noting the silent ranks of gladioli and tulips along the Main Street boulevards, acknowledging the waves of friends, squinting at the peaks that with cupped hands offered up the glacier for inspection, I pondered the profound impact one person can have on an individual's life. Sedro's influence should have faded with his departure, yet here was Patsy Jillian — and Audrey Weeks, for that matter — casting me directly into the path of his legacy.

Could he not leave me alone? More accurately, could I not escape? My early goals of flight and fancy should have carried me clear of the carnage. I should be sailing the Indian Ocean on a research vessel, or examining the results of pollution at the mouth of the Orinoco, or doing anything other than the prosaic business of running a hardware store in the same town, with the same friends, in the same environment as my youth.

In those days the pairing of Sedro and Audrey hadn't seemed logical, not that logic has anything to do with it. I freely admitted there was a lot about love that eluded me. At sixteen categorizing the things around me was of paramount importance, coinciding with unsettling flashes that it might be impossible to do so. I kept trying, but conviction has a way of branching into new conflicts. And I had nothing if not conviction.

And conflicts.

But Audrey and Sedro — I couldn't figure. She seemed to be all right in a general way, though through the eyes of a teenager she was particularly uninteresting. She shared little of Sedro's appetite for discovery, and of course that was bizarre, but I think what disturbed me most about Audrey was that she seemed incapable of pleasure. She was not mean-spirited, but she was a hard woman who shunned spontaneity and clung stubbornly to a lifestyle that was unrewarding in simple mirth.

What I held against her was that she managed to strip Sedro's certitude. The old man had all the answers, in my book. Lord of the tidal flats, master of the forests, purveyor of history and philosophy, and Merlin of the teenage id. But be damned if he could explain his attraction to Audrey.

He could expound on love with the same certainty with which he lectured on natural history. He was decisive enough when it came to advising me on my nascent stirrings, and he knew more than an old-world matchmaker about the relationships of the people we knew. But he did a lot of staring when he talked about Audrey. His sentences came in jerks and starts.

"I think it's something that defies explanation," he said one day, the first time he had ever uttered words of such evil portent.

I kept my distance from Audrey, for anyone with the knowledge of how to confuse Sedro had to be dabbling in voodoo. Taxonomy was more my speed — it provided neat labels I could slap on the creatures of low tide or of the forest. Even the creatures with the power to do me harm had a name, were recognizable. This love shit was the monster in the closet, the kind only covers over the head can keep at bay.

Which more or less leads me to the lowdown on my folks. Their characterization in my mind came to an abrupt halt that summer. I tried to label them as I did everything else, but it was a mug's game. I did it easily enough, but then I'd have to answer for my smug intolerance and rip off the labels. I wasted a great deal of energy switching my appraisal back and forth in this way, never realizing that I shouldn't have been labeling them at all.

Whether it was genetics or environment that had the upper hand in pushing my father down the shitslide, I don't know. His parents came from an up-Island town similar to Salish Spit and he never talked about them. I think of his problems as stemming from rigidity. A small bullet-headed man who gave no one a break and never received one, living a marginal life beyond the pale of happiness, fighting the world while occupying the space it provided.

His periods of unemployment were such crushing indignities that he felt the pursuit of a job only called attention to the idle times, so he would give up and lapse into episodes of brooding malevolence. I can see him sitting on our old brocade maroon couch with the strips of wood on top of the arms, glaring and unspeaking. His sullen black moods tore him apart, for even to these he wouldn't yield, just brood and play with his work gloves. Play with the gloves and speak lowly so Mum or I had to ask him to repeat himself, giving him an excuse to hurl the gloves and slam out the door.

For years he never hit my mother or me, and even this seemed a calculated ploy, as if by giving us the back of his hand our presence would be ratified. Rather, he would leave for days at a time in cathartic flight.

He drank a lot. Oddly enough the alcohol did not deepen his despair, seemed instead to release him from his violent moods and provide him with a brief roseate view of his lot. He would bring cronies home from the pub at closing time and my mum would drag herself from bed to prepare a feed for them. She enjoyed this, for the more humane of his pals would praise her lavishly and even my father would thank her, though later his drunken state would prompt displays of affection that would chase my mum back upstairs and leave him prostrate in the kitchen or out on the porch.

But his bitterness burst out one day. When not steeped in silent self-loathing he became inchoate with hate and struck out with fists and boots at my mother and me and the furniture.

A number of people in the Valley thought him genuinely insane and I guess we'll never know for sure. I never loved him, though I pitied him so deeply I would have done anything in my power for him. But I never knew what to do and he never let me try. If he had lived till I was a man I might have been able to help, if I had still wanted to.

But Sedro shot him.

After the funeral there was a small bunch back at the house and the prevailing if unspoken sentiment was one of relief for me and Mum. But I wasn't all that relieved. My father had been a heavy pack on my back, and although the burden had been removed I had had no hand in its removal. I wanted him gone but I also wanted him solved.

My mother died two years later when I was on the ferry, going off to university on the mainland, and she died still missing my father. Mum was a simple woman, untouched by any of the movements urging independence and individual rights, untouched even by plain ambition to get the hell someplace where she could be happy. She took a fatalistic view of the world and never said much about her perception of her place in it.

I felt sorry for her all my life, but looking back I sense her resentment of that very concern. Acceptance was her strength, and she embraced it as her cardinal virtue.

Strange, that I should stand here today feeling less affected by the love of an unworldly woman who was concerned only with me and with survival than I do by the abuse of a mad, miserable human being like my father. But I guess it takes too much painful self-analysis to remember what was sad. It's always the serious scar tissue that hits like a hammerblow.

I didn't attend Sedro's trial, couldn't. Besides, the tsunami was felt charging up the bay and right through the town. Eagle desperately wanted to go but stayed with me in Salish Spit.

They said my father was hunting illegally, which was probably true enough. They said Sedro was sighting his rifle and accidentally smacked a .303 round into my father's forehead. My old man's vicious character was promenaded — by the prosecution trying to show motive, and by the defense to establish some sort of misguided Tolstoyan sense of retribution, though Sedro had no part in that. By all accounts he had no part in anything, sitting stoically throughout the trial, testifying without his usual volubility, accepting the verdict with no sense of triumph.

About a month after the trial, with Sedro long gone, Eagle and I broke into his cabin. It was damp and musty. His dog was nowhere around. We drank a little bit of Plainsman Rye and I spent a long time running my hands over the spines of his books and looking through the stacks of leaves he had pressed and sealed in acetate. We went outside and sat on the porch awhile, looking out at the bay, at the spit and the water and the straggling line of kelp marking high tide.

Then we carefully shuttered the windows and locked the door and left.

I drove past the access road to the house, letting my thoughts rattle along with the machinery of the '66 Merc, and eventually pulled into the parking lot of the Fanny Bay Inn. I was of no mind to go inside and share my time with the regulars, so I sat in the truck with the window open and smoked a cigarette, staring sightlessly at the front door as people came and went in slow motion.

Nothing seemed to be working these days, except the truck, so I started it and headed back on the winding Island highway. I pulled into the gravel driveway and got out and went inside the house.

With all its welter of collectibles, the place yet managed to feel roomy. Haida art and Mexican jugs and African masks and baskets, but plenty of space, elbow room to fry up a big mess of eggs or slaughter a few dance steps or punctuate a story with wild gesticulations. Tatamis protected the floor from the sand and the forest duff that was impossible to keep from tracking in from the surrounding acre of scrub wood and broom and beach grass. We were thirty yards from the shore, but winter storms would bang water, wood and kelp into our yard, even depositing its flotsam under the dog run. That was my idea, the dog run, and Elizabeth hated it, having to traverse twenty feet of open veranda to get from the bedrooms to the main part of the house. I regularly did it naked, sending her into brief seizures.

I built a fire in the big old stone fireplace, using the discarded committee notes to light the kindling.

I considered going to open up the store, but once again it was too late in the day. One of the reasons I was unconcerned about losing it to the Big Project was that it made me no money. I was always off on some seashore foray, or climbing to the glacier or occupying my position on a stool at the Square Rigger. I never posted a sign to indicate whether the place was open or closed, so oftentimes it was only Snuffy wandering around and pitching shoes that gave it a fragile edge over a condemned building.

People would wave at Snuffy, take what they needed to fix a toilet or patch some drywall or string a fence, and leave payment on the counter. Then it depended on which event occurred first: Snuffy going inside and seeing it there, in which case he dumped it into a paper bag; or Eagle coming by and seeing it there, in which case I was left with no more than twenty bucks. Were it not for the blind loyalty akin to a small town's patience with a useless but familiar doctor, the place would have come crashing down around my ears a long time ago.

I stretched out on the couch and picked up a back issue of *Scientific American* from the coffee table. I heard the door swing and Elizabeth came in with three bags of groceries. Without a word she began tossing the contents into the fridge and the cupboards. When she finished she came to the entrance to the living room, the boundary established by a cotton runner and three blooming clivia, as there was no formal demarcation of rooms in the rambling main area.

"Will you look at this place," she said.

The article on genetic engineering was demanding more concentration than Elizabeth would allow. I had read the same paragraph four times. I dropped the magazine on the floor and gave her my attention.

"Will you just look at it."

I glanced around. "Looks familiar, all right," I said. "Weren't we at a party here once?"

"It's a dump."

"I like it."

Elizabeth growled. Her assaults on the house were episodic and predictable. It had been seven years now, so she had trouble coming up with fresh observations on the place. The furnishings

were so insulting that they failed to register without elaborate
scrutiny.

The three bedrooms, the kitchen and the bathroom were
hers to decorate, but I held sway over the main room and of
course the lab. Not much of a lab — an addition out back that
held my collection of minerals and fossils, part of my library
and whatever it was at the time that most interested me. I had
been lazy lately so the only projects were a bed of ferns I was
growing hydroponically and a clutch of snake eggs I was trying
to hatch in a terrarium.

"It's too … too *heavy* in here."

"It ain't heavy, it's my —"

"What we need is something contemporary," she said. "That
Swedish furniture would be perfect. There's a sale on now. We
could pick it up cheap and assemble it ourselves."

"It's called contemporary furniture because it doesn't last
long enough to become traditional."

She shook her head. "That's what I mean about you."

"What?"

"You know."

"Oh," I said. "That."

"Yes, that."

"I don't know what the hell you're talking about."

"There — that's what I mean."

"*What?*"

"Jesus, Jack."

I went to the window and looked out at the beach. It was lightly raining, that senseless orographic patter. The broom bushes were losing their little yellow blooms. Without them the bushes were more weed than anything, but I liked them. If the West Coast hadn't much of a non-native history, at least the imported flora indicated discovery on some level. Not much to brag about, but I liked the specks of yellow the bushes cast up in the spring.

I could see Elizabeth's reflection in the window and it was pretty magnificent. Bulky sweater over khaki shorts, wide hips and smooth legs, her anger making her vital and vibrant. A Kwakiutl mask on the wall grinned at me from over her shoulder.

"I guess we could get something new," I said.

"Really?"

I turned back to her and she smiled. "Maybe next week," I said. "I'm heading up to see Sedro tomorrow."

"It's important to you, isn't it?"

"Yes, darling, it is."

"How long will you be gone?"

"Couple, three days," I said. "If I can't settle things and convince him in the first hour I might just as well head on back."

"Will I like him?" she asked. "I'm afraid to meet him."

"So am I," I said. "Petrified, if you want the truth."

"But you have to."

"I have to."

"Do you think he'll be able to help?"

"Hope so."

"You don't feel too good about the way things are going."

"I can't help feeling responsible if the bridge comes in. I should be doing more. Audrey tried to throw me out of her office today. She said I had no new arguments and she's right. I'm acting on gut feel on this one. The bridge will help in the short run and that's the way I've always punched through. Solve what's staring you in the face, then press on. Yet here I am thinking of the future. Me! Funny, eh?"

Elizabeth came over and kissed me and we held each other. "If it's any consolation, Audrey didn't have much time for Donna and me, either. She can be intimidating."

"Who knows."

Elizabeth let go of me and went to the kitchen, and while she puttered around making something to eat I stood out on the dog run smoking a cigarette.

I had to grant her the courage of her convictions. For the first five years of our marriage she had been a management consultant in the Valley, but when the management fled so did the consulting. So what she had left was her craft classes and a husband who had abandoned all but a pretense of a career. The bridge coming in could hand her back a position of responsibility, so to take arms against the proposal showed a lot of strength.

She called me inside and we sat at the coffee table. She poured two mugs of some turgid health drink while I bit into a hot dog. Back out it came.

"What the hell?" I said.

"It's a hot dog."

I probed into the bun and held the wiener aloft. "What newt gave his life for this?"

"It's tofu," she said.

"Tofu."

"Tofu wieners. They're healthy."

"What would possess any rational human being to use soybean extract to make a wiener?" I asked. "I eat meat, and I don't stay up at night carving a turkey to look like a turnip."

"Nasty, Jack."

"You force your ideas on me as if I were helpless."

I don't know when it changed. Initially Elizabeth's critiques of my behavior and my approach to life I had considered the natural fallout of her concern for my well-being. She was heavy-handed, to be sure, but the fact that she was usually right helped mitigate the broadsides. But somehow, over time, the roles had been reversed. Now I was the one taking exception to everything she did, and my criticisms were based far less on substance than on impatience. Faults are part of the fabric of love that should warm you, but lately I was spending all my time kicking off the blankets.

"Before you launch into a tirade," she said, "let me show you something."

While she went to the bedroom I ate six plain hot dog buns. She returned smiling.

"When's our anniversary?" she asked. She was standing in front of me, her hands held coyly behind her back.

"It was two months ago," I said. "The eighteenth."

"Right."

"So?"

"So I got you a card."

"Uh, thanks, but ..."

"I got two, actually. I couldn't decide which one you'd like more."

"Okay."

"This one," she said and held up a card in her left hand.

"I like it, I really do." It was a sleigh scene that looked like a Christmas card.

"Or this one," she said, reversing hands.

"I like that one, too." It was a picture of a fly fisherman in full extension.

"I wrote a poem and put it in both of them," she said.

"That is thoughtful."

"I know it's late," she said. "But I had trouble rhyming some of the lines."

"Better late than never," I said helpfully.

"Which one do you like better?" Both cards came out, bracketing her smile.

"Uh … that one," I said, pointing at the fisherman.

"I thought you said you liked this one." She waggled the Christmas card and the sleigh bells jingled.

"I do like that one."

"Then why did you pick this one?" The fisherman danced.

"Because you asked me to pick. I like that one and I like that one, but you asked me which one I liked more and I said that one."

"You think I have poor taste, don't you?"

"Your taste is impeccable. Look at those corduroy swim trunks you bought me last year. I wear those with unbridled pride. I like both cards and the sentiment is touching but you asked me to pick between the two and I picked that one."

"I just want to know what's wrong with this one," she said. The sleigh horse was starting to sag in its traces.

"There's nothing wrong with it. I almost pissed myself with pleasure when you first held it up. If it were up to me I'd frame both of them and send the poem to a literary magazine. But you asked me for a decision and I picked that one. Now gimme it before I wad both of them into my shotgun and blow them across the fucking bay!"

"God, you're nasty," she said. "You should have eaten those wieners." Crying, she ran to the bedroom.

I sat very still while considering a leap into the fire. A while later I picked up the dishes and threw them off the dog run into the broom bushes. Back inside I squashed a ballcap on my head and was putting on a jacket when Elizabeth came in from the bedroom.

"Darling," I said. "I'm sorry."

Nothing.

"I'm to blame."

"I agree."

"I have to go down to the pub to tell the guys what happened with Audrey today."

"How late will you be?"

"I have no idea."

"Phone if you're going to be late."

"No."

"Why don't you ever call? Is it too much trouble to perform the simple courtesy of phoning if you plan to be late?"

"I want to cut the arguments in half," I said.

"What's that supposed to mean?"

"If I come in late we fight," I said.

"I know that only too well."

"If I call we fight over the phone. Then when I come in late we fight again. A fifty percent reduction in gunfire is worth skipping the call."

"God damn you," she said.

"I'm sure it's crossed his mind."

The rain helped. It pattered and dripped off the peak of my cap and hissed as it settled on the chuck. It was about three miles to the pub if I took the shore the first part of the way. Just as the house disappeared the spit came into view. Along with the glacier it gave the town its geographical identity. A long, curving comma of rock and sand, slightly gibbous at the base then tapering and slicing like a fadeaway half a mile out into the Straits. Heaped volcanic rocks decorated with bladder kelp and eelgrass, barnacle-speckled, home to oysters and bay mussels, at high tide a jumbled, barely submerged highway, at low tide a mountain range in miniature clasped by undulating striations of sand. Dark sand, volcanic, that burns your bare feet when the sun's been on it.

Up and over the spit I scrambled, close to the shore. The heels on my cowboy boots didn't help as I climbed up across and down, slipping and scraping my hands and my shins. On the northwest side was the bay, the tidal flats Sedro and I used to prowl. I followed the concavity of the shoreline and passed his old cabin, slack and senile. A quarter mile farther I cut inland through the salt grasses and plantains and climbed the embankment.

New world at the top. A fairly level field that had been cut from the bush years ago. The wind was always stronger up here. The tang of the conifers took over from the pungent stink of decaying kelp. I was across the field and into the first line of trees, bald eagle roosts far above in the snags. Just me and what rain filtered through the canopy, then I was over the ditch and onto the shoulder of the tarmac road leading to town.

Passed up two ride offers, cut right at the main intersection and crunched up the oyster-shell driveway to the Square Rigger.

N I N E

B edlam!
    To the left a grand-scale argument at the pool table. Salish
Spit residents play pool like soldiers play poker — rules invented
on the spot, a barrage of interpretations. From the jukebox Jimmy
Buffett was crashing out "Livingstone Saturday Night." Dale
James was playing shuffleboard with a small, scruffy man who
kept yanking him back by the belt, but Dale kept playing as if
this were part of the game, flinging the rocks into the gutters and
looking confused at his inaccuracy. In the far corner a bucket
brigade, being fed by an arm through one of the windows, was
passing cordwood along to the fireplace. It was already three
hundred degrees in the place, so the smoke in the air might have
come from jeans and jackets spontaneously combusting rather
than from the cigarettes and the fire. I counted four separate
groups in softball uniforms, and from the way one team tiptoed

back and forth to the bar on the tile floor, it was clear they had left their spikes on. Trays held high, the waitresses were invisible as they snaked through the crowd at the bar and around the tables. I folded my cap and stuck it in my jacket pocket.

"Jack!" I saw Eagle ice-breaking his way through the mob.

"Your fly's open," I said when he reached me.

He waved his hand. "No time, no time," he said. He thrust his big yap close to my nose. "It's turning into one hell of a night."

"So I see."

"Well, let's get you a beer. I got good news." He started chucking people left and right and I followed his blocking to the bar. "Don, give us a couple, will you? And get anybody else what they want. Keep that tab going."

I couldn't see Don past Eagle's back but the beer came promptly. I raised my mug. "Cheers."

"Lots of them," Eagle said.

"How did you talk Don into running you a tab?" I asked. "You win the lottery?"

"Yup."

"Get away."

"Found out this morning," he said. "Ticket I picked up last week, found her in my pants when I was cleaning up. Maybe my luck's changing."

"No maybe about it. What did it come to?"

"Four hundred and something."

"Four hundred?"

"Had to share it with thirty-six guys got the same numbers."

"Oh, well," I said. "It's free money."

"Don't let that fuckboat Don know, but I only got about eighty bucks left."

"That'll disappear quick with the tab you have going."

"Oh, I must be through her by now," Eagle said. "We been in here since eleven this morning."

"He'll kill you."

"Naw — I didn't blow the four hundred. I invested it all. Soon as I make my profit I'll pay up the tab."

"What did you invest in?"

"Pope stuff," Eagle said.

"Pope stuff?"

"You know, when the Pope come over to Vancouver a few years ago. Guy from Burnaby has a cottage north of here. Sold me all sorts of shit. Hats, T-shirts, dashboard Popes. You can mark stuff like that up two, three hundred percent. I'll kill. Must be millions of religious fanatics on the Island couldn't get over to the mainland to see him."

"Beautiful, Eagle."

"Yeah." He was stunned by the sublimity of the project.

"So that's the good news," I said.

"More than that."

"Do up your fly."

"No time, no time," he said and plowed away through the crowd.

I watched him go. I loved the man, but around Eagle love was a parlous topic. He had made one mistake in his life, so he claimed. He fell in love with a married woman. Oh, he screwed a lot of wedded lasses to be sure, for there was no category of woman exempt from his bed. But this was love, it was real. Her name was Jean. They met by chance on a job site when Eagle was working for the lumber company for which Jean did secretarial and purchasing work. The affair progressed rapidly and the intensity of their passion bowled me over the few times we were together.

It was a Sunday. Elizabeth was with a friend, Hammerhead Bernice, in Vancouver for the Labor Day long weekend. I was feet-upping it in the living room when Eagle, slogging up from the beach, appeared in the picture window. It was a wild man I let in and poured a drink for. He was encrusted with salt and sand and dirt. He took the bottle and threw the cap behind the stereo.

"You look like you were raised by goats," I said.

His hair was sticking up everywhere except on the left side, where it was matted down, blending into his beard, which was festooned with windblown debris. His shirt was open to the waist and he was wet from the knees down. A long scratch on his right arm was tentatively leaking blood. His hands were black and he smelled like Sam Riley's St. Bernard.

"Wow," he said.

I waited.

"I kicked her out."

"Yeah?"

"Yeah."

He drank. "I love her," he said.

"Yeah?"

"Yeah."

I drank.

"She loves me."

"Then what's the problem?"

"The problem? You want to know what the problem is?"

"Yeah."

"I'll tell you what the problem is. What it is is that ... awww ... "

We both drank. Eagle dug in his tin and stuck a pinch of snoose in his yap.

"The problem is ... the thing — you know."

"Yeah."

"Okay. Let's say she hated him ... or didn't love him, anyway, even if she didn't exactly hate him."

"All right."

"But she does. I mean, she doesn't. Doesn't hate him.

Doesn't … or does, I mean. Does love him."

"She loves two men at the same time," I said. "You and her husband. It can happen. It does happen."

"Right. Okay. And let's say she loves me more. Or is *in* love with me more."

"Yeah."

"But maybe it's because she … or I'm new, you know? Like, she loves this guy — they been married fifteen years — but wants to be with me. We're more suited, I mean. We got so much in common and we're friends and shit and it's great in bed and just … better. Better, yeah."

"It's better with you."

"That's right. So it's better. But how much better does it have to be before you leave someone you've spent fifteen years married to? She's comfortable, well taken care of and her husband — there, I've said it — her husband loves her. Really loves her. Like the guy — her husband — needs her in his life, needs her. Maybe he's not like you and me, we can keep going no matter what, press on, like you always say. But maybe he can't. Maybe the poor bastard falls apart, she leaves him. And I'm the motherfucker that did it to him."

"The last time I talked to Jean she told me she was unsatisfied with her marriage," I said. "Unfulfilled if not unhappy. That says to me she'd eventually leave the man in any case. Why beat yourself up?"

"She wouldn't leave him now," he said. "If she hadn't met me she wouldn't leave him *now*."

"You can't plan on love," I said. "You can't hang around waiting for her to leave and snatch her up then."

"But wait. Okay. She's got two kids."

"I know."

"Now the kids have a good home. Well provided for, good mum and good dad."

"Mmm."

"So if … I mean she can't take them right away."

"Eh?"

"I can't keep them. Hey, I got no money coming in right now, I got a little dump of a place with hardly room for the two of us, never mind four. I want them. I want the kids to … I think it's important for kids to be with their mothers. I know, 'cause I didn't have one."

"So move into a bigger place sometime down the road."

"But that's sorta like sticking the guy with the kids in the meantime. I'm taking his wife and running, I do it like that."

"Does her husband know about you?"

"Shit, yes. He guessed and she told him and then she said she's moving out, even if it's on her own for a while. Jesus, Jack, what am I going to do if I have to see him face to face? I mean, he's just a skinny little guy and I'm going to have to let him get the first few licks in but I can't keep my hands in my pockets the whole time."

"Avoid him for the time being," I said. "And I think it's a good idea, her moving out on her own. She'll need a period of adjustment to assess the situation. There's too much emotion between you two, or three, to be able to come to any rational decision."

"She doesn't have the money to move into a place of her own. And she'd have to keep going back home to help with the kids and to keep close with them, right? And every other minute of her time we'd be together, so she might as well move in with me right off the bat. Even if she spends lots of time back home. Then she'd be living in two places, sort of, instead of three. Plus that'd help us figure out if things'll work between us."

"You have doubts about that?"

"The normal ones. But I know it'll work. It's too good. Except what if it doesn't? Then I've busted up a marriage and the end of it is that five people go through all this and nobody gets what they want. I feel guilty, Jean's high and dry, the kids got their parents split up and the husband's left sucking hind tit. So what then?"

"Would that be any worse than dropping the whole thing?" I asked. "This isn't a fling. So she stays with him and still loves you and everyone marinates so long in frustration it destroys your lives anyhow. Besides, you're talking worst case. What if you and Jean click like you think you will? And she still spends time with the kids, and they get to know you, and eventually you all make a decision about who lives with whom?"

"Her husband still gets the shaft," he said.

"This must be the real one," I said. "You don't exactly have a great track record for giving a shit about injured third parties."

"Right on both counts."

"It's too late, man. The problem is *in situ*. Someone's going to get it."

"I caused it."

"This may be a cliché, but life's not easy. If you can't work with the big guys don't pick up a hammer."

"That's real helpful, Jack, you fuckboat."

I shrugged and went out to the kitchen to get ice. The bottle of Plainsman Rye gurgled as Eagle made sounds of anguish back in the living room. I returned with the ice and stood looking at my friend. Poor bugger, sitting there as if he had been mauled by a silvertip.

"You said off the top that you kicked her out," I said and sat back down in the wing chair.

"Did the honorable thing," he said. His great shaggy head was bobbing and weaving. "Told her how I felt then sent her back home. She belongs there."

"No," I said. "No, she doesn't. She won't stay. She needs more, and nothing is more powerful than a person who awakens to possibilities. One day she'll leave — for someone else or just on her own."

Eagle ponderously rose to his feet. He stuck his thumb up his nose and probed around a bit. He spit snoose on the area rug at his feet. "Get your boots on," he commanded.

"I'm not going anywhere."

"Ain't been to the glacier since I was a kid," he said. "Want to see why you keep climbing up there."

"You're piss drunk," I said. "You'd never —"

The look on his face did it. I retrieved my boots and followed the sad giant out the door.

We hashed the subject to death for the first part, but as Eagle labored ahead of me up the mountain we grew silent. It was late afternoon when we reached the terminal moraine and stood in hushed reverence. Didn't stay long. The glacier stared Eagle down. He was frozen with buck fever, and when he broke the mood it was to shove past me and start back down.

Sad part was, I was right. Jean did leave her husband, fleeing for Toronto, now doing Christ knows what with Christ knows whom, and Eagle had never gotten over her.

Although usually it was hard to tell.

I filled his wake and elbowed my way to the bar. Robert was two stools down, dragging on his pipe and talking to Don as the owner pulled the taps on a parade of mugs. Robert's hunted look was barely in evidence, submerged by the energy in the room. He was telling Don some story the bartender wasn't interested in. When he saw me he paused.

"Jack," he said with a nod. "Did you hear about Eagle's good luck?"

"Just now," I said.

"How much do you think he won? He won't tell us."

"Didn't tell me, either, but he's celebrating up a storm so it must be substantial."

Snuffy squeezed in behind Don and dumped a double handful of lime slices into a bowl. "Hi, Jack," he said.

"Hey, Snuffy, you old ape."

"Old ape, he says! You kill me, Jack."

"How are you?"

"Great! Eagle won a bunch of money today."

"I heard."

"And you know what? He said he's going to buy me a boat. A rowboat, he says, cause they're good and safe and he'll teach me how to work the oars and everything."

"That's super, Snuffs."

"A boat. Lots of guys around here have boats. Remember when we went out last year on that boat? Right out on the water. Boats are great."

"What a guy," Robert said. He leaned forward to see me better. "He's going to pay for the new fence around my outbuildings and buy me that horse trailer I need."

"He sure is something," Don said, slapping mugs of beer on the bar. "He's flat out giving me the cash to expand the brewery out back. You can't help loving a guy like that."

"You can't," I said.

"His good fortune will affect us all," Robert said. "He's planning to fund a huge campaign to stop the bridge coming in."

"The meeting's next week," I said.

"We were supposed to have three more weeks!" Don screeched.

"Audrey moved it up," I said. "That's what I came here to tell you."

"We'll just have to push like hell," Robert said. "Eagle's talking about a van with a loudspeaker, posters, TV and radio ads, the works, just as soon as he picks up his cheque. I think I'll go over and see the look on her face."

"Where?" I said, whipping around.

Over by the far bay window Audrey Weeks and her daughter were sitting at one of the round spruce tables. Patsy Jillian was in profile, leaning back in her chair, away from Eagle, who was standing and roaring and waving his mug, a huge shaggy-beast slopping beer in scything swoops of his arms. I could see Audrey's face under his hairy hand. The tables around the mayor's were packed with people delighted or shocked with the floor show. Eagle stretched his arms up over his head and screamed at the firmament, petitioning some higher authority or, with the shape he was in, merely addressing the cedar planks of the ceiling. When he realized the extent of his audience he pirouetted and the ceiling fan caught his mug, flinging it into the middle of Audrey's table.

I had allowed myself the luxury of flight too often lately, so I grabbed a mug at random from the bar and went to intercede, though on whose behalf I didn't yet know.

Dale James was digging his shuffleboard rocks out of the wax in the gutters. A bearded softball player skated along the tiles on cleated feet while his teammates pelted him with ice cubes and lemon wedges. A few friendly voices tried to penetrate the din as I passed. Denise, a waitress recently arrived from Victoria, had consumed her daily ration of homegrown, which had joined hands with her defective brain, prompting her to grab the crotch of anyone handy. As she snaked her hand out to me I tipped her back into the bearded softball player, who went to ground in a death spiral of spikes and uniform.

"Eagle!" I yelled. "Eagle!"

The big idiot was pointing at the ceiling fan and screaming something about the Pope's intervention. I grabbed his arm and spun him around and he tripped and sat down flush on Patsy Jillian's lap. She squirted out of her chair and sprawled on the floor. I helped her to a new seat.

"Eagle has been painting the big picture for us," Audrey said after I nodded hello. "Using an enormous canvas." She was dressed in a Johnny Carson ensemble.

Eagle hadn't heard. He was gasping in his chair, pretty far gone.

"What are you doing here?" I said. "I've never known you to slum like this, Audrey. Campaign tour? Press the flesh, kiss a brat?"

"Don't start on me," she said. "There's nothing barring me entrance to the lounge."

"Lounge."

"I thought it was time to experience public opinion first hand. I've been lax in that area of late."

"So you have."

"So I have," she said, and I liked her for that.

Eagle leaned back and choked on his saliva. The coughing broke loose the lining of his recently shattered nose and he began to bleed copiously. Audrey ignored him.

I apologized for everything to Patsy, maybe because she deserved it, maybe because she looked so sensational in her attempt to appear phlegmatic. Soft and firm with a little set to her mouth and I thought about oysters. She had tried to dress to fit the surroundings but had as much of a knack for it as her mother.

"Eagle doesn't know the big picture," I said to Audrey. "And that's nothing to aim for anyhow. All we're trying to do is keep pasting snapshots together."

Denise arrived to clean up and left in a swirl of mindlessness after doing nothing more than mix Eagle's blood and the spilled beer. In a grand gesture the bearded softball player spread his jacket over the table and clattered away after patting Eagle like a puppy. Eagle came to with a start.

"Jack!" he screamed, looking at Audrey. "Jack!"

"What?"

"Jack!"

"What is it?"

"Jack! Get my truck started right now. No more pussyfooting with pussies. Jack! We'll winch that fuckboat bridge out of its moorings. Jack! Tie up to the pilings and rip her out by the roots. Right into the chuck with the pisscutter. Jack!" He collapsed back onto the table, his ugly yap neatly covering the jacket's team crest.

Audrey smiled at me. "If, as you claim, I am in cahoots with my ministers, have the good grace to admit I am more adept than you at selecting them."

I had to laugh. Audrey was in a good mood and it wasn't going unappreciated. I was trying not to stare at her daughter, trying very hard. I was excited and flushed. Patsy Jillian had walked into my life and stuck a rolled-up newspaper down my throat. I didn't know what to say, so I grabbed a chair and back-straddled it with such an inflated air of confidence I'm sure my insecurity was on the table for all to examine.

The conversation was impersonal for a while, but at some point it shifted and damn me if it didn't feel as if the three of us — and our grounded Eagle — had planned the night out together. So long as the enemy remains faceless it is an exercise of little effort to hold them in contempt. But hey, you can't keep your bag in a knot when you're staring at the enemy across a table full of beer, blood and shaggyhead and the enemy is telling you about a vacation to Puerto Vallarta during which they were jobbed buying a blanket on the beach because the first time it got wet it fell to shreds, and the beer is flowing and softball players are recreating the seventh inning with a pool cue and a pair of underwear swaddled in elastic bands, and from the juke Tanya Tucker's telling you she don't know if they let cowboys into heaven but that Texas is as close anyhow so what the hell, and so much wood is jammed in the fireplace that it extends out onto the hearth and a few cedar ceiling planks get scorched.

Somewhere along the line I got to thinking about the first time I climbed to the glacier at night. I was about twenty and wanted to raise my glacier-hiking to a new level, so I waited till it was dark, the dead of night, a new challenge, with the moon quilted in cloud and the trees and the deadfall all feral and threatening, and when I made it and stood triumphant on the terminal moraine at its mouth, bleeding and tired, I waited for the surge of accomplishment. But it never came. I stayed there till morning and retraced my route, furtively making my way back home.

So you can never tell just how things will turn out.

All I know is that an hour after closing time I was in the storeroom and Patsy Jillian was on the floor in front of me, gripping the edge of the daybed, her ass upthrust, and I was behind her squeezing her tanned hips, heaving and shuddering. I pride myself on good judgment. Yes, I do. Then comes something like this. I swear, sometimes I drive myself fucking nuts.

T E N

It was something I had never done. Adultery in a general sense was not up there on my hierarchy of evils, but it was despicable where I was personally concerned. Because physical love is so linked with emotion — at least in my appreciation of the act — I had never considered cheating on my wife to be anything but low and foul. The ramifications were infinitely more important than a few moments of carnal release.

So what was I doing?

When a time of change is in the air, I tend to shy from careful scrutiny of the new conditions. Rather I prefer to clear the way for new growth by torching the forest. But fire adds unplanned-for variables to the equation, and is by nature impossible to control past a certain point. It's easy to start one, but when you have to call the men off the fireline and hope for rain and a change of wind you quickly realize you're not in charge anymore. This bit of domestic arson could very well torch my marriage, just as the firebug in me had initiated it.

From the time Elizabeth and I met I knew my old existence was close to extinction. It came to a head one day as I was sitting at my desk, sifting through papers and staring out the window at the dock that extended like a fragile Meccano toy out from the catwalk surrounding the institute.

Ronny Digs stopped by. I must have been on his mind for some time, as normally at work he would not acknowledge anyone. Ronny was all concentration, with an enviable capacity for detail, but only for what he deemed important. Personal concerns were seldom important.

"Get in," he said. "Get in and sit down."

I preceded him into his office, pulled up a chair and positioned myself amid the flea market of papers, instruments and junk that at first glance appeared unrelated but, taken as a whole, had a colligative personality of its own. Ronny followed me in, closed the door and waited for me to start.

I didn't.

"You look sick," he said.

He poured two weak coffees from a thermos. Out of his desk came a paper bag, and after picking through its contents he offered me half an egg-salad sandwich.

I shook my head and looked over his shoulder out the window at the dock and the larger wharf with the research vessels tied alongside. At the end of it one of the marine geologists was jigging for rock cod.

"I'm fine," I said.

"Middle of July and you have the complexion of Casper the Ghost."

"I found the perfect sunscreen," I said. "It's called Neighborhood Pub."

"I'm serious, Jack. You need a rest. Or a change of lifestyle."

"I'll get my rest," I said. "I'm pulling out."

"Old news," he said. "Ever since you arrived you've been sending out signals indicating this is all some sort of trial period."

"At first it was hedging. Now I mean it."

"What is it with you? You take seriously the things you should be shrugging off and piss around with anything of importance."

"Helps maintain balance."

"You have no balance. Everything is extreme in your view. Yes, no, black, white, share my last piece of bread, buy your own lunch."

"I gotta get outta here."

"We've covered that ground."

"This is the real one. I'm quitting, Ronny. Gone."

"What is it this time? The deal with SCO?"

"Nothing in particular. This time is in cahoots with all the other times. The institute's gotten too big, or I'm too small. There's no love left in it for me."

"Research is hard work. That's something you have to come to grips with."

"It's not the work and I don't *have* to do anything. I'm an amateur at heart. I like the romance of science and the learning and all that, but it's no fun anymore. The politics and the bureaucracy and the cutbacks and the internal bickering and what the hell I'm bored and don't want it. Head back to Salish Spit and cruise the tide pools and play some ball."

"You've published three papers."

"I'm bored."

"You're my top young guy."

"Bored, Ronny."

"You shouldn't have stopped fucking my daughter."

"I'm getting married."

"Idiot."

I slumped in my chair and shrugged.

"Marrying that woman won't cure your boredom," he said. "Add to it, more likely."

"I love her."

"She told me she likes you because you have a nice turn of phrase."

"So?"

"So she has no grasp of substance. Jesus, man, you can't marry someone who just likes the way you put things. Nice turn of phrase — there's the foundation for a successful marriage!"

"You don't know what you're talking about. Things'll be fine."

"She's in management, for god's sake."

"As you are."

"She wears sunglasses with a string that goes around her neck!"

Shrug.

"Her luggage has those tiny wheels on it."

Stare.

"She has personalized license plates."

Nothing.

"I caught her reading an abridged novel."

Light a smoke.

"She thinks red tide is an enzyme detergent!"

"Leave her alone."

"You know, West Point cadets are not allowed to marry till the end of their senior year."

"How deep did you reach to pull that out of your ass?"

"The point is, there's such a waiting list to get married in the college chapel they have silly bastards who book a date before they've even met the woman they want to marry. They're so scared to go alone into the real world that they latch onto anyone showing a pulse rather than have their asses shipped unattended to Fort fucking Dix."

"If forced to draw a lesson from that, I'll point out that I grew up in Salish Spit. It's no new world to me, and I'm not doing this out of fear."

"What a waste," Ronny said. "My top scientist going to Fort Dix with a woman who likes how he turns a phrase."

"Want to give me away?"

"I'll give you to the night nurse at the bughouse."

Elizabeth's decision to accept my proposal was a bit unsettling. Her past of ricocheting through life might have told me I was just another way stop before she spit off in a new direction.

She was born near Toronto to parents much too successful for anyone's good. Both were high-powered investment brokers, members of that class of delightfully rich people who get where they are on their own merits while producing not one goddamn thing that has any merit of its own. Pictures of Elizabeth as a child show clear signs of a youngster brought up by people determined to raise an heir, not a daughter: hair just so, clothing expensively tailored, always posed, no candid shots, nothing to suggest the glee of a child covered in mud and holding up a frog or clutching a puppy that's trying to lick the kid's face right off.

Different from my own, but a tough life nonetheless. Always under scrutiny, freedom a word that only applies to others, tossed around at election times or when reading an article on a Third World country. Sent to private schools and etiquette lessons while all the time living in a tacky monstrosity of a house in a pissant bedroom community where everyone gets into their car just to go get a quart of milk.

When she rebelled she spent a short period in Toronto, on Queen Street West, living a bohemian existence short of authentic due to her trust fund. But hell, she was trying. She was married for a time to an actor, by all accounts an evil little shit, who eventually found his calling at a dinner theatre in Houston, playing a gay civil engineer opposite a homophobic fireman in a minor extravaganza called "Don't Burn Your Bridges — At Least Not the Ones You Designed" that ran for five years to abysmal reviews and full houses.

The night of the wrap party she washed three peyote buttons down with a six of Lone Star and wound up in the penthouse apartment of a vice president of South Central Oil. A week later, after a scrubbing and a change of clothes, she was working as a minor headhunter for the company, putting her education and heritage to good use, if anything like that deserves the description, and eventually parlaying her position into a private management consulting operation with close ties to our man at SCO.

In essence she was following the path foreordained by her upbringing, but with the devil in her yet, a devil I put my arm around when we met at the press conference. Besides, who among us is unable to convince himself he could reform even an ax-murdering road whore, given half the chance? So I ignored our differences and proposed marriage and she accepted, leaving the vice president from SCO to figure it out as best he could.

I like to think I adapted well to Elizabeth and to marriage, but in light of our recent clashes perhaps it was just tolerance that eroded into tightlipped frustration.

But those early days were wonderful, so good that it made the present more terrifying. I didn't know who was hurting the most, but I knew for the moment who the son of a bitch was.

I was an adulterer now. Whether more plagued by the sense of its injustice or the fear of being discovered, I don't know. But it created conflict and that, as I've said, I abhor. Or revel in. I'm such a cesspool of opposing demons these days I can never get that one straight.

Ronny and I kept at my quitting the institute awhile, slapping the subject around till it was good and bruised. I would miss him, with the sense of emptiness that makes you both frown and smile when thinking back on a favorite teacher, a mentor.

I would also miss him on a personal level. I wasn't exactly cutting the ties, but I knew with time the rope would fray and part in the dark while neither one of us was looking.

Good guy, Ronny.

Patsy Jillian and I woke up on the daybed, twisted in clothing and sheets. Deep embarrassment effaced any attempt at normal conversation, and while she waited for a cab I farted around the store pretending to prepare for another day in the retail trade. I watched her go off in the taxi, then started the walk home, hoping that time would provide me with the courage that had been in such conspicuous absence the night before.

When I reached the house I jumped in the shower. Fifteen minutes of spray and half a bar of Irish Spring failed to convince me I was free of Patsy's scent. I wanted nothing more than to sandblast myself clean, but then to rush back to her and love her until her smell became part of mine.

I toweled off, grabbed the saddlebags from the porch and padded naked to the bedroom to pack. When Elizabeth came in I tensed.

"I wish you'd let me go with you at least as far as Vancouver," she said.

I dodged her embrace, using as an excuse my need to get on the road and cover some miles while it was still daylight. "I'm not stopping in Vancouver," I said.

"You just hate it because of the tunnel," Elizabeth said.

"Urbanites shouldn't have free access to Salish Spit. They'll bugger it up. You come from Toronto and Houston — you think Vancouver's like this place, a small lovable town."

"That's because I adapt, Jack. And you've never even been to Houston, so don't judge it."

"You know how they let blind people know when it's safe to cross an intersection down there? They have a guy across the street hold a cat up on a rope — the seeing eye dog bolts for it."

"Just drop it."

"Cities!" I snorted. "Artificial pieces of shit."

Was I starting a fight out of guilt? Oh, yes.

The saddlebags were packed and draped across the seat of my 900 Norton Commando. Long thermal underwear made my jeans fit tight. It was cloudy but dry. I mumbled something to Elizabeth and left without a kiss or a hug or any respect for myself, shot out onto the porch and gunned the bike off the concrete pad out back. I hit ninety on the road leading to the highway before the cops stopped me, but it was only Kelly Clark and he let me off with a warning.

I was back up to ninety before his car vanished in the rearview mirrors.

E L E V E N

The drive down the Island Highway barely registered, and it wasn't till I was cursing the traffic congestion at the ferry terminal in Nanaimo that I realized I would be halfway through the tunnel to Vancouver by then, and had to laugh at the irony.

Good thing I was on the bike — I pulled past the long ranks of cars and RVs and transport vehicles to the head of the line with the other motorcycles. A few travelers glanced over as I rolled past and by the time I braked the other bike owners had checked out my machine.

I nodded and shut down the Norton. Two Honda Gold Wings stood gleaming on their center stands, each with its bags and fairing and radio and cigarette lighter, only lack of a roof and a washroom keeping them from lining up with the tour buses. Their unisex riders sat on their machines, the four of them in identical red leather jackets with "Traveling Funsters" slashed in chenille across the back. They still had on their helmets, conversing through the boom mikes attached to the skid lids, I guess:

"Things okay back there, honey? Over."

"Still with you. Over."

"Any sign of those Messerschmitts? Over."

"No — they peeled off over the railroad yards. Over and out."

A gorgeous Harley Softail was crabbed sideways at the front of the herd. The owner looked like one of those executive types who gets a wild hair around thirty-five and takes up hang gliding or rock climbing or buys an expensive machine to take to the office once a week:

"Did you see what Henderson showed up on this morning? A motorcycle."

"No!"

"Big black thing — parked it right out front."

"Crazy. He'll kill himself."

"Well, you know Henderson."

"Some guys are born to die young."

He was promenading along the chainlink fence, trying not to limp in his new boots, staring down a squirrel, probably toying with the heretical notion of having a cigarette. He wouldn't appreciate the Norton.

A young kid sat astride some Japanese behemoth with more cubic centimeters than a Saturn rocket, impatient to launch himself into space.

Two guys on bikes built of four thousand spare parts ambled over, both of them in outfits similarly rigged from bits and scraps, getting the same stares as I did when I went skiing and flung myself down the mountain looking like a patchwork quilt out of control.

We gabbed awhile about bikes and the weather — not an idle topic among riders — and I thought that if most men who go on boats call themselves brothers, as Hemingway maintained, then the same is at least as true between bikers and pilots and anyone whose activities elevate them even briefly above the shit.

The big *Queen* reversed her screws and rumbled into the slip. We were soon chocked in place. I went up to the passenger deck and bought a coffee and took it to the stern lounge area. A dollop of Bushmill's from my hip flask sweetened the coffee and I stared out at the churning wake as the ship made its way out into the Straits.

Leaving the Island behind triggered thoughts of the project again. I hadn't tried very hard to save the hardware store. Every town tells the legend of some lone wolf holding on to his house in the face of progress, an old eccentric living in a shack smack in the middle of a cloverleaf.

But there are paths around that these days. Legislators have a way of forging weapons from terms such as "In the public interest." Aside from that, anyone who knows anything about wolves will tell you that the loner will take any course of action rather than run brazenly toward its pursuers. Even the Light Brigade wouldn't have charged without the stupidity a mob induces.

Odd as it sounds, I didn't want to keep the store in the event the project went through. It would be too much like coming away with your luggage when everyone else died in the train wreck. Looting, really.

I was trying not to get too personal about the project, focusing on what was best for Salish Spit as a whole. But it was difficult, as I felt that very human reaction to people brought low by their own hands: Fuck 'em. You can't force someone to admit to facts, and if the bridge came in and didn't prove to be the panacea everyone hoped for, it would serve them bloody well right. Too much self-righteousness, I know.

Already the hand-rubbing was starting, in anticipation of a windfall. I don't think the community realized that the profits from an outside-generated project go back to the source as surely as the glacier's ice will someday return to vapor up at thirty thousand feet, as certainly as if the developers carried carpetbags in lieu of briefcases. Native golf and country clubs do not spring up when a dam is built in the Sudan.

Maddeningly, there were townfolk who outwardly opposed the project while welcoming its completion. These were of a group that stood to profit, yet knew a little ineffective protesting would allow them to ride the gravy train while bitching about the smoke from the diesel.

I dozed awhile till the docking announcement brought me awake to rub my head where it had been plastered to the bulkhead. I pawed at the line of drool on my jacket.

The Norton howled beautifully as I climbed the hill to the Upper Levels Highway and made my way along the North Shore. Vancouver looked wonderful down there, nestled between greenery and ocean. For a city, it was doing its best. Goofy, but that was to be expected when you commingle an economy driven by primary industry, environmental awareness, a place to sleep in the streets without dying of exposure, a tourist destination, a haven for foreign investors, venomously militant unions, and a political base dopier than anything outside of Québec.

My lectures to Elizabeth aside, I liked the place. Cities don't sit well with me, but periodically I need the sense of energy they impart. The mix of success and seediness underscores the continuity that runs through the history of civilization, and where millions of people collide there is little room for boredom.

I just wished Vancouver could take pride in its daffiness and treat rectitude as a vice eastern cities peddle as a virtue. Back in the 1850s Edward Gibbon Wakefield's theories of economic planning for Britain's westernmost holdings included this stirring pronouncement: "The Committee believes that some of the worst evils that afflict the colonies have arisen from the admission of persons of all descriptions, no regard being had to the character, means, or views of the immigrants." He labored against this weakness and, in a masterstroke of misdirection aimed at hand-picking the newcomers, concluded, "The principle of selection, without the invidiousness of its direct application, is thus indirectly adopted." Not much had changed.

But I was cheered by the knowledge that in Salish Spit, at least, the most successful automotive dealer, Branch Smiley, annually consulted a crystal ball to determine which line of new cars he should emphasize in his ads, and that Rodney Klimezewski, owner of the Fairy Kingdom, the most abominable of the roadside tourist traps, was a card-carrying Communist and kept eighty-nine cats in his yellow house trailer.

By the time I was across the Patullo Bridge I had settled into a driving pattern, and the ensuing miles of Fraser Valley countryside slid by pleasantly. The cold didn't gang up on me till almost the end of the Coquihalla Highway, and I was glad to rest in a tiny coffee shop in Kamloops.

Then it started snowing. I stared out the window at the hills bracketing the loose junction of the Trans-Canada and the Yellowhead. They had been drying out, small wildflowers and grasses getting their legs in shape and enjoying it till the hell-fire summer temperatures burned them brown. Now they were being asked to start over.

Starting over.

Sedro should have thrown my letters out, for his chicken-scratched "Return to Sender" was unmistakable, broadcasting his location like a homing beacon. He might have been slipping, but I told myself it was his way of leaving the door open. And surely he would remember telling me the stories of his place up north — that's how I tracked him down in the first place.

So I convinced myself he was waiting for me, talking myself into it with one-sided arguments.

Hope, Fear and Desire: The omnipotent troika.

I phoned the weather office at the airport and listened to the bad news. No hope of going any farther on the bike. I drove through the beginnings of the storm to the terminal and hopped a 737 to Calgary. The airport bar was on last call when I clomped in, so I had one quick scotch and went to spend the night on a waiting-area couch.

In the morning the plane punched through a layer of stratus and had barely leveled off before it was time to throttle back for the enroute descent into Edmonton. No change of plane. Short wait, then into Yellowknife on Great Slave Lake.

An hour later we were off for Davis Flats, Sedro Tuckett's home these many years. An isolated company town sixty miles north of the Arctic Circle on the Mackenzie River. The pilot greased the landing and we walked to the terminal.

After a forty-minute wait the only taxi in the area sort of

happened by. The driver was a laconic, boozy veteran of the world's first bar fight, driving his own '67 Biscayne, no meter.

"Never seen ya before," he said, lighting a cigarette. "Workin fer Esso?"

"Nope," I said. "Just visiting."

"Nobody visits here," he said. He had a distracting manner of speaking, looking everywhere but at you, staring off into space over your head or off to one side, as if pontificating on some great truth. "Apples're a buckanahalf a fuckin' piece. No roads in or out. Town ran outta cheese yesterday, couldn't even get a pizza."

"Drop me at the main hotel," I said.

"All we got, only is one." He squinted through a scud of smoke. The taxi drifted onto the shoulder and we raced pleasantly along through the gravel awhile. "What business ya in?"

"I'm a spy."

"That right," he said. "Knew ya wasn't only visitin'. Brother was a spy fer a while. Quit. No fuckin' dental plan."

The hotel was a hollow square of trailers on two-foot stilts, perched above the permafrost like a stranded houseboat. We almost pitched it onto the frozen river before sliding to a stop.

"How much do I owe you?" I dug in my wallet.

"Jeez … whatever. Mostly deal in flat rates here."

"Fine. What's the rate from the airport?"

"I like them boots ya got on."

"C'mon, buddy."

"Five bucks is okay," he said. "Make it an extra fin, I won't tell anybody what yer doin' up here."

The spartan lobby was empty and I checked in without having to present a credit card.

I dropped my saddlebags on the bed. A small room, utilitarian, the hotel obviously constructed for newcomers in town, roughnecks just signed on, or management up to check on company affairs. Over the bed was a print of the northern lights, the aurora looking like bad cottage draperies, while below on the tundra a wolf, or a badger, or a marmot, some critter vaguely mammalian anyway, poured out a love song. The whole contraption shook and swayed whenever a door slammed or someone climbed the steps. Late-morning ice fog hung in limbo outside, sublimation from vehicle exhausts and the tiny steam plant attached to the arena up the road. I shaved and jiggled the door till it opened and went down to the coffee shop that was in its own trailer off the lobby.

"What's up?"

Reluctantly but automatically I took a seat at the cab driver's table. There was no waiter in sight, no one at all. The cabbie went over to the coffee machine and brought back a mug and the pot. He filled the mug, shoved it across to me and put the pot down on the table, where it set to melting through the cheap oilcloth.

"How's the room?" he said.

"The jacuzzi's broken."

He snorted. "Jimmy Crews."

"Jack Thorpe." I reached out. "What else do you do besides drive cab?"

"Most anything," he said. "I'm one of the only guys up here who doesn't work on the rigs. Little of this, little of that. Pest control is the best job. Scare off the animals at the dump, keeps the meat comin' in. Town used to be a pimple on the ass of the arctic till Esso come in around '81. Found out most of the oil is under the river, so they built them islands out in the middle fer the drills and pumps and fly the workers back and forth from the shore all day in a chopper."

I was caught not caring — a link is hard to establish with a group of people who don't fit into your agenda. Like the bridge group. Get in and get out, money in the bag, drop a little on local charities, attach your name to a hockey team, call a press conference and praise the stunned locals. But I should have been more interested in Jimmy Crews and the people up here. I grew up in Salish Spit, so my people I believe to be a distinct, peculiar, special group, when most likely they are not.

Or at least no more special than anyone else.

Jimmy Crews lifted the pot, removing a neat circle of color from the tablecloth, and refilled our mugs. "So what else is it yer doin' up here? Other than the spyin'."

"Looking for a friend," I mumbled. "Haven't seen him for a long time."

He waited.

"Sedro Tuckett?"

"Ha!"

"You know him."

"One of them guys — you know, see him everywhere then don't see him at all. Like a hermit, only now and again ya can't turn around without runnin' into him. Everybody calls him the Professor, 'cause he's always goin' on about somethin'."

Sounded like Sedro. "What does he do? I mean, does he work?"

In my heart was the wish that Sedro had replicated his life on the Island, was up here ruling a vast domain of wilderness, cynosure of Davis Flats, lecturing and leading and fostering legends.

"Pissall, far as I know," Jimmy said. "Made a bunch of money off Esso, I think."

"Oh."

"So how come yer sittin' in here?"

"It's been a long time."

"Like me and my sister. Went all the way to Winnipeg to see her then turned around and come back."

"Couldn't face her," I said.

"Owed her money," he said.

The door opened and three men came in. The waiter was still nowhere in sight so they helped themselves to coffee.

"Lunchtime," Jimmy said and drained his mug. "Bunch of guys are gonna want a lift."

"How far is it to Sedro's?"

"Them boots'll cover it."

We went out to the cab, Jimmy waving at men getting out of their trucks and trooping into the coffee shop. It was a short drive.

I saluted Jimmy Crews as he slewed his cab back onto the road. I walked the twenty-seven steps to the front porch. Instead of going straight up I squeaked through the snow around to the side. It was a small place, not much bigger than Sedro's cabin in the Spit, but with none of the mystery. Planning on getting a good feel for the place before I banged on the door, I laughed as the ludicrousness of the situation struck home.

Fifteen years not enough, have to squeeze in another ten minutes.

I leaned against a tree that bordered the path leading to the back of the cabin and lit a cigarette. When it was close to burning my fingers I carefully field-stripped it and dropped the remains in the snow, crushing them fiercely under my boot.

My first feeling was of bathos. But then what could I expect? What had I expected? I had built up the reunion in my mind by carefully plotting an orderly sequence of events, assuming this would lead to some sort of glorious epiphany. You would think I had never experienced the disappointment that inevitably was my reward whenever I planned anything.

So I had stretched my anticipation to the breaking point, but upon seeing Sedro it didn't snap. It just contracted slowly back to where it belonged.

We went inside. He was old and very small. Bony bare ankles crossed, waggling black Converse All Stars. He wore a beard, perhaps in deference to local custom, or to the cold. It looked bad on him. He was never a man to be pitied, yet plunked down in a swarm of randomly selected humans he would look pitiful. He was tired. I was no sprite lately, yet still I felt embarrassed at my vitality, sitting across from him in the three-room shack, sipping on a glass of Plainsman Rye.

There was no scene. I had knocked on the door and he had answered it. We shook hands firmly but with no lingering over the action, no drama. He invited me in and pawed through the clutter on the counter and found a couple glasses and there we sat.

There was no immediate catching up, and I was glad. After any absence a good rollicking recap is fun but serves mainly to trivialize the present, two blank faces hiding dreams that somehow escaped, bust the chain on the leghold trap, laughing and shooting you the finger from a safe distance.

He told me about Davis Flats and I nodded and listened and gradually, like a cat creeping along a limb, the old feeling came back. The old feeling but paler, not so flush with excitement, the capillaries not so engorged. But the old feeling, yes, with me standing on my hind legs, big gumboots over my knees, listening to the mayor and fully expecting — not hoping, but expecting — the day to last forever, with the glacier looking down and grunting with approval.

Sedro used to look at the glacier with eagerness, up on his toes, as if waiting for it to become ambulant or flash him a sign, never treating it as a river of ice, perhaps feeling that a life cycle implied life.

The life of Salish Spit, that is the collective energy of the place, he controlled as if managing the nozzle on a fire hose. The best definition of a leader I have come across is someone who gets people to do willingly what they don't want to do. Sedro used to run town meetings so that by the end people were not only willing but positively enthusiastic.

Or maybe it was simpler than that.

Eagle and I had hitched a ride with Sedro to the hall. It always seemed too small for a meeting, but Sedro kept it that way, describing it as a funnel for energy, the same as the rebuilding of the British House of Commons along its old, cramped lines rather than the spacious austerity of modern legislative seats.

Eagle had been working on his dad's car so he looked like a creature that had barely escaped La Brea's tar pits. People filing in for the meeting grimaced as if a kid of sixteen should be anything but a mess.

There was no reading of minutes. Anything that had been agreed upon at the last meeting Sedro would already have implemented, and proposals that had been voted down would have been quietly circumvented, so the mayor started right in.

He talked about nothing in particular for a few minutes, allowing people to get settled. At least, as close to settled as they ever got at town meetings. It was hard enough just keeping people on the main topic.

"Riverside Park is home to two baseball diamonds, a rugby and soccer field, and the picnic area back along the trees," Sedro said by way of introduction once the din was manageable.

He didn't get any further. He was in control, but that never stopped anyone from jamming in an opinion. Salish Spit town meetings were panel discussions, not formal debates.

"What did he say? What is he saying?"

"Quiet. Sit down and listen to him,"

"Why does he always start on time? Common courtesy would let us get comfortable."

"Gimme that chair over here. This bloody thing's gonna tip me on my ass."

"If I can have your attention," Sedro called. "A lot of you are opposed to the idea of giving over the park to the Sylvan Fair on the August long weekend."

These were tremendous affairs. Every year, at a different spot on or around Vancouver Island, a wonderful variety of people assembled to sell their wares, enjoy the sun, cavort and mingle and play for three days and nights, simultaneously attracting thousands of visitors and scaring the hell out of others who looked upon the fair as some sort of traveling gypsy show intent on stealing their children for a blood ritual. No question that there were a few Sixties Children still in place on the Gulf Islands, but there were also a lot of rednecks who had claim to a much longer heritage. It was these latter idiots with whom Sedro had to contend.

"There's never enough chairs at these meetings. Why don't they bring in more chairs? Can't anyone on the council even count?"

"I believe it is time," Sedro said, "for us to —"

"It turns into a zoo, Sedro. Every place that hosts one of their fairs is destroyed."

"Destroyed?" Sedro said. "Where are you getting your information?"

"They don't destroy anything. That's just nonsense. What the problem is —"

"You'll have your say," Sedro said. "Everyone will have their say." He waved his hands to settle them down.

"Who was that?"

"I don't know — he's up at the front. There's always someone talking out of turn at these meetings. I don't know why I bother coming if parliamentary procedure isn't going to be enforced. How can you accomplish anything if people don't shut up and recognize whoever has the floor? Christ, I hope this doesn't take long. I'm supposed to drive Bert to Campbell River tonight."

"They've been rotating locations," Sedro said. "Every year they hold the fair at a different spot around the Islands. I think it's time we gave them a permanent home here in Salish Spit."

"They'll wreck the playing fields! That's bottom land with poor drainage —"

"August!" Sedro boomed like an aroused Jove. "That time of year we have to water daily to prevent the fields from turning into a dust bowl."

That had happened once, about the time Algeria gained independence. But now someone else was in full cry.

"I seen that fair last year in Comox. Three thousand old hippies trucking in with their Volkswagen vans with chicken coops on the tops. Half of them with moons and stars painted on their faces, the other half dancing bare-assed under the trees. That's what we have the Gulf Islands for — to keep them out of the towns and cities. Bloody hippies. Where the hell do they get off raising their kids like that, anyhow, that's what I want to know. They want to be hippies this long after the Sixties, that's okay — though just try to tell them how stupid they look now they're all old and burned out from drugs. But they shouldn't be allowed to influence their kids like that. It's morally wrong. Children should be allowed to learn what's right and what's not from the world, not from an old wrecked hippie mother with hair under her arms and a dad stoned on marijuana capsules."

"Do you take your kids to church?" Sedro asked.

"Of course I do. What do you think, that I'd let my children run free without showing them the difference between good and bad? Hell, Sedro, if you had kids you'd know you can't let them stuff up their heads with just anything. Parents have a respon- sibility to pass on what they know is true and proper. That Darlene of mine will thank me one day. She'll look back and realize you can't spend all Sunday just reading books — you got to learn things!"

Sedro reached for his water glass, which looked amber in this light. "Good," he said. Apparently the first point had been dealt with.

"Next point is the contention that they will be selling their crafts without permits. Flat-out wrong! Everyone with a booth will have a vendor's license and must display it just as every retailer in town displays —"

"I don't have a belt I bought off one of them two years ago on Texada Island!"

This piece of nonsense prompted a swiveling of heads.

"I had it, but not anymore."

The remaining heads pivoted.

"I mean, I still have a belt I bought in Victoria over ten years ago. The beads that made out the shape of a totem pole wore off, but the leather's still good. It works, is what I'm saying. But I got one of them handmade ones at their Sylvan Fair and it hardly lasted a year and a half. That goddamn Sidney of mine tore off the cold water pipe in the basement doing chinups, right? Then when I cinched the thing back up with the belt I bought off the hippies, the thing broke and he just about cracked his skull. And wouldn't that be a pretty sight for my wife to come home and see her son's brains dashed all over her preserves. If Kindersley wants his players to work out like weightlifters then the team should provide proper training facilities. That's what we should be voting on here: a weight room for the junior rugby team."

"I disagree. I still have a vase I purchased from a lovely young man who turns out beautiful work. He had a stall with flowers all around the posts and the valance board, and I stepped right up and said, 'I'll have that vase, young man. Not that one, no — what would I do with that monstrosity in the kind of place I have, I mean, really. But that one. And I won't pay a penny more than what it's worth, either, and from where I stand it's a little off-center. But lovely nonetheless, so wrap it up, please.' I have put fresh wildflowers in it every day since and it doesn't show a bit of wear."

"The craftsmanship of the artisans is not at issue here," Sedro said. Even he was looking pained.

"Right. 'Cause if you want to see shoddy work all you have to do is take a look under the hood of my Land Rover."

"Nobody calls me a liar! Or a cheat! You get what you pay for, and if you want a mechanic to do a top-dollar job, you don't lowball the man. People think auto parts grow on trees, for chrissake."

"It's the labor. That's where the gouging comes in. That's my bitch — the cost of labor."

"So you see my point," Sedro said. He allowed his conviction to quash the confusion. "Now that we've agreed on the main items, there remains only the opposition to the outdoor music. There will be two stages erected, the acts alternating sites throughout the three days. It will be folk music —"

"My bloody Geoffrey listens to *Anthrax*! Can you imagine the mentality involved in naming a band after a cow disease?"

"Folk music," Sedro emphasized.

"Is it Peter or Paul who's dead?"

"Mary, isn't it?"

"No, no, they're still alive. Mama Cass is dead."

"Mama Cass?"

"Plane crash, I think."

"Patsy Cline was the plane crash. And Amelia Earhart."

"Jesus Christ."

"Valdy might come. Didn't he play at the fair on Texada Island a couple of years ago? He's from around here somewhere. Doesn't he own one of those little islands, or is that Michael Jackson?"

"We don't need any Michael Jacksons hanging around the kids at Riverside Park for three days."

"Jesus Christ."

"The rugby team has agreed to practice on the high school field," Sedro said.

"Silvertree shouldn't be playing *and* coaching. Stick with what you're good at, though that fool isn't any good at either one."

"*You* try it, you fat sonofabitch! Let's see *you* get on the cleats and head out on the field!"

"So there's nothing left to discuss," Sedro said. "Audrey Weeks has graciously accepted the responsibility of overseeing the setup and cleanup."

"Tell her to get plenty of portable toilets. Every softball tournament they stampede across the road to the hotel and clog up my bathrooms without so much as buying a beer or a sandwich."

"You sell sandwiches and beer in the bathrooms?"

"Jesus Christ."

"So if there is no other business —" And Sedro Tuckett was gone out the side door.

A few people blinked and looked at their watches, and other than those involved in internecine tiffs, the main body was stunned. They knew they had missed something but couldn't get a handle on what it was. Eventually they shuffled out, vaguely unsatisfied, and Eagle went under the chairs to see if anything of value had been left behind.

In any case, Sedro did no leading or steamrolling that night in Davis Flats. He tailed off in the middle of a description of Game Night, when for five bucks a head you can sit at a folding table in the Davis Flats Arena and gorge yourself on caribou and bear. He looked at me until the silence grew oppressive, then rose and pointed at the couch and went into the small bedroom at the back of the shack. I didn't want to stay the night but felt compelled to and, once compelled, wanted to after all.

I wrapped myself in a Hudson's Bay blanket and lay down to sleep.

The dreams came. In various guises they railed at me, demanding to know why so many questions had been left unasked, armtwisting bastards giving no quarter, as little disposed to grant me control as I was to relinquish it.

I awoke feeling in great concert with the losers of the world, the plain old sad sacks who never see anything but the back of a hand, who can't seem to get a break or grasp one when it shows up.

We've all felt it: Standing in the rain with wet feet, baggy-ass pants sliding off your hips, food stains on your shirt, need a haircut and a shave and you're soaked to the tits and tired and uncomfortable with your clothes and your looks and your life and the wind whips the top off your umbrella and you're left holding a pathetic handle like a lightning rod, and hoping lightning will strike, or wishing you were suddenly eight months old so at least you had another kick at the cat.

It is so common it even has a name: One Of Those Days.

There's a marine organism called *Volvox* that has the curious habit of entirely everting itself. Poke your finger into a loosely inflated balloon till you touch the far inner side, then imagine a hole forming so your finger keeps going and everything reverses, the inside of the balloon now the outer surface. That's *Volvox*, and that was me.

Or look upon it as becoming such a huge asshole that you fall down through it and hang yourself.

Learning is my life but it can lead to disillusionment — it robs certainty. I longed to be experience-free, packed with ignorance enough to be sure again, childish and innocent and positive and convinced and unquestioning and unquesting. Simplicity and clarity, me hearties, and get your backs into those oars!

The toilet flushed and Sedro came padding out into the living room. He drew on a pair of gray cotton rugby pants from a pile of clothes that were hibernating on a wing chair opposite the couch. Lifting my head, I watched him out of one squinted eye until he looked squarely at me and started talking.

"The love is gone when you let her cry on her own," he said.

I fumbled with the blanket and with my wits.

"Last night," he said. "You were talking about your wife — Elizabeth, I believe — last night. Do you still comfort her when she cries?"

"Let me get awake, here," I said. I sat up and raked my fingers through my hair and trolled through the glasses and papers on the coffee table for a cigarette.

"Do you?"

"Do I what?" I said. "Yeah, I guess so."

"Do you?"

"No. But it's not because I don't love her."

"You're wrong," he said. He went to the kitchen, filled the kettle and popped the gas range into life.

"Thanks," I said. "Thanks a hell of a lot. That solves everything."

"Not trying to solve anything. That's your job. I'm merely commenting."

"Trouble is that even if she forgives me it will still be there between us. True forgiveness is hard to give or receive."

"She hasn't found out yet."

He looked so small, so ineffective, standing there like a stranger I had heard of all my life.

"Thanks for trying," I said.

"I already told you, just commenting."

"You've always used that as a defense. All the same, you are trying. Don't know that I need it anymore. Or if I want it, or if it even works."

"Cold out there today," he said. "This time of year the snap won't last long, though. We could head out and roam around if you like."

"That all you do these days?"

"Do what I want these days. I made a pile when Esso decided to buy up land to tap the oil and gas in the area. I do what I want."

"When haven't you?"

The kettle whistled and Sedro made a big production out of serving the instant coffee.

"What's got you pissed off, young Jack?"

"The great innocent!"

"I'm serious."

"I'm not doubting your sincerity, just your innocence."

"I figure it's not my place to initiate the conversation. This is my home. You're a welcome but uninvited guest. You broke the ground and you still wield the spade."

"Save the homespun aphorisms."

"Have it your way."

"Fucking right." I set the mug down on the old trunk he

used as a coffee table and went to take a piss. When I came back Sedro had on a sweater and was building a fire.

"Last night wasn't the time," I said. "But you know I have questions."

"That's why I asked," he said. He touched a match to the newspaper. "It's your nickel." A flicker of concern marred his face.

I poured a dose of Old Bushmill's into my coffee. "Why the hermit act?" I said. "Why the running and hiding?"

"Who says I ran?"

"The facts."

"Facts are speechless. The conclusions you draw speak."

"Don't play games," I said. "You owe me that much."

"I didn't run," he said. "That implies heedless flight, escape. I created a situation that required I remove myself from the scene."

"Stop it!" I cried. "Cut the semantics, cut the bullshit. You didn't create a situation, you shot my old man in the head. In the fucking head! If it was an accident there was no reason to run, to be so gutless."

He snapped to his feet and looked me hard in the eyes and I saw his age and his fear.

"What if it wasn't an accident?" he said. "Is that enough of a situation for you?"

"It was," I said, my own fear tempering my voice. "It was an accident. It had to be."

"For the sake of argument —"

"Negative. This isn't a debate. Was it an accident?"

It was cold in the room, glacier cold.

"No." It barely escaped his lips. "It was not an accident."

I was the first to avert my eyes, though Sedro was looking right through me, focused on infinity.

"Is that what you wanted to hear?" he said after a while.

"Wanted to hear? *Wanted* to? You murdered my father. Sedro, you killed him. But … why, man? Why?"

Never in my life have I seen anyone whose internal anguish so distorted their expression.

"Not now," he said. A tired old man. "Not now."

I had slept the night fully clothed, so there was nothing to pack. The saddlebags were heavy on my shoulder and the walk to the hotel was long. I couldn't rustle anybody up so I dropped fifty bucks on the front desk. Jimmy Crews was in the coffee shop and I pointed through the glass out to his cab.

"Short visit," he said, cutting off a Volvo as he pulled onto the road. "Spyin' not so good up here, eh?"

"Slow season."

"Yeah," he said. "Gettin' warmer, except for today. I guess spys're like anyone — itch to get the feet movin' and sow the oats come spring. That's one thing my brother always used to say about spyin': slack in spring."

"Wish I was as dumb as you, Jimmy."

"Lots of my friends say that. Can't see it myself. Anyhoo, here's the airport. Six bucks."

"That's a buck more than it was going the other way," I said.

He turned and blew a jet of smoke at me. "Headwinds."

T W E L V E

It took me the rest of the day and the next morning to retrace
the air route back to Kamloops, and the time allowed me a
chance to be alone even while surrounded by fellow travelers.
Introspection winning out over interaction.

Damn, I felt good. I didn't really know why, but I did.

The concept of facing the demon was clearer, standing out
in harsh relief amid my other concerns. I didn't have to beat the
Monster. Letting it know I was in the neighborhood and wasn't
running was sufficient for the time being.

The snow had melted in Kamloops. I wiped the water off my
Norton and set off on the highway through the mountains. I
drove the machine hard, slinging it into curves and slamming
out so sharply the wobblies continued until the next turn.

My mind was operating in such high gear that the rest of the
trip slid by like a hallucination. By the time the ferry disgorged

me onto the shores of the Island I was more affected by the fact that Sedro was capable of what he had done than by the actual homicide. Obviously the old man had a side to him I had never seen, while the murder itself had been so long ago it had lost the strength to horrify.

Besides, if my old man were resurrected today I'd want him around only so long as it took to solve him, after which the pain he inflicted on me and my mum could very well prompt me to dispatch him myself.

I hadn't asked all the questions and Sedro hadn't explained his answers to the ones I had the nerve to dish up, but a certain simplicity had been established. Sort of a negative, backasswards way of going through life, I know. As opposed to building toward a desired end, I was paring away the trash that didn't work. Creating a sculpture rather than a painting, I guess.

The last part of the trip up the Island Highway I tackled under pristine skies, a keenness in the air, no transition between mountaintop and atmosphere, but a hard crystalline razor's edge that had me countersteering wildly into the bends of the road and all but screaming with joy. If I could ever remember the words to a whole song I would have sung up every song that driver knew, but contented myself with about twenty opening verses and a couple hundred refrains. As I got closer to home the last chorus of "Brown-Eyed Girl" faded and blended into engine noise. Back to the real world. A Crusader having conquered the Holy Land, now safely home.

But with no G.I. Bill.

I knew it was all wrong, I felt it.

Usually my optimism overwhelms the willies, with the result that bad news is able to sneak up and belt me in the head with impunity. But this time as I braked the bike and yanked it up on the center stand I knew Elizabeth was not in the house. The pickup was in the driveway, but I knew she was gone.

Vertigo had hold of me as I wandered through the place. Funny how it didn't look different but was, with Elizabeth gone. She had taken few clothes. Probably waiting till I came back, or teaching me a lesson, or so far gone she cared for nothing but flight. I stood on the dog run, smoking, and figured if she was still in town she would be with Bernice. I had to try.

"Listen, Bernice, it's Jack. Elizabeth there?"

"No, I haven't seen her for days. How did your trip go?"

"You sure she isn't there?"

"Are you accusing me of lying?" she said. "Of lying to you?"

"All I want is to find her."

"Maybe she doesn't want you to."

"If you haven't seen her in days, why would you jump to that conclusion?"

"Intuition," she said.

"Come on, what do you know about this?"

"I merely said she may not want to see you."

"Let her tell me that herself. Put her on."

"She's not here," she said, adopting her Aunt Bea tone. "But if I happen to run into her I will leave a message. Maybe you and I could talk about it."

"I can't talk to you about it."

"Why not?"

"Because you're an idiot, Bernice. The worst kind — a meddling idiot, a socially irresponsible idiot. And if I find out you're hiding Elizabeth I'm going to beat the shit out of your idiot husband."

"James has never done anything to you!"

"He married you," I said, the red meat kicking in. "And I don't hit women, but someone at that house of yours has deserved a beating for a long time."

So Elizabeth had heard about Patsy Jillian. No need to ask how. There is always someone who knows, someone who finds out, someone eager to tell all out of maliciousness or simply because knowledge like that is power to little people who have never experienced power in their lives.

I didn't feel bad for abusing Bernice. Even my wife thought she was a fool and couldn't explain why they remained friends. The woman spent most of her waking hours figuratively peeking through the curtains, and her gossip had on several occasions wreaked havoc in the community. A tabloid life, yet another person consumed with trying to do something for someone else's good.

I left the house and soon had the old halfton rattling along as if there were two skeletons humping in the back.

Just past the main intersection I saw the apparition: a huge bearded man in work boots and long red underwear with a button missing from the bumflap. Perched on his head was a scarlet cardboard dunce cap festooned with gold ribbons and sequins. On the sidewalk in front of him were three tables overflowing with trinkets and odds and ends. The man behind the tables was spitting snoose on the sidewalk and pawing at the crotch of his long underwear. He was unsteady on his feet, possibly a drinker. He was massive and ugly.

He was Eagle.

I parked in front of the stand and got out of the truck.

"Hey, Jack!" he said. "Need any Pope stuff?" He flung his arms open, turning and baring one cheek through the bumflap of his thermals.

"What's with the getup?" I asked.

"Nearest thing I could find to a Pope costume. Had a cape a day, maybe two ago. Somebody stole it last night or the night before." He heaved his bulk into a lawn chair, settling in with a shrieking of aluminum and a groaning of plastic.

"How long have you been manning the stand?" I asked, fiddling with a Pope fridge magnet.

"Since you left," he said. "Too much stuff to pack back and forth to my place so I plan to stand guard over it till she's all sold. That fuckboat Don found out I only had eighty bucks lottery money left to pay the tab, so I got to make a good profit on all this." Again the arms opened, proudly bracketing his wares.

"What have you sold so far?" I asked, picking up a basket full of Pope bottle openers.

"Nothing," he said. "Slow time of year for Pope stuff, I guess. Some kids come by last night and pretended they were interested, but they were just all drunked up and tried to steal some T-shirts. I run them off and the bastards drove by throwing beer bottles. I heaved one of them Pope doorstops through their back window."

"How do you expect to unload all this junk?"

"Junk? That's blasphemy, I think. Can you imagine how long it took for the Pope to pose for all these valuables? I know you're no Catholic, but show some respect, for fuck sake."

"You want me to genuflect?"

"Jesus did that at Easter. The Genuflection."

"Fine, fine."

"That Pope-on-Black-Velvet would look good over your fireplace."

"Sorry."

"Remember when the Blue Jays were playing in the World

Series in Atlanta and the Marines brought in the Canadian flag upside down? Guys made millions selling T-shirts about it."

"They did nothing of the kind. The idiots are still trying to unload them."

"Anyhow, the Pope's bigger than the Blue Jays."

"Bet he makes less in endorsements."

"Take one of them Pope cocktail glasses. On the house. When it gets wet his robes melt away, big Pope pecker sticking out."

"Pass."

"Whatever."

"How much do you owe Don?" I asked.

"Nine hundred."

"No."

"And a couple hundred to the cab company."

"What?"

"Aww," he waved. "Couple ballplayers and me had a few drinks and decided to take in a drive-in movie."

"In a cab?"

"Didn't want to drive drunk," he said indignantly. "Anyhow, the hack hadn't seen the third feature so he gave us a discount. Got one of them car speakers out of the deal, too. It's under the corner of the table, there. New cord and you got yourself a big Walkman."

"Aren't the other guys kicking in for the cab?"

"Out of work."

"So are you."

"But I won the lottery."

"You're a mental case."

"Probably."

"I'm looking for Elizabeth," I said.

"I guess you are."

"You sound like you know something."

"Just that she took off on you."

"How did you find out?"

"Everybody knows."

"Oh."

"Shouldn't have screwed that young thing."

"How do you know about that?"

"Everybody knows."

"Great!" I said, slamming down a pair of Pope baby shoes. "What are you laughing at?"

"Just tickles me to see a man shit on his own doorstep then try to step around it. Or maybe I'm glad it ain't me for a change."

"I'm going to the Square Rigger. Maybe Elizabeth's staying with Don and Donna."

"Hey — how did the meeting with Da Vinci go?"

I stared at his big dopey face a moment. "We're on our own."

"Fine," Eagle said. A brown stream hit the sidewalk.

I drove off. Obviously Eagle wasn't too concerned about Sedro, and I used that to help suppress my own thoughts about the man. I had mentioned the project to him, but asking for his help would have been too transparent a ploy. That's not what I had been there for. Sedro had dismissed the whole thing the same way he had written off the town years ago. I had gladly dropped it.

There were few vehicles in the Square Rigger's parking lot. I pulled up beside Don's old Impala. Already I was ashamed to face him. I hoped none of the regulars were in the pub but of course they were.

The trouble is friends are inept at dealing with marital discord. They don't quite know how broken up you are, whether you want commiseration or the hearty good-riddance bluster that passes for wisdom. I wanted neither. I wanted Elizabeth.

Don's disapproval leaped from his eyes. He gruffly let me know Elizabeth wasn't with him and his wife. No one in the place would look at me for more than a second except for Snuffy.

"Thanks anyhow," I said. I trudged to the door. "See you guys around."

Mumbles and yeahs.

"Bye, Snuffy, you old hog."

"Old hog, he says! You kill me, Jack."

So I was off for where I knew her to be all along. I don't know how Bernice had fooled me, although I am easily lied to. Sedro once told me it was my ego. He maintained that people with large egos are easy to dupe; they can't imagine anyone being less than honest with such a magnificent creation as themselves. The way I felt now, the reason was more along the lines of stupidity.

"Open the door!" I yelled, slamming the flat of my hand against the frame.

"Go away!"

"I know you have her, Bernice!"

"She's not a prisoner."

"Tell her I'm out here." Keep control.

"God, she knows by now."

"Tell her to come out. Or let me in."

"She says she needs time to think."

"She's had over thirty years and hasn't taken advantage of the opportunity." Why does that woman make me say things like that? Elizabeth, not Bernice. Bernice, too, for that matter.

A man's voice. "Jack? Go away, now!"

"James!" I yelled. "You gutless prick! You've been hiding in there all along. Get your wife away from the door and open up."

"I can't," he said. James couldn't do anything. He wasn't a bad man, just a dandruffy, dogeared human who worked inefficiently at the bank and who pissed me off only because of his uselessness.

"I want my wife!"

"Don't make me call the police!"

The rage took hold. The nausea, the red and the shakes. Not just at Elizabeth or Bernice or her dumbass husband. At myself and my life and the bridge and the tunnel and Sedro, who shot my father, who probably deserved it, but who hadn't built himself, hadn't planned for the world to reject his world.

I'm in the truck and ramming it into the house again and again and again and the wood and the stucco flying and me wishing the mortar and the boards could scream as the people inside the house are screaming.

Then the engine died. The cops came but by the time I saw their lights turn off the main road I was out of the truck and into the woods.

Running without plan or pattern, I concentrated on escape. Wiping the tears, I left the lights behind me to probe into the bush, my bush, and I found my way to the foot of the stream bed and followed it up, and hours later, all the while flagging but pressing on, I finally stood on the terminal moraine and looked up at the river of history, the expanse of wastage and resupply, of growth and death and constant rebirth.

But it wasn't right. There was no communion, no oneness. I did not belong up there that night because I had come for the wrong reasons. I was bleeding from a hundred scratches and scrapes and I'd probably get slung in jail tomorrow and my wife had left me and Da Vinci had murdered my father.

The glacier didn't want me in this state. I bowed my head in acceptance and some understanding of the ice monster's feelings and started back down, crashing and bursting through the brambles and the deadfall, back to some kind of home.

T H I R T E E N

I crashed for the night on the couch, drifting off after a couple
hours of staring out the window at the ocean. A restful,
dreamless sleep, my mind able to embrace only so much. Upon
waking I showered and used half a bottle of hydrogen peroxide
on the cuts and abrasions from my charge up and down the
mountain. With no agenda, I set out on the bike for town.

I cruised by the mayor's office, then pulled a U-turn and
angled the Norton against the curb. The neat rows of pansies
and peonies on the boulevards were struggling to hang on,
planted a little early it looked like. I sat on the curb to catch
as much of their scent as possible and watched the cars and
trucks roll slowly past, counting out-of-province plates like
a kid, listening to the faint sounds of a morning ball practice down at Riverside Park, sitting and thinking, sitting and
relaxing, sitting.

Audrey Weeks came out of the drugstore down the street and strode up the sidewalk and through the double doors. She hadn't seen me, and I let her have a few minutes to get settled before I followed her trail into the civic building. I could have given her a couple of years to get settled without much effect. It didn't take long for the action to heat up.

"I'm too old to apologize for getting laid," I said. I mashed my cigarette out in the nephrite ashtray. "And I'm tired of women thinking it involves them relinquishing something that the man takes."

"Fine," Audrey said. "That's fine if it's nondestructive. But not only are you married, your sense of timing is atrocious. Did you do this deliberately, Jack?"

"No, I was forced into it by a Mongol horde."

"You know what I mean. Did you do this to stir things up?"

"Would I deliberately bring a live toaster into the bathtub?"

"You might," Audrey said. "If you thought it would satisfy your craving for a challenge."

She had started raging the minute I walked in, and stood there now behind her desk like a raptor waiting for any sign of weakness or inattention.

"My wife left me," I said. "That's hardly the result I'd chance merely to feed some sense of challenge."

"You really screwed up this time."

"I made a mistake."

"No," she said. "A mistake is when you put *i* before *e* in 'neighbor.' What you did is screw up."

I stared at her.

"I'm the one who told Elizabeth," she said.

"You vindictive — !"

"Fifty people saw you and Patsy make fools of yourselves in the pub then leave together. News would have reached your wife by noon the next day. You know what this town is like. I wanted her to hear it up front."

"Good morning, madam. Just wanted you to know your son fell out of his office window."

"It wasn't like that."

"It was a disgusting thing to do," I said. "You did it out of spite."

"You hurt me," she said.

"Hurt *you?*"

"You were only trying to get at me through her."

"That's not my style. Besides, Patsy wasn't forced into anything."

"She cares nothing for you."

"Then what was she doing — sleeping her way to the bottom? I have nothing to offer her."

"You never nibble at the edges, do you?"

"What's that supposed to mean?"

"You go right to the heart of the situation. That's admirable if your intent is to find a solution. But it's never that simple. If you can't solve it you still stir it up. You love to see the fur fly."

"Let's get something straight," I said. I rose from the couch and went to the sideboard, staring at her law degree while pouring a glass of rye. "What we did stemmed from mutual attraction. It was no frivolous attempt to get the fur flying."

"I don't believe you."

"Don't you ever get laid?" I asked. She flinched so visibly I thought she might shoot out through the bay window. "Did Sedro poison you on men to that extent?"

"Get out!"

"You're always telling me that. Everyone tells me that these days."

She looked at my glass. "You drink too much."

"No shit."

"Why?"

"Because I have to deal with people like you."

"You're intentionally being cruel and I don't appreciate it."

I slammed my glass on her desk and leaned over as close to her as I could get. "And you didn't intentionally pick up the phone and vomit your poison into my wife's ear?"

The beauty of the glacier and the mountains and the trees through the window; the ugliness of a running sore in the room. The standoff continued till I broke it off and sat on the arm of the couch. I wanted to split her skull with the ashtray.

"Can we drop this?" Audrey said. No apology, but a note of contrition in her voice.

"I don't know why we picked it up in the first place."

"Maybe I was wrong."

"You'll have to do better than that or I'll toss you out the window."

"Get out!"

"Again."

"No matter how much fur flies, it won't stop the bridge."

"Don't you know anything?" I said. "That fucking project — the whole thing makes me sick. I don't care about the bridge anymore. At times I think I took up arms against it as a way of relieving my boredom. It should not be built, I am certain of that. But will it really change anything? Salish Spit won't boom as a result. These aren't the old days when a town's life or death depended on the railroad coming through. With a PC, a phone and a fax machine you can run a business, put yourself through school and order Chinese food from a whorehouse in Moose Jaw.

"What they are proposing is blind progress, forging ahead because that's how it's always been done. But I trust this town. I think people around here are finally starting to measure progress by quality, not quantity, of life. We'll make do, as we always have. That's why a connection to the mainland won't sink us. It may set us back on our heels, but it won't put us on the canvas.

Even the dumb buggers in England realize the tunnel to the continent isn't going to tear apart their world."

"So you're giving up?"

"No, no," I said hastily. "It's part of the Great Game, isn't it? Have to see it through."

She stood up and sat on the edge of her desk. "Sedro won't help one bit."

"Don't worry about it," I said. "He's not coming."

"I told you he wouldn't. But ... why not? What went on up there?"

"I didn't ask him to come."

"You didn't ask?"

"No."

"What about ... What did you find out?"

I thought for a second, then put down my glass and went out the door.

Back on the bike for the short trip to the cop shop. They threw me in the jug. I felt safe in there but Bernice and James wouldn't press charges and I convinced the boys — or they let themselves be convinced — that I couldn't have been resisting arrest if we hadn't even seen one another. Kelly Clark came in and we talked sports awhile. He remembered twenty bucks he owed me so all in all it was a profitable experience. Our local RCMP like to see your face now and again. If they can nab you on minor offenses like drinking or fighting they feel they have a handle on you. It's being a sneaky type who never gets caught at anything but *must* be up to no good that irritates them.

Also, it helps if you've been the emcee at three of their weddings and play rugby with two others. I waved and was on my way.

As I drove the Norton through town I saw Eagle in a sleeping bag behind his Pope stand. A big ugly wiener sticking out of a down-filled bun, the red dunce cap pulled over the tips of his ears. It had rained briefly before dawn and Eagle's head was resting in a puddle of red dye that had leaked off the hat. I was tempted to stop but kept rolling over the bridge and cut left, paralleling the stream leading from the glacier, till the road ran out at Audrey's house, hard at the foot of the mountains.

An orderly cedar place with large bay windows and a wraparound porch. There was smoke coming from the chimney. The air was still, so it was going straight up, losing cohesiveness and spreading into a thin veil.

The driveway was unpaved, so I propped the side stand of the Norton on a cedar shake and approached the house. I could see wisps of smoke leaking through an open window, then the door was flung wide and Patsy Jillian charged out choking and swearing. She was wearing oven mitts and holding a smoldering chunk of poplar. She chucked it off the porch.

I stared and smiled as a sexual heat rash spread out over my chest and down to my groin. This could be tough. I knew any attempt at conversation was going to be either a formless broadside of bullshit or a halting attempt to say the perfect thing in the perfect way, which would eventually render me mute.

I looked at her standing on the porch, stripping off the oven mitts. Tan skin and caramel hair and muscular body and I remembered having her and still wanting her and hoping Audrey was wrong — Patsy must feel something for me, she must care, or I must find a way to make her care. I didn't like the look on her face. A sign of recognition and a trace of a smile, but that's about it. She went back into the house and I followed, hiding my big grin of greeting, trying to purge thoughts of Elizabeth.

Patsy had piled too much wood in the fireplace and left the screen open. The chunk of poplar had tumbled onto the hearth rug, scorching off the nap and smoking up the room. She finally started laughing and I joined her. Much too heartily — a condemned man parading his nonchalance.

The coffee was strong and hot. I was weak and hot. Patsy was strong and cold. Bad news all round, except for the coffee.

"I hope you aren't thinking too much about the other night," she said. I should have fled right there.

"Of course I am."

"I guess I got a little drunk."

"Give me a break," I said. "I felt more than a mating instinct coming from you." I was already angry and knew I had no right to be.

"Jack, it was wonderful, it really was, but you and I ..."

"You and I ...?"

"It's the wrong place," she said. "At the wrong time, in the wrong company."

"You can't always choose those elements."

"You're happily married."

"Let me be the judge of that."

"No."

"Fine, take it out of my hands. Evidently I have no say in anything affecting me these days."

"Don't whine," she said.

"I'm not."

"You are."

"Calm down. No sense in both of us being pissed off."

"I'm just trying to tell you we should nip this in the bud before we get carried away."

"You feel enough for me that getting carried away is a possibility?"

"I didn't say that."

"You haven't said anything."

"You won't let me. I've seen you in action, Jack. You twist things. You strip a person's confidence."

"Yours seems intact."

"Don't be so sure."

"I don't want to twist things with you," I said.

Maybe my feelings for Patsy were being sucked into a black hole, but sometimes one-way love is good for you. It hurts like hell but it can bring a sort of bizarre contentment. You sure as hell know you're alive. Love creeps in, is borne along, then is lost to melting and evaporation. Elizabeth and Patsy and the snow falls and the love lives and dies in perpetuity. "You remind me of a deer," I said.

She wouldn't look at me.

"Like that," I said, leaning forward with my elbows on the table. "If you come quietly on a deer in the bush it looks at you but away, keeping you in its peripheral vision. Come a little closer and it moves to keep you in the same spot — not away, exactly, but at an angle, maintaining distance but not yet running. Another scent or noise will make it bolt, but God, while it stands there sniffing and looking at you but away, every tiny fiber alert and dancing on its flanks, it is a beautiful thing." I stopped and sighed and she looked at me, not away.

"I have a lot of problems right now," she said. "I don't need another."

"You?"

"Yes."

"It shouldn't surprise me. Everyone does. But you seem so … I don't know. Happy."

She toyed with her coffee cup. "It was only last year that Audrey told me who my father was, told me anything about him. My whole life she merely said it was someone she once was close to. She's so shut down with me, so enigmatic. Don't you think it's strange that she's lived almost all of her life in this town yet nobody knew she had a daughter? I grew up in Victoria with my aunt. Right from the beginning Audrey denied me, all the while hiding the identity of my father. You don't know what it's like to be abandoned by both parents — both of them!"

"You never tried to track Sedro down?"

"He was never legally registered as my father. My aunt knew nothing and my mother wouldn't say."

"Then if you don't mind my asking, what are you doing up here in cahoots with a mother who denied you a normal upbringing?"

"I don't care about the bridge and tunnel."

"I guessed that by now."

"I have to solve some things and this might not be the way to do it, but what choice do I have?"

"Choice?" I said. "Wipe your nose and kick Audrey in the ass and go find Sedro and kick him in the ass, or just say howdy and dust them both off your coat and press on. All we can do is press on or we beat ourselves to death. You're happy with your life in general, and if you're not happy with your past it's only because you've been screwed by other people. Let that part of your life die or you die yourself."

"You don't speak with much sympathy about my father. I thought you two were close."

"Were close," I said. "He's a part of my past I have to let die."

"I know some of it. That is, Audrey told me about Sedro and your father."

"It was an accident."

"You had to confirm it for yourself, though. Your trip up there was the same as mine to see Audrey."

"Yes," I said. "And now it's all confirmed and is laid to rest. It was an accident. An unfortunate accident."

"And he's coming back here for the first time since."

"He is not."

"Oh."

I poured more coffee and cursed myself for cowardice.

"I like what I saw of your store," Patsy said.

I laughed. "The old thing isn't all bad. Well tossed."

"Pardon?"

"The way a hardware store should be. Big jumble of unrelated items side by side. Workingman's place. The proprietor should know where everything is, but nobody else should. If you can't sniff it out then you belong in one of those new hardware emporiums that has bold signs and arrows and neon. Loses all the romance. A hardware store should look and smell like one."

"It's right in the path of the access way to the new bridge."

"They can go around it," I said. "They want me to sell, of course, but they've designed the thing so as to isolate the store in a circle of ramps. The isolation will sink me, but I guess stubborn pride or sour grapes or some goddamn thing is keeping me from capitulating."

"You could start another one."

"Romance is gone. I guess you're really impressed that my idea of romance has to do with a hardware store and squishy sea life."

"Romantic notions are all beautiful."

"Worst part is the bridge site slashes through land the natives are contesting is theirs."

"I didn't know that."

"There's so much in the news these days about natives gaining concessions and winning land claims and re-establishing a toehold, but it's mostly empty journalism. They're still getting jacked around large. Seeing Ovid Mercredi on TV is about all the government needs to convince themselves an equitable redress of aboriginal title is in progress. It's criminal when you think of the cultural richness that has been lost. Look around on the Island: food was so plentiful and the supply of wood and other materials so abundant that the people prospered like no other native group on the continent. Their religion was intense and complex, their art was unparalleled. Ah, you don't want to hear this." I grabbed another cup of coffee from the tin percolator on the stove and went over to boot at the fire.

"There were also slave-keeping tribes," Patsy said.

"You can't use present-day standards to judge people in the past. If you do it's easy to make a case for locking up every group of people on earth."

"You also can't excuse their atrocities because of their antiquity while trumpeting their virtues for the same reason."

"Romantic license," I said.

We laughed and the talk died.

"What do you want?" I asked.

"I don't know."

I sat back down at the table. "I want you."

"Jack, I've been trying to tell you —"

"All you've told me is that I add to your problems," I said. "Having no problems implies an empty existence and an empty head. I'm glad you have problems."

"So you're telling me you want to leave your wife?"

"She already left me."

"And you don't want her back."

"No. That is, yes."

"No or yes what?"

"Yes, I … I do want her back," I said. "But I honestly don't know whether I still love her — I do in some ways — or if it's habit and pride talking."

"You are something!" she said. It was the first time I had seen her sneer. "You break in here and do everything but declare your love for me then tell me you want your wife back out of habit. You're crazy!"

I was out of the chair and around the corner of the table. I pulled her to her feet and kissed her. It went on for some time, at least the time it took for me to realize she wasn't kissing me back. I let go of her shoulders and stepped away, right into an enormous pit of embarrassment. I doubt there's anything worse than that in the immediate sense — unrequited love aches deeper in the long term, but one-way lust makes you want to run screaming away like a mad bastard. It was as if I had worked like hell to get used to Elizabeth's tofu wieners then been hit by a bus — there I'd be, dead *and* dopey.

I looked closely at Patsy, hoping for a sign that it was only her common sense overriding her heart. But as the seconds collected it became plain I was accomplishing nothing but prolonging our mutual agony.

"Can you give me some time?" I finally asked.

"Time for what, Jack? That will just make it later, not better."

"So this is it?"

"I guess."

"Well, shit," I said. "I must look like a sorry sonofabitch standing here."

"I'm sorry."

"I don't need your sympathy."

"Then quit asking for it."

"Yeah."

What the hell to do now? I had to salvage some pride, but the chances were slim I'd think of an idea for a grand exit.

"I'm glad you came, Jack. It would have been worse if we had bumped into each other in public."

Now there, I thought. Not a brilliant closer, but I should have been able to come up with something like that.

"Uh," I said. Or maybe it was, "Mn."

"I'll remember that night," she said kindly.

"We'll always have that," I said. "I'll remember every detail. The Germans wore gray; you were nude."

At least I left her laughing.

FOURTEEN

I raced back into town, not knowing whether to love the whole world or jump off its edge. Eagle had no trouble with such decisions, for he had long ago fallen off the edge. But there was something about him that acted as a salve to my wounds. A sense of completeness filled me in the man's presence, a sense I needed to keep from fragmenting.

The tables were still there and the lawn chair, though sprung and twisted, rested against a fire hydrant. But Eagle had bolted with his wares. I knew he'd be at the Square Rigger, and I hesitated for some time before going to talk to him while surrounded by the regulars, to whom I hadn't exactly endeared myself lately. Nonetheless I cranked up the bike and set off, wondering how it was I had reduced the bulk of my life to a triangle with the three points being my store, the house and the pub.

Eagle was back in civilian clothes. He was standing beside four army surplus duffle bags. The dye from the dunce cap had stained the right side of his beard a bright red and left an ersatz birthmark the size of a saucer on his face. Robert came in from the brewery out back and took a stool. Don and Snuffy were roaming around, getting the place ready for the happy-hour rush.

"Give up the souvenir trade?" I asked Eagle.

"Taking a break," he said, rubbing at his new birthmark.

"Did you sell anything?"

"Got rid of about twenty pounds."

Don slapped his hand palm-up on the bar. "Then let's see some cash."

"Got rid of," Eagle said. "Some guys stole it when I was asleep. Show's there's a market, though."

"You'll never pay that tab," Don moaned. "I can see it now."

"Have this," Eagle said. He slid a huge, elaborate Swiss Army knife down the bar. "I traded a guy a Pope plunger for it."

Don picked it up. "You owe me nine hundred dollars and you give me a Swiss Army knife."

"It's one of the old ones. Got a knife and fork on her."

Don unfolded the thing. "Great," he said. "A knife and fork, but when you open them up they're six inches apart, facing opposite directions. How are you supposed to eat with something like this?"

"Yeah, I know," Eagle said. "Fucking Swiss'd go extinct if they couldn't make watches."

"Can we go over to the store, Jack?" Snuffy asked. "I want to practice with the horseshoes. We haven't played in a long time."

"Haven't done anything normal for a long time," Robert said. "I wish I had my law practice back."

"Wishing never got a horse his own car," Eagle said.

"What time's the general meeting tomorrow?" Robert asked.

I had almost forgotten about it, buried as it was in my mental compost heap. "Seven," I said.

"Gives us plenty of time to get our case straight," Eagle said.

"It gives us nothing," I said. "We don't have a case. We have zip going for us and frankly I don't care anymore. Let them tunnel in, let them stick up a bridge, let them drop tourists from balloons. You guys figure it out."

"Don't go getting pissed off at us," Eagle said. "You jump some little bimbo, your wife takes off, then you badmouth your friends. Fine way to act."

"Shut up, will you. You useless buggers wouldn't fart at a chili cookoff if I wasn't there to tell you when. You want the bridge sunk? Go to the meeting and tell them all about it. I'm fed up with this town and everybody in it. I am not going to stand in front of a room full of ungrateful, shortsighted cocksuckers and spoonfeed them sense. Count me out." I tossed a ten on the bar and headed for the door.

"Jack!" Snuffy called. "Can we go pitch the shoes now? I gotta keep in practice or I'll never get to finish the batch. I still need a crossways line through the other four on the blackboard to make five and a batch. I got to practice."

"Leave him go!" Eagle roared. "Who needs a quitter? That's right — you're a yellow, shitass quitter, Thorpe!"

I kept walking. I heard Snuffy following me.

"Snuffy!" Eagle yelled. "Get back here, you old goat!"

Snuffy's shoes scraped to a stop. "Old goat, he says! You kill me, Eagle."

Needless to say, I was feeling like a right royal prick. I had let it build too much. Usually I can't even shoo a drunk away in a bar. I end up listening to every cockeyed theory and opinion that frustration and alcohol ejects. I guess everyone wants to be liked, but at times I cultivate it even from people who have no business parading their power of speech. Trouble is, it's all fine if you can keep up the game indefinitely, but you can't, and when it all becomes too much and you're losing sight of yourself, the floodgates open and the innocent and the damned, friends and assholes, are swept thrashing indiscriminately together along the waterway.

Good thing I didn't have to worry about Eagle — never had anything I said hurt him. We were too close, linked in some unfathomable way that goes beyond friendship.

Eagle had just turned fourteen and I was close on his heels

both in age and literally as we trudged along the railway tracks leading back to his house. Eagle's dad had sent us out on our first unchaperoned hunting trip. Not hunting, really, for it was out of season, but he wanted us to get the feel of tramping through the bush armed and alert, observing safety rules and getting accustomed to the presence of someone else whom it would be bad policy to treat as a deer.

Dale Stingley had done something like that the year before. Out bow hunting, his partner was leaning against a pine while he took a leak. Stingley mistook his hand for a squirrel and pinned it to the tree with an arrow. Way I figure, you go bow hunting for squirrel, you deserve everything you get.

Eagle's dad was keen on guns but fanatical about firearm safety. His wife was to leave him four months to that day, and the resulting titanic binge found him being pursued by the police at three in the morning, down on the beach, blasting crabs with a shotgun. Fanatical zeal about anything slips the bonds on occasion.

We beat it off the tracks and through the scrub to Eagle's place, a tumbledown log house with a dog run that I would copy years later when building my own house. The old man was sitting on the porch, elbows on his knees, shiny steel safety toes poking out from the leather of his work boots.

"Hopped the bus," Eagle said to his dad as we approached. "Rode along shooting from the windows. Must be six hundred

dead animals scattered from here to Victoria. Jack got a mountain lion — thousand yards running shot. I got two rhinos."

Eagle's dad said nothing. He never did, and maybe that's
why Eagle was always so full of it: he could never get his father's
attention. I didn't know his name, and wasn't sure if anyone
knew. His wife called him any of a dozen diminutives — none
of them particularly endearing — and Eagle had a slew of nick-
names for him. He was an odd man, a little mean, but not in
my old man's league.

We broke and cleaned the unfired guns in view of Eagle's
dad then put them in the rack on the living-room wall. When
we came back outside the old man had hold of Sodbuster by
the collar.

Sodbuster was their goofy golden Lab. The dog was ancient
and senile and couldn't be trusted in town anymore. He never
attacked anyone, but just let him see an open door and he was
through it and going nuts in the store, raking things off shelves,
peeing everywhere and scaring the bejesus out of everyone. Eagle
and I loved it, but when he dropped a large turd on a batch of
Mexican rugs at the import store the council banned him from
the town limits. He had lost an eye to a raccoon a few years back
and the other was sad and rheumy.

"Eagle," his dad said.

"No way!" I could see the fear on his face.

"It's just time, son."

I didn't know what was going on, but clearly they had discussed the matter before.

Then I knew and didn't like it any more than did Eagle or the dog. The old man's attitude toward some things had little to do with present reality, clinging to beliefs from his upbringing that were impervious to logic. To Eagle's dad hunting was not merely a way of providing food — although they did eat everything they killed — but was a prerequisite for coping with the world. In his mind it was important for a man to get used to dealing death, as if it were a criterion for becoming a man, a symbolic ritual not powerful enough to cut it. If necessary, it must be done, but is not an act that should be deliberately sought out. As if needless killing does anything but strike terror of its repetition in the thinking and diminish its consequences in the witless! But the dog had to be put down and Eagle's dad wanted his son to be the one to hurl the bolt.

"I ain't doing nothing," Eagle said.

"I'm not asking, I'm telling."

"And I'm telling you to shit in your tackle box!"

Eagle came up slowly, ignoring the blood leaking from his nose. The old man wiped the blood off the back of his hand by trailing it down his shirt front.

"Hold him, Jack," he said, and for some reason I took hold of the dog's collar. Eagle's dad went inside.

"With that?" Eagle said when his dad returned. The old man

held a thirty-ought-six in one grimy hand. "At close range? It'll blow him to pieces!"

"Do what I tell you."

Eagle caught the rifle at the breech. The old man went back in the house.

We were a hundred yards behind the place, on the edge of the property against the tree line. I still had hold of Sodbuster's collar. Eagle held the rifle as if it were alive and squirming.

"This is wrong," I said. "He can't make you."

"He can," Eagle said. "God, I hate this. I hate him."

"Your own dog," I mumbled.

"Yeah."

"Fire a shot," I said. "Fire into the air and we'll let him go."

"He'd come back."

"Then I'll keep him, or we'll find somebody else to take him."

"He's got to be put down," Eagle said. "Better now than letting him suffer and get stuck with a needle at the pound. That'd be a gross way to go — he ain't a fucking cat."

"Start walking," I said.

"Eh?"

"Back to the house. Gimme the gun and get out of here."

"Aww, Jack, thanks," he said. "But you can't —"

"The gun."

Eagle was halfway back. Sodbuster sat there uncomplaining. He had a few burrs in his coat and I tugged at them and they came free. I tossed them in the grass. There was a five-round magazine on the rifle and I checked and saw one in the spout. Six rounds. Was the old man crazy? I was scared. Scared and wondering why things had to end. Death was normal but not natural. Yes, it happens to every living thing, but that didn't make it natural. Life is natural. Death is the end of nature, whether it chucks us into something better, something worse, or something nervously awaiting the judge's decision. Maybe I feel different now.

Maybe I don't.

I shied as the rifle roared. The round tore off half the dog's ass. I had turned and could hear him howling right behind me. Then the fever had me.

I looked back at the house and raised the rifle. My next shot shattered the latticework on the porch and punched through the wall into the pantry. Eagle and I found the bullet later in a sack of flour. With me jerking at the trigger, the next three shots went wild. Eagle's dad came running out onto the porch and went to ground as the last bullet smashed out the bathroom window. The barrel was hot but I ignored it, swinging from the heels, trying to smash the stock against a sitka spruce. The wood cracked in a couple places and I kept my grip and bust into the trees and ran.

Twenty minutes later I was in a field, paralleling the mountain range, going nowhere, heading vaguely south, walking along with the rifle in the crook of my arm. I slid the gun under a split-rail fence and climbed over. I bent to retrieve the weapon and saw something move a ways back along the path I had made in the grass. I was back over the fence and scared as hell and it was Sodbuster. My loss of control had rubbed out any thought of him. I was weak and I started crying as I looked down at the sad old guy. He was just about gone, limping and trailing the remnants of his hind leg from a hipless haunch.

And there were no bullets in the gun.

He licked my hand and I scratched him and waited till he died then I carried him to the tree line and raked through the duff and buried him in there and piled rocks on top. Then I took the rocks off and placed the gun beside the dog and piled the rocks back on.

I had Sodbuster's blood all over me and I left it there and went home. Mum told me to get changed and cleaned up before my dad saw me like that but I said no and waited for him. He asked me what happened and I wouldn't tell him, flaunting the blood. So he beat me up some, but I didn't cry or yell that time, just let him have at me, and I saw how it scared my mum. It wasn't the last time he hit me but I think my lack of reaction rattled him, and after that he really had to get a hate on to take his hands to me.

I stood outside the pub and finished a cigarette. Eagle wouldn't stay angry at me, and I had too many troubles to worry about the others. I couldn't go home, not with Elizabeth gone. The truck was still up against James and Bernice's house, for all I knew or cared. Leave the pub, press on, jump on the bike and off for the store.

I sat on the daybed, and it took a while but finally I laughed. It was all so trivial. All of it real, yes, and important, oh yes, but so trivial. I went out front and served some customers, and by six o'clock had a total of about seventy bucks in the old cash register. If I hadn't owned the store outright the bridge coming in wouldn't have been an issue at that point. My savings were almost gone and the business had never paid any decent money. I locked up like a real proprietor and pride of ownership actually squirmed in somehow.

Time to head home.

FIFTEEN

Elizabeth was inside. I pulled the bike in beside Bernice's vehicle, one of those new-age jeeps designed for cuteness with a tiny wheelbase and artistic splashes of pink and mauve along the sides, a pretty little surrey with a fringe on top.

I had known the issue between Elizabeth and I would draw Bernice into the fray. A few years back Bernice had engineered a breakup between Luke Postma and his wife, and I do mean engineered — an artfully planned and carefully developed campaign of destruction, veiled in claims of disinterested concern, like an ichneumon wasp planting an egg in her victims, allowing the hosts to be devoured from the inside out.

What began as a serious but not impossible situation, Bernice turned into a brawl that tore apart a marriage. Luke's wife, Phoebe, had been friends with Bernice for years, but Luke should have known better than to listen to an outsider. Hell,

Luke never listened to anybody. But Bernice was good, and through counseling of the "you are the victim" variety, she managed to develop in them a therapy-induced loathing of each other. Over time she repeated the procedure on other couples, so I knew the minute Elizabeth sought shelter with her and James that my relationship with my wife was no longer just a two-way dynamic.

"Get out of here, Bernice," I said before I was through the doorway.

She turned and stared at me, her waspish face pinched as if staring at a squashed raccoon on the road. Her face really was waspish: big compound eyes bracketing a nonexistent nose and a mustache like cilia. She made a tsking sound with her mandibles. "I am here to help Elizabeth pack," she said.

I brushed by her and let my keys drop to the floor. As she reflexively bent for them I tipped her backward onto her fat ass. Her shriek was accompanied by a shattering of glass coming from the lab.

I pushed through the door and stared at the mess. The heat lamp was broken and the terrarium's front was bust out and the snake eggs sprouted a hammer from their midst.

"That's all," Elizabeth said. "That's the end of it. I'm not going on a rampage."

"I've given you reason to," I said.

"Yes, you have."

"Are you really going to walk out on me without talking about it?"

"What do you have to say?"

"Not much," I admitted. "But give me a minute. Some time alone with you."

"Aren't you going to start off by begging my forgiveness?"

"I probably don't deserve it."

"But you're not going to try?"

"Forgive me."

She shoved past me. "Fuck you, Jack."

I freed the hammer from the terrarium. Only six of the twenty snake eggs had been flattened, their pliable skins oozing what looked like ointment. Maybe I'll switch to a proper incubator next time — more uniform heat than the lamp provides. But here I was thinking about snake eggs.

I went back out to the kitchen. Elizabeth was clattering around in the bathroom. Bernice was standing on an Afghani area rug and I yanked the edge of it, sending her on her fat ass again. Elizabeth came out with a plastic bag.

"I left you all the soap and towels and things," she said.

Bernice was back on her feet. "The All Nature Store is closing down, Liz. You'd best bring along your goat's milk shampoo."

"There you have it," I said. "There you have it. You won-der why no right-thinking human being can keep his temper around you two. How do you expect to be taken seriously when you use goat's milk shampoo?"

"It's rich and natural," Elizabeth said.

"Yeah, sure," I said. "Just leave me the last case of turtle shit deodorant, will you?"

Elizabeth set the plastic bag down on the table and headed for the bedroom on the far side of the dog run. "This will take two minutes," she said to Bernice, who smoothed her dress and lowered herself into a chair at the table.

Before storming after my wife I yanked the back of Bernice's chair and her ass became her perch again. Through the living room, across the dog run, I found Elizabeth sitting on the edge of our bed, crying, clothes piled on the counterpane, their hangers tangled and twined. I stood at the door, my thumbs awkwardly hooked in my belt. I couldn't concentrate on the situation. My mind was veering and orienteering. I watched her till she stopped crying and wiped her eyes with the back of her sleeve.

"Do you know," she said, "that I have never once slept with another man since we met? Not once. Not when you'd be gone for days on end on some diving trip. Not when you'd go off on a rugby tournament and stay a week longer than you should. Not when you'd get on one of your drinking jags and spend the night passed out in the storeroom. Not when you'd embarrass me by bullying everyone in an argument over nothing at the pub. Never have I done that. Never. Do you know?"

"I know," I said. "This is the first time for me, too."

"Don't you dare say it that way! It implies we're equals."

"Sorry."

"How could Audrey Weeks have phoned me about it? How could anyone do something that sick?"

"We agree on one thing," I said.

"Oh, God. Does that woman mean anything to you?"

"No."

"Tell me the truth — you owe me that much."

"I don't know," I said. "I barely ... a little, I guess. I just met ... "

"What happened to us?" she said. "Do you remember the fight we had in our first year together? You told me you thought I had married you on a whim, that some day I'd leave you, fly off in a new direction is how you put it. But I haven't."

"You haven't flown off — you've drifted off. I know I'm to blame for this situation, but that doesn't negate the harm you've brought to our relationship. If you'd only realize how inconsiderate you are to people, particularly those close to you, specifically me. Consideration for others is the only thing that binds all us suffering bastards together. I don't care how much of a failure a person is. You have great warmth, but you use it as a tool. You have great love, but you wield it as a weapon. I love you, but —"

"That sums up your personality," she said. "You're the worst kind of romantic. The kind who speaks glowingly of brotherly love while practicing fratricide. You claim my inconsideration has ruined our marriage — right after you've been pounding some slut you met a week ago. You don't see the irony in that?

"And you never used to feel the way you do. My so-called inconsideration never surfaced until the knots you've wrapped yourself up in took control of you, of us. There are so many things in your past with which you are incomplete that you've latched onto my 'weapons' as an excuse to shut me out, so you can brood about Sedro and your mother and your father and the career you won't admit to missing so badly.

"Jack, you are the greatest guy in the world if it results in personal benefit. Your stance against the bridge is symptomatic: selfish, selfish, selfish. You know it will help the town, the Valley, but it will disturb *your* ideals, *your* life. You're a hypocrite. The most insufferable type of hypocrite: a speech maker."

"I don't have the strength for speeches these days."

"You've never been able to taper off, have you? From wild elation and optimism you shoot right down past a normal state of being into a barrel of shit. Don't you realize how that leaves me grasping and groping? How outside it all you make me feel, how little a part of the process? I don't feel so bad now about Pearly Thomas."

She let out a barely audible squeal and stared at me in horror.

"What about Pearly Thomas?" I said as clearly as possible.

"Jesus," she said. Then, into the electric void, she whispered, "It was two years ago."

"Pearly!" I cried. "You fucked Pearly Thomas? *Pearly Thomas?*"

"It was an accident," she said. "Just one night when —"

"That's vicious, that is. That is vile, my dear. You rake me over the coals, playing the martyred wife, all love and innocence and incomprehension, you lie to my face and rub it in and tear me down and, and — Jesus monumental fucking Christ!"

I laughed like a bughouse lifer.

But hold on. Pearly Thomas? He got his name from his big white choppers, enormous dentures that stuck out of his face and curled his lips back like a whickering nag. He was a boring man, who when feeling particularly wild would eat an apple without rinsing it off. Wearing the horns was bad enough, but being cuckolded by someone who just wasn't, well, *worthy*, was too much to live with. Had it been Pavarotti, or Robert Duvall, or Chuck Yeager, or Richard Feynmann, rest his soul, or ... hell, anybody with an ounce of ... But Pearly Thomas?

"What are you thinking about?" Elizabeth said. "Your mouth is open and you're drooling. Are you going to say something, or is your mind gone? You're not the type to be deranged with grief."

"Liar," I croaked.

"Shut up." Elizabeth was looking entirely too composed.

"O! Jezebel!"

"I said shut up, you moron." She lit a cigarette from my pack on the nightstand.

"And you started smoking again," I said. "What else aren't you telling me?"

She shook her head and laughed and carelessly flicked the ashes beside her on the bed.

"Where does this leave us?" I asked after a bit of silence.

"It leaves me to stay with Bernice — don't roll your eyes — and it leaves you to think about what you want. I'm not making any decisions right now, but I can't stay in this house with you. I can't."

I walked back across the dog run, through this strange house, and out into the kitchen, where I leaned against someone else's counter. Elizabeth came out with an armful of clothes, dragging one of those suitcases with the asinine little wheels. Bernice had been keeping her distance, waiting to spirit my wife off to a place of safety. She backed toward the door, chattering away, her pea brain interpreting this as some sort of extended pajama party. I stuck out my foot and down she went again.

"Goodbye," I said tightly to Elizabeth.

Her eyes were clouded over. She stopped and looked at me and I thought she was going to say something. But she didn't.

I made it through the night, neither eating nor drinking, doing nothing but thinking and walking the shoreline and returning to the house then hitting the beach again. I slept some. In the morning a sense of inadequacy drove me to seek out the familiar and I found myself at the Square Rigger talking to Eagle.

"So what's with the tie?" I asked.

Eagle's big hands were tearing a coaster apart. A plain blue silk tie was knotted around his massive neck, splitting the middle of a grimy Pope T-shirt.

"Just come from a new fancy restaurant down in Nanaimo," he said. "Got to have a tie to eat there."

"So you put it on over a T-shirt."

"No, no. I went in without one and sat down. The waiter-d' come over and give me this one to put on. I ordered coffee to go and buggered off. Cheap tie, eh?"

I shook my head.

"Think I'll drive down again tomorrow. Go in naked and see if I can pick up a suit."

Robert tapped his pipe on the bar. "Let's go," he said. "We have only twenty minutes till the meeting."

The meeting. Right.

"Don!" Eagle yelled. "Give us a couple cases of beer for the road. This ain't going to be easy to sit through dry."

Don shuffled two cases onto the bar and Eagle's hams snatched them up. Don and Snuffy came out from behind the taps and Denise, the hazy waitress, sidled in.

"Put the beer on Thorpe's tab," Eagle said to Denise. "If that quitter won't even help us out, the least he can do is buy us a couple drinks. Or are you still on our side? Are you?"

Sixteen

I talked to Denise for three minutes, but the odd looks she was slinging my way meant I was making no sense. Hardly an expert at following the trail of a conversation, Denise at least had mastered the waitress shuffle, the bland agreement with whatever the customer is saying that is necessary armor against vacationing salesmen trying to grab her ass while handing out personalized ballpoints. But in the three minutes her responses had changed from agreement to incomprehension to total confusion, even alarm, so I flipped a five on the bar and went outside.

Figured I should head on down to the meeting. I knew full well I had to put in an appearance. Patted myself down, but the rough notes I had been carrying around for two months must have been in my other jeans. It was only half a mile to the assembly hall, a big barn-like deal with a shake roof and a series of small windows, sitting in the middle of an oyster shell parking lot.

Knots of men stood outside, getting in one last smoke before the meeting. Couple hands went up in greeting and I nodded. I lit a cigarette myself, and as I took a deep drag and stared off at the tree line, trying to make some sense of what I wanted to say, Patsy Jillian drove up and braked in a spray of oyster shells.

She leaped out and in her haste got her briefcase wedged between the doorframe and the back of the driver's seat. She was still reefing away on it by the time I arrived. I flicked the release with the toe of my boot and the seatback slapped forward.

"Thanks," she said. "I'm already late. Audrey will be having a conniption fit."

"Can I talk to you?"

"Later, Jack." She stopped and looked at me. "What are you doing? Aren't you supposed to be part of this? You're on the agenda."

"I feel like Bambi's mother at an NRA convention."

She broke into a brisk walk and, as if realizing the pot was finally starting to boil, there was a general flipping and crushing of butts and the men followed her inside. I trailed a ways behind, and as I passed through the outer doors, Patsy came charging back out into the small foyer.

"What's up?" I said.

"They're in there," she said. She looked scared and I felt a feral, protective tingle right up to my ears. "They're on the dais with Audrey. The two men who came to see me in Victoria."

"I'm not following."

"Damn it — the men who threatened me. No, not threats, really. More a vague warning."

"About queering the proposal? The government guys?"

"I don't think they're with the government," she said. "They're the only ones on the stage I haven't met, so they must be the contractor's reps in from Vancouver."

"I heard someone was in town," I said. "Same guys, eh? What exactly did they say to you?"

"I can't remember. They were concerned about my ties to Audrey and they knew all about my committee work for the government, but the entire conversation seemed designed just to put me on edge."

"What did Audrey say about it?"

"You remember talking to her when you and I first met. She was worried about it as well."

"She's not still worried about being your mother?"

"I don't think so. She feels that with me on board and the town — whoever really cares — knowing about me, there's no worry."

"She's right. These goons sound like they have a mandate that goes beyond PR work for a bunch of concrete layers and hammer swingers, but they were probably just being overzealous in covering all the bases. Come to think of it, that does imply government ties — misguided priorities, trimming your fingernails after you lose your hand in a bandsaw."

"Well, there's nothing I can do about it now. I just got frightened, that's all."

"I'll be at the back," I said. "You better get in there."

"Thanks," she said. "And about —"

"Go on."

Patsy went up the center aisle and took her place between the two strangers and the town council. Audrey Weeks was at the far end of the dais, rising now and going stage right, approaching the lectern. I was impressed and depressed with her preparations.

A rear-projection slide unit was already flicking images on a huge screen. Stage left was her collection of weasels: a good-looking but unctuous stranger, a menacing-looking man to his left, Patsy Jillian, and then the town council — six men and four women sitting there with their hands on their laps and the same fatuous look of triumph Uncle Clem wears when holding up his championship squash.

I readjusted my attention to the two strangers. Even from this distance it was clear they felt this was all a little beneath them. The slick one studied the audience and gave Audrey no more than a cursory glance as she adjusted her notes. His partner was plainly uncomfortable — he looked like the type to pull his jacket over his face at the first sign of a camera.

Audrey started speaking. At first she was a bit jerky, glancing over her shoulder at the screen, trying to catch the rhythm of the visual presentation, but she soon fell in step. The opening slides were various scenic shots of Salish Spit and the Valley, tourist stuff, then smoothly and professionally they switched to statistics and charts and graphs, matching Audrey's narrative flow. She was on a roll, working the room, interspersing personal observations, little quips — hey! I never said she wasn't good. She sat down to a roar of approval.

One of the insectivores from the council got up and introduced Patsy, who gave a concise speech outlining the government's position, praising the whole scheme, simultaneously pissing me off and giving me an erection. I assumed the strangers would speak next.

I felt the visceral unease that goes with facing someone from outside the fold. It's like when our rugby team plays against a foreign side — you can outweigh them to a man on the field and have the utmost confidence in your own abilities, but the very fact that you've never seen them before and they come from a far-off place invests them with a portentous substance that cannot be ignored till the first collision.

I switched back to thoughts of Patsy, how she felt beneath me, on top of me, mentally judging and juggling her and Elizabeth.

Then my name was called.

What the hell was this? Was I a witness for the prosecution? Surely the guys in the suits were there for more than moral support — it shouldn't be my turn yet. Trust Audrey to arrange things so she got the first licks at the jury as well as the closing remarks. I looked guiltily around as more and more people turned to stare at me at the back of the room. Audrey was on her feet, hands on her hips, waiting like a grizzly for me to swim within reach of her paw. My boots on the wood were far too loud as I headed for the dais.

I had no slides, no statistics, no clue. Our strong suit — the environmental issue — I played briefly. I was the oceanographer, one of the experts, but BAT GUANO was scheduled to send its people to the stage with what promised to be a painfully detailed report, and I knew full well the perils of beating a subject to death at any public gathering in Salish Spit. So I did no more than sketch an outline of the problems.

I started in on the aboriginal land claims at the bridge site till Audrey stood up and said had I been listening earlier I would have heard Patsy Jillian describe the deal the government was working on by way of compensation, so whether it was eventually accepted or not, it at least was being addressed.

"Oh," I said. Or something brilliant.

I looked out at the crowd and wondered if I was on the right side. Bunch of friends and enemies and neighbors and relatives, just trying to get by and maybe get the kids the new clothes they need and try to pass them off as Christmas presents because there sure as hell ain't any money for toys. Goddamn truck needs a whole new rear end and where does a man get the time to enjoy the beauty of where he lives when he's trying to make a dollar to pay for vehicle repairs? Brenda's over there — her mother died and Brenda had to borrow money she can't repay to go to the funeral in Prince George. Barry Peters there hasn't used his backhoe on a paying gig for two years. The five fishermen at the back are down to two boats among them, deckhanding for one another in a loose co-op and drinking and bitching the whole off-season.

Why shouldn't we accept something that can get us off our asses? This is B.C. — gold mines and ghost towns, baby. Boom and bust and make hay then press on. No need to purposely opt for any sort of continuum. Clear cut and fuck 'em all.

I realized with a start that everyone was waiting for me to get through my reverie. Elizabeth and Bernice were staring at me, my wife with embarrassment and Bernice with enormous satisfaction. A couple of people figured I was done so started clapping, and Audrey Weeks rose and approached. With a glare I drove her back to her seat.

"Okay," I said into the microphone. "Okay."

I breathed deeply and loosed off a weak grin. Not much of a grin, more a tired smile from a drained, beaten fighter, an opening so the trainer can remove the gumshield, prelude to an overnighter in the hospital and another couple months of flinging your fists and your life at a heavybag and at a dream.

But as I said earlier, I hadn't been getting many breaks lately, so maybe I was just looking for attention.

"I went into the store the other day for some coffee," I said, looking down at Linda Beetleman. "Your place, Linda. Monday, I think it was. Tuesday, maybe."

"Is that a question?" she said. "Do you want an answer or something?"

"Monday. It was Monday."

"Okay," she said. "Monday."

"I was in line behind a guy with a T-shirt that had some kind of joke on it."

"So?"

"Can't remember the joke. But you know the type of thing I mean — kind of joke that's funny first time you see it, but wears thin real quick. Tell a joke at a party, everyone laughs, and you can keep telling the same joke over and over, years sometimes, everybody knows what's coming but being in on a good joke makes you feel part of the action, privileged, like you and the guy telling it are partners. What about this T-shirt thing, though? It's the same as telling the same joke continuously: hit the punchline, start again at the beginning and keep going, no break, nothing, just over and over and over, till the joke isn't so good anymore. You start thinking, not even a joke, really, kind of stupid, harmless but stupid, could get on your nerves, actually, the same joke over and over. Gimme a break, buddy. Besides, there's a time and place for a joke. Leave off with it already, we're getting tired. Hell, I only laughed the first time to be polite, and you don't even tell it very well so shut up now. I never really liked you, just put up with you type of thing and if you don't like hearing the truth maybe we should take it out in the parking lot.

"So you see what happens. A joke's a hell of a good thing. It makes you feel better, but after a while it's too much — a damn fine thing that made you feel better, but after hearing the same thing over and over you start wondering if it isn't time to start thinking about dinner. Buddy made you feel good for a few minutes, but he didn't know when to stop. Now you don't have anything ready for dinner and you've spent all this time listening to the same joke and you're ready to take the guy out to the parking lot.

"So they build a mall on the edge of town and everybody feels good, like hearing a joke. About six months later you real- ize you haven't been to the new mall since the first week it opened, because who can afford to go to a men's specialty shop and buy a big onyx chess set or something frivolous like that? And the shoe store next door is too expensive because they're paying the same rent as the specialty shop. You start thinking, hey, isn't that mall right on the field where the high school kids used to hold their Thanksgiving bonfire and corn roast every year? That's right. The kid's are still there actually, but they can't roast corn beside the fountain in the middle of the mall, but I guess hanging around spitting in the fountain ain't so bad, at least you know where they are.

"So with the mall dying, they build a new highway right past it, because it's no wonder there's no business — nobody can get to it. And everybody feels good. Only trouble is for the families whose kids and pets have to be more careful now that there's a great bloody freeway out front of their yard, and trouble aplenty for the folks on the old spur line that have to sell their gas station and their three stores now that nobody takes that route into town anymore. The highway's good, though, because with that kind of access it's worthwhile for the Vancouver developer who's never lived on the Island to buy up the mall for a song.

"And if people are going to drive in to have a browse around the mall, might as well stick up a motel with a swimming pool so they can stay overnight and spend some money, which they do, at the mall and the motel lounge and gift shop, making enough for the motel owner that he can stop driving up from Victoria, which is good because he has to be available to supervise the new waterslide park he's building in a down-Island town that used to be like ours. Everybody still feels all right, but looking at their watches because it's time to start thinking about dinner.

"That waterslide idea is catching on, so if they extend the highway we can have one of our own on the north side of town, and the investors from Hong Kong and Los Angeles have a point when they say that the low land off the road just breeds mosquitoes, and the fishing isn't all *that* good in the feeder creek, and we shouldn't be shooting ducks anyhow, so it's a perfect place for the waterslide, so let's fill in the marsh, and if we're going to have a park no sense in going small — we'll need the facilities for whatever you want to do, and the people who don't like water can play miniature golf right beside the thing, then cross the new pedestrian overpass to the wax museum on the other side that has all the stars of *Melrose Place* in wax.

"But now you've missed supper. And you aren't feeling so good since you found out that the view of the waterslide and the new Taco Bell and the fake antique store out your window — pretty as it all is — is going to cost you an extra fifteen-hundred in taxes now that your property has been reassessed.

"So it's time to do some figuring. Because you stopped laughing some time ago. And the way you have it figured is if anyone at all starts telling you that joke again, it's going to be you and him out in the parking lot."

I had been aware for five minutes that Audrey was fed up.

"Thank you, Jack," she said.

No sooner was she out of her chair and making for my redoubt than someone yelled, "Sit down. Just sit down, you!"

It was the only voice of protest, but there was an air of agreement in the drafty old barn.

"So off went the guy in the T-shirt," I said to Linda, who was smiling and nodding warmly at me. "It still took a while to get to me."

"That's right," Linda said.

"The woman ahead of me was buying a lottery ticket and needed help picking the numbers."

"She kept changing her mind," Linda said.

"Of course, she never played the lottery. Waste of money, is what she claimed. But nobody had won for a few weeks and the grab was up to seven million. Now, as a sometimes gambler myself, to which a few of you can attest — shut up, Darryl, you're off duty — I can understand the thrill of the competition and the hearty camaraderie of trying to win Eagle's truck off him again."

The crowd was loose, and there was a groaning of metal as people slumped and reclined in their folding metal chairs.

"We must put a time limit on the speeches," Audrey said.

"Shut the fuck up!" someone yelled, then added, "Your Honor."

The laughter told me I was on the right track. I didn't really think I would get anywhere with all this, but then even though Scopes was found guilty, the Monkey Trial achieved a sensible and wholesome shift in attitude. I continued.

"Makes me wonder. When the lottery stands at a million bucks only the regulars drop a fin for a ticket. Get it up to seven million and everybody with a pulse and a last name lines up to put down his money. What the hell am I gonna do with a million — hardly worth the bother. Now, seven million, a person can eat and maybe get the old man something for his birthday.

"In any event, there we have it — going for the Big Seven. Sure, the odds are so enormous I could play every week for twelve lifetimes and still have no more chance of hitting than a one-legged rodeo clown of saving his ass. But it's only five bucks a week. First couple times it was fun, and I don't really expect to win anyhow. Then I won ten bucks, so I'm only down a fin, you see. Harmless fun, dreaming about the Big Seven — where'm I gonna go, what'm I gonna do? Damn it! Missed again this week. Better get a couple of tickets, double my chances, right? Damn! Nothing again. What I'd do for that kind of dough: get out of debt, pay off the mortgage, junk that bloody truck. If only. Nothing again — this is getting ridiculous. If only. See who won this week? Eighty years old. What's she gonna do with seven million? How much Poligrip can you buy? *I'm* the one who needs it. If only. Aww, no, not again! Just one break, that's all I need. Lost again? That's it, I'm playing one more week and then … what's going on here? This ain't right. I could fall in a barrel of tits and come up sucking my thumb. It's not right." I stopped and looked out at them, staring hard.

"Fine," I said. "Perhaps I'm laying this on a little heavy. You are not stupid people. But I am going to spell it out: Quit waiting for it to happen. We have to do it ourselves or we die. Don't wait for the lottery. Don't count on the big inheritance or you'll end up suing your brother for his share as well. Don't piss around digging for gold on your back property or you'll wind up with a lot of holes and a bad back. Don't buy a painting hoping the artist will die before you do. Don't hang on to your favorite hockey player's rookie card for any reason other than because when you were a kid he was your hero.

"And don't — at all costs, don't — wait for people like this." I pointed directly at the oily stranger. "Do not wait for people like this to come along with a scheme and a bag of money. Because sure as shit we'll be left with the scheme and he'll be going home with a bigger bag.

"This is our town and our lives. We can and should fix it ourselves. I don't want to live anywhere else, and by letting other people transform Salish Spit into their idea of what it should be like, we will find ourselves living somewhere else without ever leaving home."

As the hall erupted into hoots and howls, I stepped off the dais. Linda pushed into the aisle and tugged at my sleeve.

"I'm with you, Jack," she said. "I really am. Wow — who would have thought I'd be looking at things this way just from you coming in the store?"

"Jeez, Linda," I said. "I haven't been in your place for six months."

She laughed and I laughed and I went to the back of the room feeling pretty fucking good. I went outside while the speaker for BAT GUANO was being introduced. Two of their members had got themselves up as coho salmon with steel bridge girders seemingly plunged through their chests, like Steve Martin's arrow-through-the-head gag.

I lit a cigarette and heard a creak. I should have been shocked, but wasn't, when Sedro Tuckett came out the door and joined me.

"Lookit here, kids," I said.

"How are you, Jack?"

"You tell me, old man."

He laughed. "Where'd you learn that style of speechifying?"

"From the master," I said. "Have you any idea of the number of times I hid in the back of that very hall listening to you bullshit and rant and get what you wanted without ever making a clear case?"

"I always believed you could fool all the people all the time if only you left them thinking they hadn't been fooled."

"Good to see you," I said. "I thought you had no interest in this."

"When you were up north you sort of mentioned it in passing," he said. "Treated it as inconsequential. So I knew how important it was to you."

I smiled. "Want to go grab a beer?"

"Have you seen enough fur fly?"

Chuckling, we went back inside and positioned ourselves against the back wall.

BAT GUANO was lustily cheering their spokesperson as she finished her speech, while the rest of the crowd sat bemused and uncomfortable.

Audrey Weeks introduced the greasy stranger, who smiled down at the audience like a substitute teacher specifically chosen to control an unruly classroom. He removed his tie, probably thinking it gave him something in common with the blue-collar mob it was his job to crush or suborn. He gave a well-rehearsed speech, painting a rosy landscape, all but assuring us that every eager beaver in Salish Spit would be able to work merrily away on the project and henceforth live forever snug and secure on its benefits. Visions of Cecil Rhodes danced in my head, alongside images of sweating Xhosa workers half a mile down a mine shaft.

I heard little of it. Sedro's presence beside me was too strong, too strange.

But then, lads, the fuse was lit on the dynamite, the carbon rods were exposed to the air, the monster broke free of his wrist shackles and climbed off the operating table.

Audrey Weeks should have taken control of the question period. She had dominated the room while speaking and she was the mayor. But she lapsed. Smug in apparent victory, Audrey was counting her pilings before they were sunk. She let the stranger — I still hadn't caught his name — field the first set of questions.

Sedro raised his hand and shouted for attention. With his beard and the crushed straw hat he had on, no one immediately recognized him.

"You claim the project will provide work for all the men in Salish Spit who want it," Sedro said. "And that the spinoffs after completion will continue to boost the economy upward. Yet why should this time be any different than what has occurred in the past? The Island has always pulled the short straw when it comes around to reaping the benefits of outside investment."

It didn't take much more. I joined in and between the two of us we played our game, going on about the government, nothing specific, just playing the grousing, intolerant, indignant civic boosters, not letting the stranger get in a word, leaving no space for answers, slinging rhetorical questions around with abandon. The kind of bitching every right-thinking person should ignore. The belaboring that rabble-rousers with no facts to back them up get into at every gather of decision makers, be it the House of Commons or a Kiwanis luncheon.

My money says when an African termite mound holds its annual fundraiser there is one insect who stands up on his hind legs and complains about his work party having to take the long path to the job site, then scuttles away laughing while the meeting erupts into frenzied bickering and the Arthropod of Ceremonies is pelted with buns.

It is called disclaiming responsibility, pointing the finger, fighting truth with volume. And it was working. Maybe I do like to see the fur fly.

Sedro and I finally ran out of things to say, and the contractor's rep dealt with the situation in the worst possible manner: he attacked. And that's when the shit accelerator kicked in. The whole crowd was unleashed and took to screaming questions and demanding answers and making claims and hurling denunciations and even introducing personal grievances. Fist-beating and footstomping and Audrey Weeks yelling in the microphone and the town council shifting in their chairs like guards at a prison riot. No sense was made. It was vendetta time, and every old conflict was hauled out for public inspection, with the crowd eventually turning on itself and pretty much ignoring what was going on at the head of the room.

It didn't stop at that. Sedro and I were standing and laughing at the back. Audrey took charge but the contractor's rep, maintaining a sliver of personal dignity, snatched the mike back from her and was trying to pacify the mob when his menacing-looking assistant strode up beside him. The din in the hall subsided with remarkable timing to make the assistant's amplified remark audible to everyone.

"Fuck these hicks! Let's get outta here."

That's when Eagle charged the mound.

"Yep," Eagle said.

We were in the Square Rigger. The mudslinging had carried on from the meeting and was only now dying down as everyone relaxed in more familiar surroundings. Eagle was leaning back in his chair, shaggy head against the glass of the bay window.

"Yep," he said. "He was pretty big for a guy in a suit, but I don't think he judged my speed right. I gave him the old bulldozer move — head down and drive right into the chest. Down he went." He gulped at his beer and scratched at the red patch on his cheek. The dye was almost gone from his skin but his beard still blazed scarlet. "Who do you think got me with the chair?"

"I was at the back," I said. "All I could see was a pile of bodies thrashing around."

"Thrashing's the word," Eagle said. "More like a baseball fight than anything, guys jumping on the pile ass-first just for the fun of it. Bunch of kids!"

Sedro laughed. He sat there with his legs crossed, feet waggling black Converse All Stars. He was still aglow from the battle. Eagle, of course, had recognized him, and Audrey Weeks must have been stung by his voice, but it wasn't till we were back here in the pub and it started to fill with the survivors of the melee that the local folks began to suspect.

And Sedro had carried it off, all right. A fifteen-year absence he had wiped out by the simple expediency of shaking each person firmly by the hand and speaking as if he had never been away. Don greeted him shyly then went behind the bar in self-defense. Robert was stiff with him, but pleasant. Eagle squeezed him by the shoulders and looked him hard in the eyes.

"Da Vinci," he said. "Good to have you back. How's it up in Eskimo land? All-day parking lot owners must lose a bundle half the year, eh? Ha! Well, let's get you a beer. You'll have to buy. Seems I went over my credit limit a couple bucks and Don cut me off."

There were tentative stares from all corners of the room and occasionally someone would sidle up and shake Sedro's hand and say a few words of welcome, or stumble over his tongue and leave with evident relief.

Sedro looked tired. He had shrunken and there was a clear lack of life force about him. In the past his curiosity lent his eyes the look of a town snoop — let's see, what do we have here and what's this now and how do you like that and by God that's exciting, now that's exciting! Oh, he was confident enough and as of old when he spoke he commanded attention. Someone who didn't know the man as I did might call it serenity. But it was something lost, not gained. A deposit on an account that paid no dividends.

Sedro hadn't met Audrey yet but said he was intent on visiting her soon. Wish I could be in on that one. I wondered suddenly if he even knew he had a daughter. Life was getting dirty again.

"You still haven't told us what you think of the meeting," Robert said.

Sedro had dropped a fifty on the table and Robert was gulping as fast as his little English hands could capture the mugs.

"Not much to say," Sedro said. "It's obvious there's not nearly enough support to defeat the proposal."

"What?" Robert cried. "We showed all the opposition in the world."

"That wasn't opposition," Sedro said. "That was bitterness. It was good people held down too long by idleness and unemployment. Stagnation breaking out in one last belch of swamp gas. No, no, they clearly intend to connect to the mainland. And maybe it's not such a terrible thing. I've a strong inkling that defeating the proposal would merely forestall the inevitable. A great many people hollered when they connected the Florida Keys to the mainland, but the highway and railway became lifelines."

"The bridge site's partly on Jack's property," Robert said. "We still have that, and possession is nine-tenths of the law."

"Five-sixths," Sedro said.

"Huh?"

"I mean there is no rule. I thought you used to be a lawyer."

"A good one," Robert said. "A damn good one."

"Besides, according to Jack they already have plans to go around the site."

I nodded. "Any ideas at all?" I asked.

"Not at the moment. We aren't holding many face cards."

"We?" I said. "You saying you'll be sticking around awhile?"

"Might. How's my old place?"

"Don't know about the inside," I said. "Outside's weathered but sound. Wouldn't take much to spank some life into it."

"Hmn."

"Looky, looky," Eagle said. He pointed with his mug at the door.

Beautiful. The contractor's rep, or government man, or whoever the hell he was, had entered and was already shaking hands — left hand on the elbow — with anyone within reach. His assistant looked dogeared, as if he had been dragged by the heels through a holly bush. They started to take a table by the door but caught us staring and hesitated. A quick heads-down conference ensued, then they began picking their way through the crowd toward us.

"Don't pull anything, Eagle," I said. "There's no points for this one."

"Wouldn't think of it," he said indignantly.

I stood as the men approached.

"I'll be direct, Mr. Thorpe," the rep said. "I admired your speech and can appreciate your point of view. I'm Benton Firsk."

I shook the man's hand. Sedro introduced himself but Robert just nodded. Snuffy arrived to empty the ashtrays and stared. Eagle hadn't moved, wasn't even looking at them.

"Who you with, Firsk?" I asked. "Government?"

"Come now." He chuckled. "You must have been listening to my speech closer than that. I represent Pacific Rim Amalgamated. The interrelatedness of interests among businesses in these times promotes a joint approach to dealing with the points of commonality, and that is what PRA does: we assess, collate, match interests, then promote and manage the execution of a project so as to minimize impedimenta."

"Impedimenta," I said. "So what you're saying is that everyone who stands to make a buck in the construction of the tunnel and bridge has banded together and hired a bunch of leg-breakers to do anything necessary to ram the fucker through. If you can accomplish it through speeches, fine. But a few threats and a little coercion certainly aren't out of the question. Get out of here, Firsk. Go away. People like you make my beer taste bad."

"This is my assistant," Firsk said. It was as if I hadn't spoken. "Manny Parsons."

Glares all round. Parsons kept his hands in his pockets — pants pockets, for those of his jacket had been torn off in the scrap. The right side of his face was puffy and shiny. He didn't say a word.

"Jeez!" Snuffy said. "You're as big as Eagle, Mr. Parsons."

"Who?"

"Me," Eagle said, coming out of his chair.

"Eagle?" Parsons laughed. "You don't look like an Indian."

"Ain't one."

"You fight like one."

"No, I don't," Eagle said. "Indians mostly lose."

"Easy, here!" I said. "Nobody needs this."

Parsons loosened his tie. He wasn't as tall as Eagle but looked to be twenty pounds heavier, none of it gut. Bad air in there.

I turned to Firsk and said, "Tell your buddy to lighten up."

"He's my assistant," Firsk said. "Not my servant."

"That's right," Parsons said. "That's right. I'm nobody's servant. Especially for some guy with half a red beard. What's that supposed to mean, anyhow?"

"Your old lady was on the rag when I went diving," Eagle said.

"Not in here!" Firsk snapped. "Mr. Thorpe was wrong. We're merely here on a public relations mission. This is a personal matter, so take it out of sight."

Manny Parsons turned to Eagle. "Lead the way, boy."

Eagle was grinning. "Where you want to go, Ace?"

"Anywhere."

"Out back?"

"Fine with me."

Eagle spun around and plowed through the mob at the bar, yelling, "Excuse me, gentlemen, excuse me! Pregnant lady here, let us through. Pregnant lady coming through."

He headed past the pool tables for the back door. Parsons was five yards behind him, arguing over his shoulder with Firsk. Eagle halted at the dartboard and turned to face the men. Puzzled, they froze. In one blur of motion Eagle snatched a dart from the board and flung it straight into Parson's chest.

"Aggh!" Parsons screamed.

As he scrabbled to get the thing out of his body, Eagle caught him with a right hand thrown from somewhere east of Chad. Parsons was out before he hit the tiles.

"That could have taken his eye out!" Firsk cried.

"Could of," Eagle said. "If I'd been aiming there."

"That wasn't even a fair fight!"

I started choking with laughter. "Who are you guys?" I said. "You sound like his mother, Firsk. Put his eye out. Fair fight. You're too much, man. You come into town, throwing your weight around, then expect a fair fight. Maybe I was wrong. Dopey buggers like you couldn't possibly have been hired as strongarms. Could be you're government after all."

Eagle moved his bulk closer to Firsk and shoved his big ugly face at him. "While we're talking about fair … What's not fair is a couple pansy pukes coming into a place they don't know nothing about and telling us how they're going to save us from ourselves. That's what ain't fair."

He stared hard at the man till Firsk turned away and knelt beside his coldcocked partner.

"Don!" Eagle screamed, heading for the bar. "I just saved the whole town from an international terrorist. How about starting up that tab again?"

SEVENTEEN

The swallows were gone. A family of them used to nest under the gable of Sedro's cottage, tucked away out of sight, shielded from the elements by the porch roof. When it was quiet at night you could hear them scratching around at the front of the attic, up late but going about their business quietly, perhaps afraid of waking the landlord. They'd sit on the edge of their perch and let you get within six feet, but if you opened the door from the inside they would dart out and down and away, over your head and out toward the beach, accelerating and banking with high-g turns. Once a week Sedro would bang on the wall to chase them out, then hose their guano off the front of the cottage.

I had walked the shore to reach the place, along the sand and gravel and over the base of the spit with its mussels and oysters. The sky was a dull flannel sheet that yanked time back to winter — if the moderate coastal climate allowed glimpses of spring in February, then it was at least as effective operating in reverse.

Sedro was already on the porch when I arrived. But the swallows were gone. And so was a lot of the mystery that had made the place so fascinating to a sixteen-year-old budding scientist. I used to enter his domain with familiarity but with none of the contempt it supposedly breeds. I was a spelunker in Sedro's cave, a student in his lab.

Now I was a handyman in an old, leaking cottage that needed paint, soap and water and new wiring. Mildew had totaled many of Sedro's books. His various collections were intact, but somehow of another time, as if I were in the basement of a museum and looking at row after row of dead birds and mounted insects that had been sent back east by one of the western trailblazing naturalists of the past century.

I felt like hell and told Sedro to examine the rest of the inside alone. I went up on the roof. I pulled at the loose cedar shakes — a third of them were missing, ripped from their ranks by water and wind — and tossed them aside, scaling them into the bush.

Sedro had spent the night before in a hotel. In the morning I went over to James and Bernice's house and, while they watched through the window, fiddled with the truck and got it going again. I picked Sedro up and we had a big feed of ham and eggs at the coffee shop by the volunteer firehall.

Some people came over to say howdy to Sedro, but more didn't. I began to realize his absence had allowed for a lot of changes in the Spit. I bet most people in town didn't even know him. Besides, Sedro Tuckett had been larger than life in my own life, so I'd assumed he was in everyone's.

But as much as our folks know one another's business, there is also a certain insularity, a cleaving to the family unit that allows the individual anonymity even if he doesn't seek it out. I had anticipated Sedro's homecoming would prompt massive acknowledgment, but a few nods and hellos and everyone went about their business. Muhammad Ali could visit Salish Spit and a lot of men would just say howdy and ask him if he'd like to play eight-ball for quarters.

I had dropped him off at the top of the cliff so he could walk down the steep road leading to the beach, then went back home to see if for some reason Elizabeth had returned. Of course she hadn't, but I left a note by the phone out of habit, or a maudlin sense of duty, or desperation, and started the hike to the cottage.

Sedro came out and I shuffled over to the edge of the roof. "Eagle can strip and rewire the place," I said.

He looked up at me. He squinted even in the dim light, his face cracking like desiccated buckskin. "How's it up there?"

"We'll have to rip it up and start fresh," I said. "The rest of the exterior just needs a coat of paint, except for the porch. Easy enough to fix that, though."

"Why don't you come down and roll up those pants?" he said. "Tide's almost at full ebb."

The sand hadn't dried out yet. It squished and oozed as we plodded the flats. A couple of sea stars on the rocks, purple and stranded, soon to die and turn orange if washed up to the shore by the incoming tide. *Echinodermata*: Class *Asteroidea*. A bed of sand dollars a ways along. Echinoderms, too, but class *Echinoidea*. Silly little things sticking in my mind while the big things took a flying leap. We cut over toward the spit, exposed and naked, looking like the vertebrae of some long-dead monster. Tiny red crabs scuttled away as our feet sloshed through the tide pools. Their black-tipped pincers waved at us.

I soon grew bored. There was nothing new here. Rather than exploring out of curiosity, we were grasping, trying to return to the early days of discovery. Nothing fit. I looked up at the sky and felt tired. I started walking back to the beach. I turned around and Sedro was hunched over a tide pool, gently lifting a mass of bladder kelp and peering beneath it.

A pivot and I was looking up at the glacier. It was all but invisible, smothered by the low cloud that ran into the mountains a quarter of the way down. Some connection between Sedro and me must have still existed, for he called feebly and I waited till he joined me then off we went and sat on the porch, our feet digging holes in the dark gray volcanic sand.

He was the first to speak.

"You have to stop waiting for me, young Jack."

"It's been a long time," I said. "I've been doing more than waiting these fifteen years."

"In a way you've always been waiting. Waiting for me to take the lead when you were young. Waiting for me to come back —"

"Take the lead?"

"Would you have become a scientist if it wasn't for me? It obviously wasn't meant to be your life's work. You quit after a couple of years on the job."

"But I'm glad I did it."

"I never did."

"You did it the same way I did," I protested. "Got your degree, practiced awhile, then discovered there were other things out there while holding on to science as a lifelong passion."

"What degree? I earned a few credits but never graduated from anything in my life. As far as practicing goes … " He waved vaguely out at the flats that were starting to contract with the incoming tide. "That's about as far as it went."

"You told me —"

"A lot of things," he finished.

"Then you lied."

"Want to know where I earned my credits? A fine institution that allows almost unlimited study time. Outside the daily exercise periods and meal times and shower breaks, that is."

"You were in the joint?"

"The big house itself. It came out in the trial."

"I didn't follow that," I said tersely.

"You've never followed anything about me that didn't fit the picture."

We sat awhile. "What else?" I finally said.

He laughed bitterly. "Let's see … Three wives."

"Not so horrible."

"Two of them simultaneously."

"What are you trying to do, deliberately tear yourself down?"

"Yes, Jack, I am!" He stood and spun to face me. "Do you have any idea how hard it has been? Trying all those years to live up to what you expected of me, then trying all these years to live down the hurt and the anger I could feel from you across all those miles and all that time?"

"You killed my father," I said. "But I always thought more of you as my father."

"Don't say that," he said quietly. He went over to one of the scruffy broom bushes. Savagely he pulled and tore until he had ripped off a handful of sticks and leaves. "Don't say that. I've never been a man to emulate."

"The good you've done."

"The good I've wanted to do. Maybe it was all atonement."

"This town is your monument."

"This town is the glorified result of my having made hundreds of thousands of dollars," he said.

"What?"

"Why do you think I invested that much energy and effort into the place? What do you think I was doing running around the Island and bumping my gums at the government and in the media all those years? With the real estate deals and the bribes and kickbacks and every other plot I dipped my bloody fingers into, I'm surprised the earth didn't swallow me whole."

"You are not an evil man."

"No," he said lowly. "I don't think I am. I like to think I did some good along the way. But I am weak, young Jack. I am that. I've done it all over again on a smaller scale up in Davis Flats. And I did it before I ever got here."

I rose and looked at the cottage. "But this," I said. "And your shack up north. What have you done with all the money? You've never even owned a decent pair of boots."

He smiled then. "Given most of it away. Still have a lot in various places Revenue Canada will never find. I don't know. Never was the money. It was the same with my wives — something new, the chase, the striving, a restlessness that drove me to look for balance by averaging out extremes."

"Some extremes," I said.

"Some extremes."

"Audrey?"

"Hmph," he said. "She could have been wife number four, but she was much too smart for that. She didn't know the details but she knew the game. An intelligent woman, Audrey."

"Do you know about Patsy?"

"Yes."

"Then how could you —"

"Please."

I let it all whirl at its own rate.

"Drastic solutions," he said. "Never an ordered way of doing things. Wives, children, money … everything."

"And I can assume you're back looking for another solution."

"Don't know that I am."

"Absolution?" I said. "Excuse me, Father, for I have sinned. It has been fifteen years since my last confession, and I even buggered up that one."

"We always wait too long. Avoid the ugly and at some point it becomes impossible to deal with."

"Now?"

"I just had to be here," he said. "I thought being here would give me the strength to deal with it all. I once told you that comfort's a stroll once you get used to the dirt. But getting used to something doesn't mean you can deal with it. I've always let the dirt pile up until it was too late to shovel, leaving a drastic solution the only solution. I'm sorry."

"Are you sorry for my father?"

"I couldn't stand it anymore, young Jack." He looked hard at me. "The thought of him taking his hands to you … to your mother … to the world."

"Drastic solution, all right." It was too much to take in all at one go. "I still don't know why you're back. Of course that's understandable, considering you don't really have a clue, either."

"I guess we'll see," he said.

By then my back was to him as I slogged through the sand toward home.

E I G H T E E N

Alone in a house built for two. A reverberating sense of loss draining me of what strength was left. A gutful of betrayal. How does one rebuild? I suppose you start by determining what should be rebuilt and what should be consigned to the landfill site.

Did I want Elizabeth back? Yes, I was sure I did. There was something about the woman that completed the connection — I was not plugged into the world without her. Patsy I figured I was in love with, in a confusing, almost pubescent way. And Sedro — what do you do when the pedestal cracks and the bronze horseman joins you down in the mud?

I went to bed.

I had taken to rising earlier each day since Elizabeth left, and was up and about at six. I was on the dog run, heading for the kitchen, when I saw the helicopter come in low over the

Straits from the Forces base. A big twin-rotor Labrador with conspicuous yellow raiment and RESCUE—SAUVETAGE in red letters on its flanks. I waved at the crewman's head poking through the side door and got a wave in return. It banked over the spit and the pilot dropped collective, allowing his charge to drop lower still, and I saw it was heading for the hospital.

I don't know what told me, but I was inside for my keys and into the truck. The front bumper was gone, sacrificed to the fury gods and still lying in state outside Bernice's. I had wired the grille to the frame and it shook feverishly as I climbed the hill to the main road. The hood was smashed in and bent back like a pug's nose, impairing my view. The engine quickly overheated but I ignored it.

I knew in my gut it was Eagle, and that if a medevac was under way it was serious. Eagle was always getting hurt. Outstanding reflexes and the strength of five couldn't hope to cope with the way the man attacked life, treating danger alternately as fun and as an insignificant nuisance.

Soft morning light glittered obliquely off the glacier and the snowcone peaks, scattering handfuls of zircons to cascade down the slopes. It was almost blinding, striking the snow at such a high angle of incidence. The rattle of the grille was the only sound for a thousand miles. The quiet only served to intensify my anxiety.

They knew me at the emergency ward, my having tripped in so many times to be patched up after a rugby injury or a drunken stunt of idiocy, so I went there first.

The bullet had clipped Eagle in the back of the head.

No, they didn't know the extent of the injury. Yes, he was unconscious, had been since they picked him up from the sidewalk in front of the movie theatre. No, the police didn't have anyone in custody. Yes, I could explain why he was wearing long red underwear. No, he had no next of kin. Yes, I would sign for the large sack of Pope mementos. No, he wasn't there — the chopper was already on the way to Vancouver. No, the bullet had not lodged in the brain. Yes, it had sheared off part of his skull. No, too early to tell. Pardon me, Jack? Well, yes, this type of injury could permanently affect him, if he survives. Don't start that crap with me, Jack — I didn't pull the trigger.

If he survives.

Two years ago Ted Hallsworthy had taxied his Stinson float plane up to the beach in front of my house. An anchored Boston Whaler twenty feet from the shore provided little resistance as the Stinson's prop cleaved through the bow, sending the thing to the bottom. When I swam out to the plane, climbed on the float and opened the door Hallsworthy was so drunk I had to undo his lap belt and shoulder harness, lock my arm under his chin, and slosh through the water with him to shore. So he owed me one, and I said so when I got him on the phone.

Thirty minutes later he kicked the rudder, swinging the plane's tail to the dock, and I climbed in. Forty minutes after that I was scrambling onto the pier on Burrard Inlet and twenty minutes again I was manhandling an innocent orderly at Vancouver General Hospital.

"I am Dr. Haq. Please let go of that man."

I released the orderly and he scurried off. The doctor was about five-two and incredibly thin, maybe a hundred pounds when holding a small safe. He carried himself with impressive dignity and authority. He was Pakistani, had an accent attesting to his origins, and was one of those people you like immediately.

"I'm sorry, sir," I said, adopting a deferential tone. You can kick hell out of the tellers, but you don't abuse the loans officer. "My name's Jack Thorpe. I'm a friend of Eagle's."

"I am enamored of dolphins," he said.

"No, no — the man you admitted from Salish Spit. The shooting."

"Evelynn Stump," he said.

"That's him. But I'd advise you not to call him that when he comes to."

"He has come to."

"He's awake?"

"Extraordinary, really. By all manner of conjecture he should be in a coma. Or ... "

"Dead."

"Yes. You see, the injury is not extensive, there was no shattering, you understand, but it is severe in the localized sense.
Hemorrhaging, loss of cerebrospinal fluid —"

"The doctor on the Island said the back of the head."

"The occipital lobe area."

"But he is awake."

"Not for any great lengths of time. He is awake briefly, even
flirts with lucidity, then drops back into unconsciousness."

"What are his chances?"

"Difficult to say. As yet we have no idea of the extent of
neural damage. He is being prepared for the operating room at
this moment, but that is merely to deal with the wound itself."

"Can he —"

"Come," he said abruptly. "The coffee shop is down the hall.
Let us sit down."

Hospitals are filthy in their cleanliness. Antiseptic cleanliness, necessary but unnatural. Unctuous order and insidious
odor and I hate the fuckers. Even the coffee tasted of the place.
Galen's Mocha. Haq clasped his bony fingers around the cup.

"The wound is bad," I said.

"Yes, but not necessarily fatal."

"Could he be paralyzed if he lives?"

"Unlikely," he said. "Paralysis is not associated with this type
of injury. Hemiplegia — paralysis of one side of the body — is
most commonly caused by hemorrhage of a major cerebral

artery in the opposite hemisphere of the brain. It appears he has been spared that damage. There is no spinal injury and we have ruled out total paralysis. He responds to stimuli quite normally."

"Then what are the possibilities?"

"The temporal lobe, fronting the occipital area, is connected with the limbic system, the area enabling us to experience the more primitive emotions of fear, anger, lust. At this time we do not think it has been affected. Likewise the parietal lobe, above, seems intact. This lobe contains the sensory cortex and organizes, if you will, physical sensations. A lesion or injury to this part of the brain may not leave the patient without sensation, but if he is to determine whether a pinch on the foot is actually occurring in the foot or, say, his arm, the parietal lobe must be healthy."

"So ...?"

"So if your friend lives he will very likely have full control of his body."

"You're giving me lots of good news, Doc," I said. "But unless I'm mistaken an injury to the occipital lobe may leave him blind."

"Mr. Thorpe," he said measuredly. "He is blind. And will almost assuredly remain in that condition."

The gas jockey at the seaplane dock directed me to a waterside neighborhood pub in Coal Harbour, where I found Ted. He had had a few but I didn't care, and after a few jarring bumps we were airborne and things smoothed out nicely, at least in the physical sense.

On the drive back home from the dock, I saw Patsy Jillian. Without a moment's thought I braked and asked — or demanded — she jump in. When we arrived at my house I built a fire, although it was much too warm for one. I drank a bottle of Plainsman Rye as if it were water and around five in the morning, after bending Patsy's ear with everything that had ever vaguely crossed my alleged mind, I suppose I passed out.

When I awoke on the couch I was looking at Patsy asleep in the chair across the room. Around the fireplace grate were unburned strips of cedar and cigarette butts. Patsy leaped up as I came back from the fridge with two mugs of orange juice. She took one and sat back down.

"That was quite the dissertation, young man," she said.

"I'm at least four hundred years old and aging a decade a day," I said. "Sorry about all that."

"I stayed because … Well, I just stayed."

I looked out the window at Dave the blue heron out in the shallows.

"Does it make you uncomfortable, my being here?"

"Part of the reason I invited you was to see how it would affect me," I said. "Mercenary, I know."

"And how do you feel?"

"I don't want to talk about it."

"Don't be so touchy," she said. "I accepted, and to be honest, I don't know why."

"I'm only touchy about things over which I have no control," I said. "I don't like feeling helpless."

"I know Eagle's condition has you keyed up," she said. "But you have to accept it. You can't will him to survive and you can't bring back his eyesight."

"Who's to say?" I said. I rolled forward onto my knees and poked at the extinct fire. "What brings on miracles, or what we call miracles? They can only be by God's will if you believe in Him. What if it's luck and chance? In that case my wishing won't hurt. And what if it isn't? What if there is a sort of inconsistent justice at play and intense emotion can trigger it off? Fuck this world — by whose standards are people selected to be raised or crushed? All we can do is put our souls on long leashes and allow them to grab kindred souls and hang on tight. Maybe that's what cures, heals, makes our hearts dance the goddamn two-step. I must have some effect on Eagle. I must."

Her eyes misted over. We got up and while Patsy went to the bathroom I stood on the dog run, smoking and letting the sea air work its cathartic magic. There was nothing holding me, nothing but Eagle to provide focus.

I could ride a horse, hit a baseball, hold an audience. I was an expert on tidal and intertidal life, was on a first-name basis with a great many periods of history, had a working knowledge of mathematics, astronomy, geology and hockey. I knew how interferon performed its tricks and why Leon Spinks had beaten then lost to the Greatest. I could out-drink everyone in the Valley but Eagle and still work like a galley slave the next day. I could make love reasonably well, outstandingly at times, pitifully at others. I couldn't sing but did so anyway, filling the ears of anyone foolish enough to get near me when I had a guitar and a belly full of brave. But love. I was a cockup at that one.

The wind tickled my ears and I closed my eyes.

I heard the toilet flush. I went back inside and there was Elizabeth sitting on the couch.

"I was hoping it was you in the washroom," she said.

What do you say to that one? I tried. "There isn't anything going on, here. All that happened —"

"I'm sorry about Eagle," she said. She rose and didn't bang the door and I let her go. Just let her go.

Patsy came out, looking uncomfortable. Evidently she hadn't heard anything. I didn't bother with a shower or a shave. The filth felt just fine, thanks so much. We drove in effective silence and I walked her to the door of Audrey's house. Misled by the concern she had shown, I made to embrace her, but she jerked back sharply. I decided to use any advantage I might glean from what appeared to be our friendship.

"When you get back to Victoria," I said, "please do what you can. Convince the idiots you work for of the value of this place."

"I'll see. I'm very confused right now. Say hello to Eagle," she said and kissed me lightly on the lips. "He's more important than a bridge or a tunnel or anything right now."

"You got it."

"By the way," she said. "Why wasn't he registered for government health insurance?"

"He's not exactly blessed with foresight," I said. "Besides, that's not the way he does things."

"But I don't understand why you have to sell the store," she said.

"Don't be ridiculous. With no health coverage, Eagle has no money. So I sell to the bad guys."

"Couldn't you take out a mortgage on the place?"

"The bank knows only too well that isolation of the store will deep-six it. They figure the bridge is coming in, so wouldn't give me a can of cold dog food for the whole package."

"How are you going to make a living?"

"Precariously."

"Doesn't Elizabeth have a say in this?"

"Not if the money's already in the hospital's hands. I can't be worried about getting my ass kicked in divorce court while Eagle's having a metal plate put into his head."

She opened the door, keeping a hand on my chest, freezing me to the porch. "I'm not coming back," she said.

"I'll come and visit."

"No."

"What if I —"

"No."

"I'll take that as a yes," I said.

Four days passed. Four days of meditation on the ills of the world and the slow poisoning of my life. The isolation was therapeutic and when I finally roused myself and went for a six-mile run, then scrubbed myself down and drove up the road, I was feeling good.

Well, not bad.

I parked at the top of the embankment, overlooking the bay and the spit, and went sliding and crashing down the slope behind Sedro's cottage, fetching up on my ass, shirt torn and hands scraped.

"Always a kid," Sedro said. He was behind the orange snow fence at the back of his property. He had shaved his beard but looked no younger for the lack of it.

"Rain's loosened the dirt," I said. I dusted myself off and, thinking better of it, shied away from leaping the fence and went around to the gap.

"We've had no rain," Sedro said.

"Quiet, you old fart, and get me a drink."

The cabin was looking better, refreshened but not totally renovated, retaining the ramshackle feel I loved about it.

"Got tired of waiting on you," Sedro said as he tipped the bottle of Plainsman Rye. "Had a man in to do the roof."

"Eagle was going to do the wiring."

"Yes. Any further word?"

"He came out of surgery in good shape. The doctor's a good man — he wouldn't bullshit me. Said Eagle's under sedation but will be able to receive visitors in a few days. He's going to make it."

Silently we toasted our friend.

"I was scared, Sedro. As scared as I've been in my life."

Out on the porch, now, each of us more at ease with the other than at any time since his return.

"You heard they caught him?" Sedro said.

"Yeah. Hard to believe, ain't it?"

It was Manny Parsons. A sort of terrific incomprehension had set in when I first heard about it. A skull for a tooth; a bullet for a dart; a shooting for a bar fight. It was coming out each day on the news that Parsons had it in him. He had been jailed twice for armed robbery and manslaughter.

Now Eagle was supine, unseeing, and all Parsons would garner was another stint in the Tattoo Academy.

"My first thought was to get him," I said. "I didn't care. Wait till he came out of jail on the way to the courtroom and ace the bastard right there in the street."

"Revenge puts a spike in your heart," Sedro said. "It reduces a man."

"I really don't know."

"I do."

I went inside for refills. When I returned Sedro was at the water's edge. The tide was in so we stood on the shore watching a blue heron patiently wait for the morning's catch to swim beneath his poised weapon.

"You talk to Audrey yet?" I said.

"Oh, yes. We had quite the little gathering at her house, the three of us."

"How did it go?"

"It hurt, young Jack. It truly did. I have never really gotten over that woman. We were never meant for each other, we are two diametrically opposed people, but the love was real, it was good."

"I feel that way about Elizabeth," I said.

"Are you going after her?"

"Don't know yet."

"Patsy told me she's returning to Victoria. I'm afraid she feels her visit was pointless."

"Unrewarding, maybe," I said. "Not pointless."

"I hardly feel qualified to say this, but I don't think you mean that much to her. Sorry."

"No need to be sorry," I said. "I still have her boot marks on my ass."

"Let's hope it works to your benefit."

"Right."

"You've tied yourself up in so many knots you're no good to anyone till you cut yourself free. You'll flail yourself to death if you don't. Everyone knows that, even Patsy."

"How the hell have you learned so much about everyone's opinions so quickly?"

"Haven't," he said. "I just know you, and if you know someone to a certain degree you also know how the people in their life feel about them."

"So you had a good talk with Patsy?"

"It was pleasant. She's a perceptive, intelligent woman."

"Couldn't expect otherwise from a daughter of yours."

Sedro chuckled softly and turned to face me. "She isn't my daughter," he said.

"But Audrey … "

"Audrey has certain qualities that bind me to her," Sedro said. "But she's troubled and self-deluding. She's terribly incomplete with the whole issue of her daughter's birth and abandonment, but that's something she has to settle with Patsy. No, the two weeks bracketing Patsy's conception I was swindling a man on a land deal down in Victoria."

"Too weird," I said. "Hey! Didn't you admit to me that she was your daughter? Were you lying then, or now?"

"I didn't exactly admit anything," he said. "Besides, I was trying to convince you to drop it all."

"To drop you."

"Yes, to drop me."

"If you and I are ever to pick up the pieces, you'll have to stop trying to ram home your unworthiness. Goddamn it, man, even if by some miracle my own slate was wiped clean, you're the one person I would never feel self-righteous around. You've given me too much."

"I've never given anything. I've taken."

"So you didn't abandon Patsy, as Audrey claims."

Sedro struggled, choking on some internal foe, then said, "Not her, no. I didn't abandon Patsy."

"And you've never said anything to Audrey."

"People erect fantasies for reasons of their own," he said. "Who am I to shred them?"

"Patsy?"

"Still thinks I'm her father. Better to think yourself abandoned by someone than their never having existed. It allows a sort of emotional orientation, if not quite equilibrium."

"Doesn't the truth count for something?"

"Truth lies in perception," he said. "It should never be allowed to harm someone. I can deal with unhappiness better than Audrey or Patsy can. Allow me to shoulder that burden. Perhaps that is what makes me happy."

"Are you happy?"

"For some reason, with the whole ball of wax I have helped create, I am happy. Or just tired. I have lost a lot of my fire and enthusiasm, young Jack. I'm old and eroded. I've passed my peak but that doesn't mean I'm not in my prime. Nothing declares your prime can't be a leisurely glissade down from the peak."

We watched a trawler creep past the mouth of the bay, poles like antennae extended sideways — giant curb feelers. It was getting hot, the smell of our own summer-salt sweat mingling with the organic pungency of rotting kelp.

I put my hand on Sedro's shoulder and squeezed. "Good to have you back," I said.

"I suppose."

N I N E T E E N

Each day's wait was excruciating, but the doctor finally phoned with the news I needed to hear. Eagle's coming around I treated as an event worthy of fireworks and a parade of massed bands. Now it was time to deal with the fallout, and for some reason I felt up to the task.

As useless and insubstantial as I had felt after the shooting, the episode had managed to transform me into an extremely powerful creature. When faced with something of this enormity, what was of importance loses all weight and leaves you unencumbered and strong. A sort of reckless impatience with the trivial colored everything and I was feeling frighteningly close to irresponsible.

I was going to see Eagle. The desperation that had torn at me the last trip over the Straits was gone, so when Ted Hallsworthy showed up drunk at the seaplane dock I kicked him into the salt chuck and drove down to Nanaimo to take the ferry across.

I shoved through the main doors of Vancouver General. The smell of the place assaulted me again, and I couldn't even look at the patients walking and limping and rolling along the corridors. Eagle didn't fit in here. By the time I reached his room I had worked myself back into a comfortable lather.

"Course I'm all right," Eagle said.

His articulation was forced and furry but Dr. Haq had advised me it was from the sedatives and the lingering concussive effects of the bullet, not from neural damage.

"I'm in great shape. The doctor said I have the body and the constitution of a man ten years younger."

"Must have been a bitch when you were eighteen," I said.

"Yeah, yeah."

I was no good at this. I had thought I was prepared. I wanted to walk away and scream. Hold it together. Hold it.

"Bunch of the folks are coming over tomorrow," I said.

"Hey," he said abruptly. "You mind if I bunk with you awhile when I get out of this dump? Might be too strange for me at my place in the beginning. Fumbling around in the dark and all, bumping into things I used to chuck out the way."

"That's already settled."

"Maybe you can set me up my own bar out on the dog run with plastic glasses and bottles so I don't smash them up."

Hold it.

"This'll be a sonofabitch when it hits me, but it ain't yet. Just glad to make it. I feel lucky."

"You are."

"Anybody else in the room?" he said softly.

"Nope."

"This might sound stupid, but … well, there's a guy comes in every day, a wheelchair guy, and I don't think he even belongs on this floor or anything. Anyway, at first he started talking about God. Not preaching or anything, just talking, sort of soft and that. And I started talking back, 'cause what else do I do, and it felt good. But then I guess I egged him on too much, and he started getting worse and worse and brought in the thunder and the lightning and the whole Old Testament brimstone deal, and finally I had to tell him to stop coming around or he'd be the new point guard on heaven's wheelchair basketball team.

"But what I'm trying to say is some of the stuff got me thinking. I mean, what saved me, Jack? Or who? How come I ain't dead? We ain't exactly a pair of saints, you and me, but there must be something up there looking down at us. Not the guy they talk about — I mean, how can you believe there's a God who'd make a virgin pregnant without the fun of getting her that way, right? With no fun involved we might as well all just reproduce like dandelions. Turn on the fan, honey, hit me in the ass with a stick, and let's hope the seeds fall on fertile soil!"

Finally I had a reason to laugh.

"But then I'm thinking what the hell — it don't make sense to believe He saved me when He could have stopped that asshole from pulling the trigger in the first place, right?"

"Sure."

"Listen, will you talk to me like a normal human being? I can't take these one-word answers. Not from you, I can't. I know I'm blind, but before you know it we'll be screaming around town like in the old days. Just that my batting average might drop off a few points."

"Even with perfect vision you couldn't hit a horse in the head with a coffee table."

"I know it."

Dr. Haq arrived, smiling and greeting me like a friend. He checked the dressing on Eagle's head. Theatrically, he said, "Visiting hours are over, Mr. Thorpe. When you are ready to leave please advise reception that I take responsibility for your extended stay. It is time your friend had his rest leavened with stimulation."

"Thank you," I said.

"Hey, Jack," Eagle said. "How do you like this little Hindu? Ain't he a pisscutter? I always thought a doctor's job was to make sure you didn't get what you want. This guys listens.

Think when I get out I'll devote the rest of my life to saving them East Indians from floods and droughts and tycoons and all the rest of them natural disasters that get dumped on their turbans every time they squat to shit in their garden."

The doctor laughed. "Are you sure I listen to you? It could be I ignore everything you say."

"Good policy," I said.

"I am going to start weaning you off medication," he said to Eagle.

"What? I was getting to like it," Eagle said. "How about switching to something more along the recreational lines?"

"Your friend is an idiot," the doctor said to me.

"Always has been," I said.

When Haq left the room there was a momentary lull while Eagle and I considered the next move. Small talk fulfilled its duty.

"I sold your Pope stuff," I finally said.

"What did I tell you," Eagle said. "I knew there was a market. How much you get?"

"Five grand."

"Eh?"

"The folks dug deep."

"Jesus H.," Eagle said. "They wouldn't give me a nickel when I was strong enough to choke it out of them."

"Good people."

"I know that. Going to need more than five grand by the time they let me out, though."

"We'll figure out something," I said, mentally saluting the hardware store as it slipped from drydock directly into the hands of the pirates.

"Maybe I'll become a gigolo," Eagle said. "Must be lots of old broads would get their kicks outta being poked by a guy who can't see how saggy their tits are."

"I have to go," I said suddenly. I couldn't take the bantering, the light-heartedness, real or feigned.

"Jack, you ever want a kid?"

"What brought that on?"

"You know, ever get the urge to have a little guy you could teach stuff to so he turned out better than you did?"

"At times," I said. "Though lately I wouldn't trust myself with a child."

"Yeah," he said. "Be a tough job anyhow. Far as I know there ain't anybody could be better than you and me. Me, at least."

"I'll be back tomorrow," I said. "I've already checked into a hotel near here. Get some sleep." I went to the door and reached to turn off the light. I let my hand drop to my side.

"Fear does it," Eagle said. "Being scared is good, it teaches us. Fear of doing wrong, or being wrong, or hurting someone. Them little crosses on the side of the road in Montana where people have died in car wrecks, scaring you into slowing down.

Scared of being small in your friends' eyes, scared of leaving without having done something real and good. It's fear gives us energy. You don't do great things without you're scared of looking like a dickhead.

"My old man was scared. I hated him and so did most people, so maybe he didn't use his fear right. Same with your old man, Jack. You can't let the fear cut you down. You got to use it right and stay strong. Stay strong."

I was halfway to my truck in the parking lot when I broke into a run, sprinting, my boots chafing my feet. I ran as hard as I could for as long as I could, breathing in great ragged gasps. Had there been a glacier thereabouts I could have climbed to it in twenty minutes. I hit Pacific Avenue at the bottom of the West End.

Lingering daylight bathed me as I slipped from the shadows of the Aquatic Centre. I walked. Sunset Beach was awash in the vermilion remnants of the day. Sailboats trundled past under power, those on board raucously celebrating their return to moorage or, too tired, sprawling on deck, facing astern to reap the vestiges of the sun's oblique amniotic glow.

I threaded my way along the seawall, dodging mountain bikes and tourists and the elderly and the promenaders, all moving slowly, creeping, circadian rhythms gearing down in concert with the sun's last hurrah. Around the corner, looking out on English Bay. Low-lying haze had wiped out Vancouver

Island's existence, providing an uninterrupted feel of the far side of the Pacific Rim. All the way around the seawall, mind awhirl, scarcely registering landmarks — Siwash Rock, Lumberman's Arch — until I fetched up as if cast adrift on the surging backwaters of the Rowing Club. Members only, so I kept going. A small, elegantly appointed restaurant a block south of Robson Street was gracious enough not to force food on me, just let me sit at their holding table and get mildly ridiculous on their jumbo martinis.

The cab dropped me at the hotel and I rode the elevator up to my twelfth-floor room. I was buzzed from the martinis but events had conspired to force the more numbing effects from my brain — wobbly but clearheaded — and as I stepped through the door I was no more than momentarily surprised to see Elizabeth.

We were in each other's arms and we both cried a little and we tried to talk and to explain and to apologize but immediate and vital passion overwhelmed the attempts and we made love on the floor with fury and desperation and a fused single-mindedness I had never thought possible. Why had we never unchained this before and what had driven us to it? But nothing mattered except my cock in her and our lips together and the bruising intensity of flesh and heart and mind and O! Christ my love how could we hurt each other ever ever, never never again.

Naked on the balcony, smoking, unspeaking. The mountains on the North Shore, in faint exhibitionism, lifting their kilts to show the scar tracks of roads and switchbacks and houses and streetlights. Scored and marked for life by blazing malls and advertisements crawling up their bellies and their faults and folds. Rockpiles hacked right up to their — but quick, now — look left — there, between the peaks, the snaggled heads of the Lions — there you go, sharp, twin lion heads, pristine and fiercely proud but I'll be a red-assed ape if there ain't a burger stand there one day. The spoilage will win out and Eagle will never see it and ...

Nightsounds and the lick of dark; the velvet embrace of a magical mottled skyblanket around the two of us. Jack Thorpe and his wife, Elizabeth.

Cipher that one.

T W E N T Y

Elizabeth wasn't coming home. Not yet. The love we shared, as deep as it had grown, was not new, and so was susceptible to common sense. She would be staying with James and Bernice for the time being. As for me, well, it was time to get out the repair kit. I had been doing a remarkable job of pissing and moaning while allowing things to collapse around me, with the result that I was paralytic with helplessness.

Enough of it.

As I was absolutely broke, and so were all my friends and contacts, I thought about returning to the institute. There had to be something I could do around the place. I wasn't about to leap back into the scientific community — not after all this time — but just working in the environment, in any capacity, might convince me there was something I could put my hands to that wouldn't blow up in my face. I hoped I wasn't trying to return to the glory days, saddled with some idea of recapturing my youth and vigor.

I needed a job, plain and simple.

Swallowing my pride and washing it down with a warm can of Lucky Lager, I drove to the institute. It was smaller, certainly shabbier. No one on the pier. The MV *Maury*, a converted mine sweeper that was the main research vessel, lay looking terminally ill at moorage. The smaller boats — Boston Whalers, skiffs, Zodiacs and the like — were tethered or beached or missing. The place had a nostalgic museum quality about it.

Ronny Digs was the same, hoarier and heavier but lively, and he did his best to let me down easy.

"It's dried up, is all," he said.

He had taken me on the nickel tour of the place and shown me the new equipment and the addition extending into the bush out back, but all it did was accentuate the sense of despair. We were elbow-to-elbow on the pier, smoking, blowing blue scud over the gray of the chuck.

"Without the size and importance of institutes like Scripps and Wood's Hole or even Bamfield, we couldn't survive when the economic crunch came. If it wasn't for the funding still coming in from South Central Oil we would have collapsed totally. Just hanging on these days, Jack. Stranded at low tide and fighting the heat."

"In a way, I'm glad," I said. "You know how unsatisfied I was around here when I truly believed in what I was doing. Doubt things'd be much better if I signed back on out of desperation."

Ronny pulled on his cigarette and struggled with his thoughts, then said, "Listen, there might be an alternative."

"Not much interested in a handout," I said.

"Hold on," he said. "There are no research positions available, but —"

"I don't want some halfass job. I thought I did but I don't. If you can't hunt with the leopards, stay out of the trees."

"Shut up for a minute," he said. "Hear me out."

I did. And that's how I became the institute's handyman. Not a bad job, all things considered. Fair pay, slack work, flexible hours, the chance to renew my friendship with Ronny Digs. So it must have been something else that made me punch three holes in the drywall the first week on the job.

I remembered then it was almost always the Salish who were taken as slaves during the days Pacific Coast Indians favored that particular brand of economy.

There was a hitch I hadn't counted on. Camilla, Ronny's daughter. She was back, and the reacquaintance stirred up a fresh batch of uneasiness.

Camilla had married a social worker and moved to Vancouver, but the union ran aground. Then, with the usual results of those determined not to repeat their mistakes, she abandoned all good sense and ran off with the power forward from a touring basketball team that patterned itself after the Globetrotters. Now she was back, perhaps wiser, clearly sadder, but at least more adept at driving a tour bus and better versed in roundball.

The hitch was my inability to eliminate people from my life, particularly women. I had never loved Camilla, but the attraction we had shared was there still. She was certainly all for anything I suggested, and if I hadn't been wallowing in despair over Elizabeth, if Patsy Jillian hadn't come along, if my life still had some clarity ... that's right, you bet, I still wouldn't know what the hell to do about her.

So I brooded some and tried not to meet her in social situations and eventually did at Ronny's birthday party and after Ronny went to bed Camilla and I screwed like mad bears on the living-room rug, which of course simplified things immensely, and the next day at work I punched another hole in the drywall.

That amazing evening in Vancouver: Elizabeth waiting romantically for me in the hotel room, the two of us together again, love and sorrow and heart-bleeding apologies and staring off into the night and all of it so good and so real, then waking up in the morning and fighting and hurting again and off she goes and me limping home with my head down.

So Elizabeth was still with the idiot tandem of Bernice and James.

Every morning I would rise and shine and miss her and get on my bike and drive the forty miles to the institute and shoot the breeze with Ronny for an hour before getting to work fixing and cleaning and fucking the dog at a job I knew full well Ronny had created for me. Camilla came by most days and I would stay away from her as best I could, but if I didn't get out of there immediately after work I would be overcome by loneliness and temptation and we would end up somewhere together. Eventually I gave up trying to avoid her.

By then I had solved my immediate financial problems. The job didn't pay much, but I had been living on so little for so long that any regular paycheque was a windfall. So it was time to start cutting the other stuff down to size. Yeah, yeah, as fast as I was cutting it down I was reseeding, but for now the Camilla thing could wait.

Patsy Jillian would not return my calls, and trying to reach her at work through her defensive wall of bureaucrats was next to impossible. I kept trying, and I don't know why. At least with Elizabeth I knew the love was there — we just had a bitch of a time showing it.

I had always had trouble telling, right from when I was a teenager, a kid. It took me a full year of high school to get over the mortification after Eagle shoved me into Gloria and made reference to my cock in front of that most perfect of angels.

Summer holidays came along and I was out of town for the

most part, working for the B.C. Forest Service as part of a fire
suppression crew out of Port McNeil on the north end of the
Island. I was seventeen and growing up too quickly and too
slowly. They allowed us out of camp on a rotating basis. I would
hop on the bus and spit sunflower seeds on the floor as it trundled down the highway back home. Eagle and I would camp out
for a couple days in the clearing behind the fruit stand or up
toward the glacier.

My dad was dead and the house was cold and my mother
and I were strangers. All those years in common defense against
my father had convinced me I was close to my mother, but it
was an artificial bond. Now that the enemy was gone there was
nothing securing us. Herd instinct as opposed to love, I guess.
I felt guilty about staying away but that's the way it was.

I saw Gloria a few times that summer but she was always
with someone. Older guys, mostly, infinitely more mature, more
cool, with cars and money. I know all of them to this day. Most
are having a tough time of it, probably peaking too early in life.
Must be sad, but worse would be never peaking at all.

I grew four inches that summer and filled out by eighteen
pounds. Fighting fire, dragging surging linen hose up and down
forty-degree slopes, packing pumps, humping equipment and
falling spars and bucking and sweating and eating — God! the
eating. A crew of twenty up at five in the morning, steak and
eggs for breakfast then onto the fire line or, if no fire, out into

the bush to hack campsites or dig culvert holes for the out-
houses or slash overhang along miles of dusty road. Sandwiches
and pie for coffee break, pork chops and ribs and chowder at
lunch and eating right through the day. Supper: roast beef or
turkey or chicken and great gobs of mashed potatoes and turnip.
Salmon was a favorite, serried ranks laid out on the grills of the
split-in-two oil drums we used as barbecues. Thousands of calo-
ries a day in a season-long orgy of protein and carbos and not a
smidge of it going to fat, just burn her off and ask for more.

Great fraternity in twenty young willing bucks bent to labor.
Bonding, all right, and respect and blustery brotherhood, but a
good ration of macho bullshit as well. I went back to school in
the fall with confidence bordering on cockiness. So confident
and so cocky, and then came the first Couples Night and I was
brought back to earth with a body slam.

I hated Couples Nights. High schoolers organizing a night
on the town to stamp themselves with the aura of adulthood.
I never attended, though Eagle would bully his way in stag and
spend the entire evening trying to steal a date away from
someone he despised.

But I actually did it that time. My summer in the bush, doing
a dirty and dangerous job, had convinced me I could sail through
it standing on my head with a stick in my ass.

I asked Gloria. A feverish, trembling proposition if I remember correctly, and I do. I didn't have any dress pants so bought

a pair of gruesomely checked bell bottoms at the local Kmart. The sports jacket came from my dad's old effects and the sleeves were four inches too long. Eagle stole a tie for me and, inno-cent of the nuances of the Windsor family — Single, Double and their poorer relations — I lashed the thing around my neck in a bowline. My Adidas went into the washing machine and emerged without their soles. It was too late to get to the store, so I bound them up with two yards of hockey tape. I had no car so was to meet Gloria at the restaurant.

There she was when I walked in. Gorgeous Gloria, with the others in a separate section of the restaurant. Beautiful Gloria. Two dozen couples laughing and drinking and smoking. Every one of them in jeans and T-shirts and team sweaters, looking cool. I threw the sports jacket behind the hostess stand but couldn't solve the bowline so had to keep the tie. Nobody offered to shift places so I sat two tables away from Gloria and stared at my beloved with ill-disguised torment.

I had forgotten my wallet and with it my fake ID, so the waiter refused to serve me booze. There was a good deal of sniggering at my predicament, or maybe it was at my pants.

A while later Gloria started necking with Max Price. I guess it got Max to feeling guilty so he ordered a bottle of Brights '67 white wine and presented it to me with great ceremony and condescension. I tossed it off by the neck in a gurgling rush and ten minutes later, searching for the washroom, I crashed through the picture window onto the patio. I have no recollection of what happened next, but school history says Eagle arrived and rescued me, not before cutting a savage swath through the party and getting everyone bounced from the premises for his efforts.

Immediately upon graduating Gloria and Max Price were married. Max made a fortune mining jade in northern B.C. and the two of them now live amid lavish splendor in West Vancouver.

I hope they die in a house fire.

TWENTY-ONE

The weekend came and though there were plenty of things for me to do at home or at the institute, I had reached the point where I had to get Patsy Jillian off my mind. Nothing is so destructive as an issue left hanging. So south I went, on a morning filled with beauty and promise.

Victoria was its usual self, very British and immaculately sculptured, yet for all its attempts still coming off like a dowager aunt ruining the fun at a wedding. Patsy lived in a grand house in Oak Bay.

The snarl of the Norton alerted the neighbors to my arrival. Miffed old Protestants squinting through curtain gaps, shooting blasts of indignation from their noses as they rued the day flogging was abolished, pining for the times when a person of my ilk was legal prey for a company of Gurkhas. There is something about the Victorian atmosphere that converts even the most liberal, and as these folks equated liberalism with madness and anarchy, they had no chance at all.

I let the big old lionhead knocker drop home and waited. I looked back to the street and waited some more. Finally the door opened and for the first time in my life I met an actual butler. Full livery, no less.

"Cub," he said, inviting me in with a vague flapping of his hand. Not much of a butler. He was a kid of about nineteen, a rail of a thing with acne and the washed-out eyes of a cave salamander. "Lookig for Pad?"

"You have quite the cold there, Jeeves," I said.

"Yeah."

He wandered off down a long central hallway. I didn't know whether I was expected to follow but did. We passed two sets of French doors. One pair led into a high-ceilinged living room; the other opened onto a dining room out of *Architectural Digest*. An oak staircase doubled back and fled from sight. At the end of the hall the butler pushed through a leaded glass door and let it go in my face. I timed its swing and entered the kitchen. The butler was already sitting on the countertop, lighting a cigarette and banging his badly worn motorcycle boots on the cabinet doors.

Patsy was elbow deep in a mixing bowl. As she turned, her thin, brittle nose and liquid eyes and the tiny pats of flour that speckled her almost buckled my knees. I stepped over to her, kissed her firmly on the mouth and took a seat at the table, backstraddling the chair as I always do in times of uncertainty.

"Jack," Patsy said. "Whatever …?"

"Good to see you, too," I said. "Hope I haven't interrupted anything."

"No, no," she said. "Uh, Jack, this is Todd. Todd — Jack Thorpe, a friend of mine from Salish Spit."

"Hey," Todd said, flicking ash on the floor. He took a huge ragged sniff, trying to force air through his clogged beak. "Fuggid climid."

Patsy put the mixing bowl on top of the breadbox and began washing her hands in the sink. "Todd's my cousin from Winnipeg. He's helping out around here while he looks for a summer job."

"Student?" I asked the butler.

"Why nod?" he shrugged.

"Real nice place you have here," I said, turning my attention back to Patsy.

The house was gorgeous but, as with most unrenovated homes of its era, the kitchen was cramped and poorly laid out. I couldn't have lived in the place — I need a big brute of a kitchen. A table carved from a monster's climbing tree, a center island, cutting boards and hanging cleavers. A kitchen mentality is the closest thing around to a locker-room mentality, and I am blessed or cursed with both.

"I like it," Patsy said. She dried her hands on her apron,

then untied it and slung it through the handle on the fridge. "I like to be comfortable."

"Bourgeois shid," Todd said.

"Philosophy or sociology?" I asked.

"Both," he sniffed. "Why nod?"

"Why nod, indeed," I said and got a look from Patsy.

"Jack and I have some catching up to do," she said. "Could you take the dog out, Todd?"

"Stupid ped," he said. He collapsed off the counter and ambled off to one of the nether reaches of the house.

"I missed you," I said when Todd was gone.

"I was hoping it had worn off," Patsy said.

"I'm not here to plead or beg or make promises," I said. "So you can relax. I just wanted to see you. There — I'm lying already. I came down to tell you it was all over, then when I saw you there at the counter my heart went into seizure. I don't know what to do about this."

"And I don't know what to say, Jack. I can't have you showing up like this out of the clear blue."

"I'm a right royal mess these days, but I'm trying. I'm catching glimpses of the old composure and strength, and I'm doing my best to cut my way through to them."

"How can I disabuse you of the notion that your behavior isn't the problem? I like you, I truly do, but that's as far as it goes."

"Oh," I said, refusing to believe her.

"Are you staying in town?"

"No. Eagle's being released from the hospital today and I have to be at the airport to meet him."

"Audrey told me all about it. Is he all right?"

"He's handling the whole thing better than I'd be able to."

"Will you be staying with him for the first while?"

"He'll be staying with me."

"So Elizabeth and you are still separated."

"Bingo."

Todd pushed through the door. He wore a pale blue softball jacket over the livery. Down south his filthy boots poked out.

"What the hell's that?" I yelped. On the far end of the leash bunched in Todd's fist was a Scottish terrier.

"He's a Scotty!" Patsy said, with the full indignation of the overly proud pet owner.

"The sweater," I said. "The sweater."

The poor dog was bundled up in a knit tartan abortion that would have neighborhood pit bulls rubbing their paws in anticipation.

"It keeps him warm," Patsy said.

"Tartan, yet," I said and laughed. "Am I to figure the dog is proud of his heritage so picked that up himself?"

"There's nothing wrong with it."

"If you had a German shepherd, would you deck him out in lederhosen?"

"Todd, get going."

The two strange beasts departed. In scarlet letters on the back of the butler's jacket was "Save The Furbish Lousewort."

"You can be a real pain in the ass," Patsy said. She went to the fridge and returned with a bottle of wine.

"I didn't mean anything by it," I said.

She looked at me seriously. "I know that inside that cynical shell is a very sensitive man. How do you crack the shell to get at the real person?"

"Is this a clichéfest? What kind of infantile analysis is that? There is no shell and no inner core. The two aspects coexist, and sometimes one is more prevalent and sometimes the other, but they are both there *all* the time. You can't strip a person of the segments of his personality you don't like. The integrated whole is what you get, take it or leave it."

"I have trouble accepting certain aspects of your personality. It's as simple as that."

"You ain't no monument to perfection yourself," I said. "You work for the government, you can't talk to your mother, you live in a house with a grandeur that would drive me to suicide, you've hired your cousin to be your butler, you make your dog wear sweaters and I'm beginning to get the inkling that your sense of humor has been swept away by a mudslide."

"We're too different," she said. "Too different. Don't do this to me, don't try to get me going."

I took a step toward her but she shied away so violently I was afraid to reach out.

"It's over, Jack," she said. "For that matter, it never really began. You were a fun fuck. There, is that clear enough for you? It wasn't your mistake, it was mine. Okay? Now you need feel no guilt. Go back and patch things up with your wife. And if it doesn't work out, don't make me part of the reason why.

"I'm no expert at this type of thing, but if I can give you some advice, I'd say to take the time to examine what you really want from me. I'm a diversion, Jack. Not in the sense of an amusing little fling, but a diversion to keep you from dealing with everything else. Go away. Please, just leave me alone."

The clock on the wall said one in the afternoon. Three hours till Eagle's plane touched down. I'd have to hurry. I conquered my fear and moved to embrace her but she pushed past me and out the door and up the staircase.

Christ, I learn slowly.

It was raining. I pulled my rain gear from the saddle bags and struggled to jam by boots down the rubberized legs. The butler and the Scotty approached, both sodden. I nodded at Todd.

"Fuggid wedder," he said. He dragged the Scotty up to the house, boots and toenails scuffing along the flagstones.

Back on the bike and up the street. Lovely trip it had been, pure magic. I had finally got off the pot, driven down to Victoria to break everything off with Patsy, changed my mind the minute

I saw her and, to the shitkicking of my pride, been thrown out of her life like a spoiled coho. Quite the day of accomplishment.

I banked into a corner too hard and scared the hell out of myself. The simplicity of the fear cleared my head and I bore down on the throttle. Then it all became blurred: home and off the bike and in the truck and off to the airport and terrible, impersonal banter with Eagle until he demanded we go to the pub before heading home. No thoughts of women or the job or anything else. Just Eagle in my mind, Eagle alone.

I was still acting oddly by the time we hit the house. I was out of my element and keenly aware of it. We went inside. I had arranged the spare room simply. We stopped at the doorway and Eagle clamped his big mitt a little too hard on my bicep.

"This is it," I said.

"Color sucks."

I led him around the perimeter of the room, describing the dresser, the window, the night table with its lamp, the bed, the closet, and back to the door. He took it all in, running his hands over everything and feeling and prodding and trying to get a sense of the room.

"Nice," he said when we were back at the start.

"It'll be good having you here," I said. "Like camping together in the old days."

He had been taking it well so far. Perhaps prone to too much insouciance, overly casual, but that was both natural and understandable. He released my arm and retraced the path alone, familiarizing himself with the room, his gentle probings at odds with his imposing physical presence. He returned to my side.

"Only one thing I don't need," he said. With a big grin he dashed across the room, avoided the bed, snatched the lamp from the night table and hurled it out the window. I winced at the crash.

"It opens on the right-hand side," I said.

We laughed like mad whores and Eagle flopped on the bed while I picked up the pieces of glass and tossed them through the jagged hole.

Earlier his arrival at the Square Rigger had been like the reception for Nelson returning with one arm from Tenerife. Disaster was immaterial. A hero was back. Obviously some subjects were skated around and Manny Parson's name went unmentioned, but the hand-wringing and praise-singing tore at the heart and the tear ducts and it was wonderful and I've never loved a group of people as one person — mob as man — to that degree in my life. Eagle tired quickly so we didn't stay long. But the event will long be with me.

The only sour spot was Snuffy, who was incoherent. I had never seen him so affected by anything. The cruelty and the injustice had penetrated his damaged wits as logic never could. The poor bugger wept and babbled and fled at the first sight of Eagle. He was still gone when we left.

I pried the daggers of glass from the window frame and chipped off the putty. When I was done I turned back to the room and Eagle was asleep. I took the sunglasses from his eyes and put them on the night table. I unfolded the blanket at the foot of the bed and draped it over his bulk. Out in the front room I put on Willie Nelson's *Red-Headed Stranger* album, turned it low, and sat down on the edge of the dog run, swinging my feet, tickling the top of the beach grass that was poking through the sand. The wind caressed me with its salty baby's breath. Dave the blue heron stood poised in the shallows, ignoring me.

Melancholy is not my normal state. Anger, fear and several other unpleasant emotions occasionally demand their day in court, but not black bile. I sat there waiting for it to go away.

Dave the blue heron was gone. The sky was a foreboding patchwork of grays. A low line of scud was rolling toward shore, being pushed ahead of a squalling front. Unusual weather for the west coast — orographic monotony more the norm. I squashed my last cigarette into the sand and went back inside. Willie was done so I turned off the stereo. Eagle would sleep through the night. The injury, or its impact, would not soon allow him his old gusto. I roamed the house, avoiding the room where my friend lay. I was in contact with every particle of my inner world, combating the incorporeal.

I felt great loss.

We spent a couple days getting to know each other. Normally not a follower, around Eagle I usually found myself letting him put his head down and lead the way, at least until some common sense needed to be injected into the situation to save our lives or keep us out of jail. Now the roles had been reversed, and we were having trouble learning our new parts. Eagle didn't much take to orders, even when they were disguised as suggestions, so I had to be very careful about what I said to him.

He was quieter than before, more contemplative. His time in the hospital had allowed for a lot of introspection, and the tone of his conversation showed it.

On his second day back, a day when the good weather of late spring was taking a break while the cold and rain of winter visited awhile, Eagle told me about Jean. His lost love, the woman he had sent back to her husband. After their tangled moment in time, after Eagle "did the proper thing" and released her back to her family, after all the wasted years, Jean was coming back to him. He had a letter from her in his hand. As he sat there with me on the dog run, fondling the letter and searching for the right words, I fought hard to keep from worrying. It seemed to me that he was grasping at straws. The last thing he needed right now was the pain of a failed reconciliation. But eventually, as Eagle both reminisced and planned for the future, my happiness for him overcame the anxiety. Besides, to my way of thinking the best way for Eagle to get his head back to normal was to behave as he had in the past, by treating his blindness as the loss of one thing, not all things. And as recklessness was Eagle's family motto, I figured a dose of it wouldn't hurt.

"Anyhow," Eagle said, pressing the letter against his thigh. "Anyhow, she says she lost him again."

"I don't know if you can exactly *lose* Jesus," I said.

"If you can find him, you can lose him."

That had been one of the side effects of Jean's affair with Eagle, as it frequently is with the lost and lonely. Jean had gained great peace of mind from her salvation and claimed her later apostasy left her with no bitter aftertaste. It had been what she needed at the time, and that should be good enough for anyone.

"And I don't care what you think," Eagle said. "You just read the letter to me yourself. I figure if she showed the balls to write me and talk about all that intimate stuff when she knows I ain't got eyes anymore, then the least I can do is learn something about what she's been through."

"You have a point," I said.

"Least until I can slip old Elmer into her."

I sat and thought.

"So this guy's going to be at the arena the next three nights," Eagle said.

"The Reverend Harold."

"That's right. Jean mentioned his name in the letter and I heard him on the tube. He works miracles."

"Miracles."

"Sure. Every week on TV he cures all kinds of people."

"Many people," I corrected.

"Whatever," Eagle said. "Let's get us a bottle and head on down there tonight."

"You're not doing this because you think —"

"I'm doing it for Jean!" he snapped. "Don't worry about me being one of the fuckwits who charges the stage trying to be touched and healed. Just that this whole deal about there being things out there more important than the stuff you and me always thought was true has got me going. Maybe I been missing something, or maybe I gotta see what Jean saw in the whole thing."

So we finished our drinks and Eagle made a mess of the bathroom showering and shaving and we got in the truck.

I'm not exactly on a first-name basis with Jesus, and I have even less patience with those who claim to be his representatives on earth, but since he got out of the hospital Eagle had been expressing more interest in religion than at any time since we were thrown out of Sunday school for fighting.

I doubt Eagle was looking for salvation, and he certainly had no wish to place his life in anyone's hands but his own, but he did need to know there was a reason for what had happened to him. He didn't need to know the reason, necessarily, just that there was one.

I am a scientist. I revel in the fact that life is a fluke. To my way of thinking, the concatenation of circumstances that put us here on earth is infinitely more beautiful than the banal concept of a Creator.

But hell, Eagle was my friend, so if he wanted to believe in the Grand Poobah, he could go ahead and do so. If he went totally wacky on me we'd have to have a talk, but in the mean-time, let him fill his boots.

Trouble with Eagle was he had never given any indication his inner world was any different from his outer. So very much did he live in the substantial and relate to what he could pick up and put down that I didn't know where he was coming from on this one. If he were still able to see what to pick up and put down, perhaps I would never have known his thoughts went any deeper than that.

But then I have always suffered from the common fault of thinking I know more about the people I love than they do themselves.

The old rink was all gussied up. Floodlights illuminated a portable fountain with a pump driven by a generator, sending jets and sheets of water high into the night air. White-suited valets treated each battered vehicle with personal affection. We made our way inside, paid our admission, took a program each and joined the overflow crowd in the fire trap called Hodgson Arena.

People from up and down the Island were sitting with awe, reverence and curiosity as last-minute altar decorations were put in place and the orchestra assumed their positions. They packed in a few stragglers, the doors closed, and silence reigned, except for the screams of an unfortunate who had chosen cyanide rather than face the collection plate with the measly dollar remaining from the sale of his children. The orchestra exploded into hymnal ecstasy, winged angels descended on wires from dry-ice clouds and, to the crash of cymbals, the Reverend Harold, austere and humble in a three-thousand-dollar Armani suit, strode on stage. The Rev displayed a row of pearly whites and the pious in the three front rows collapsed.

It would be sacrilege to include the substance of his opening sermon in a volume not embossed with gold and blessed. Suffice to say that its conclusion found another sixteen rows leveled, those on the floor looking up with scorn at the spiritually callous who remained upright.

Songs, donations, preaching, donations, proselytizing, donations. And then began the healing. None too soon, for the greater part of the flock was now on the floor, catatonic with wonderment, covered with discarded chewing gum, and sorely in need of the Reverend's ministrations.

At first, they were hesitant to approach — that is, it took a while for the stronger of the ailing to bludgeon their way to the front — but the tide soon grew into a flash flood. Men, women, pets. Tall, short, gorgeous, homely. They besieged the stage in droves until the burly Harold resorted to a white glove on a pool cue with which to touch the penitent sufferers from a safe distance. A low rumble from offstage, and on rolled a youth in white robes astride a motorcycle that was snorting and missing on one cylinder. One touch of the Rev's hand and the machine roared with renewed vigor. The youth departed on one wheel to the delight of the crowd.

It went on. And on. People weeping, rending their clothing and hair. The orchestra flared and swooped. There was a moment of discord when the violin section defected *en masse* and hurled themselves at their conductor's feet. The program told us he was the Reverend's brother, and was thus vicariously divine.

And suddenly it was over. There reigned an air of fatalistic amusement, like the stunned relief after a major disaster: homes

leveled, property destroyed, but alive! by God alive! The chosen picked their way around discarded wheelchairs and pros-
theses and surged out the doors into the chilly night, racing for
vacant seats by the fireplace back at the pub. Great wooden
carts wheeled out the comatose.

In the two hours Eagle had neither budged from his seat nor
uttered a word. Out in the maelstrom of people in the parking
lot, he laid his big mitt on my shoulder.

"Not one fucking word, Thorpe," he said.

We were still laughing as we drove away.

Twenty-Three

Summer took charge and ran away. It can do that. The other seasons have their own imperatives, but with summer it is all to do with time. Southerners describe at great length the languorous passage of time when summer is upon them, but in Canada it is only the winter solstice that marks the beginning of the endlessness. Summer arrives in a rush, with an attitude and a harsh agenda. It's passing through, and if you need a lift then stick your thumb out.

And even at that you better have gas money.

I didn't have time to appreciate anything the season had to offer. Eagle's situation was the only focus I had. Conventional problems lost their importance, and I found myself giving up all but a token appreciation of the need for food, shelter and connection with the outside world.

As much as he needed the help and the attention, Eagle

fought against them all the way, to the point of pissing me off. Never before had I given so much of myself, and now it wasn't even being accepted gratefully. I'm afraid I was getting self-righteous about the whole thing. We fought a lot, but in general had a hell of a good time together, and other than my *pro forma* appearances at the institute, we were as close a pair as could be imagined.

Elizabeth and I had taken to calling our state of non-affairs a trial separation, but I don't know to what trial we were referring, as no work was being done toward a resolution. I was fully aware that I was using Eagle as an excuse to dodge responsibility, but wasn't about to explain or apologize to anyone.

And just like that the summer was gone.

Autumn cruised in and my work at the institute continued to tail off. There was a knock-it-down job here and a put-it-up there, but mostly I was socializing with Ronny Digs, allowing him to lament the passing of the old days of growth and scientific fervor.

Ronny didn't want to admit that he had been instrumental in creating his own situation. The environmental sciences had been a rewarding and legitimate area of study for some time and Ronny — intentionally, I think — had missed the flight. He had originally become the director through talent and hard work, but the years had taken their toll. I don't like being critical of the man, but he had a lot in common with a tenured professor: with security had come complacency. The place was getting on my nerves, so I just went in when Ronny called or I was pinched for cash.

I finally saw some money for the hardware store. Considering the badgering the government had done to get me to sell, I was surprised that the land was going to the construction company in charge of the project. I wondered if it was normal for them to be working so closely together, curious about where the line was between professional association and malfeasance, but I had grown so distrustful about anyone with any connection to the thing — especially after Benton Firsk and Manny Parsons — that I was reading conspiracy into everything.

In any event, I sold the store and started paying off the hospital.

The transaction brought with it a sense of loss, but oddly enough it was a pleasant, nostalgic feeling.

And now it was time to close it down. Crisp and windy, fall had been with us a week, October just ahead. Autumn on the Island is not as clearly delineated as back east, no riot of deciduous color, no chill evenings with children kicking through piles of leaves. More of a grumpy slide into rain and sloppy turf, people bracing themselves for a few months marked mainly by dense air. But it was clear that morning.

Sedro Tuckett was the first to arrive.

"I have to pay you something," he said. He was getting bonier by the day, crooked and disjointed, built without a plumb line, a high jumper with rickets. He was making off with some frost fence, that kind with the green plastic covering the wire.

"Look," I said, "I've had that fencing in stock for two years. People want a fence they go to the lumber yard. There's only fifty foot of it. Take the stuff."

He started dragging it through the door. I felt comfortable with him these days. Not the same reverence as when I was a kid, but fraternity. I knew now of his deep concern for me as I was growing up, and of his concern for my mother, and of his conviction that my father had been a mad thing with the capacity to turn rabid and inflict pain and suffering to a degree we hadn't experienced to that date, that date when Sedro picked up his rifle and deposited my father into whatever hell he had waiting for him. I knew the love that had driven him to such an act.

Good or bad, hero or misfit, Sedro Tuckett was some piece of work. I remember when he had his whore. All right, I don't remember. I was too young, but the incident had been retold so often that my memory has incorporated it as an experience.

For all his intellectual leanings, Sedro was not without his picaresque side. Pillbox was one of half a dozen or so hookers who worked the bars and the harbor. She was the most successful of the girls and was named for her stylish pillbox hat. After Sedro became her regular customer she would sit for hours in the Four Fingers Lounge, rejecting offers, waiting for Sedro to arrive and spirit her away. It went on, they say, for over two months, and was marked by dignity and decorum. But when Sedro called it quits the dignity and the decorum hit the road as well. Some say for retribution, others for money. Whatever, the upshot of it was that Pillbox, in cahoots with Sedro's mayoralty opponent of that fall, turned on him with the full vengeance of the spurned.

It was a wonderful week. Monday's paper carried a ribald exposé of the affair. Tuesday Sedro's opponent raked him over the coals on the town's AM radio talkshow. Wednesday Sedro called a general meeting at which he admitted everything, offering dates, times and locations. Then, in front of the town council, the media and everyone who was interested — most of Salish Spit — he denounced Pillbox uncategorically as the worst lay he had ever had. Thursday the woman left town forever on the eight-o'clock ferry. Friday it was discovered that overnight someone had broken into the newspaper office and delivered twenty-three hundred pounds of Holstein manure, and through some unfortunate oversight had deposited the stuff on the layout tables and in the main press. Saturday Sedro's political foe was found naked, gagged and bound with electrician's tape to the totem pole outside the civic center. Sunday they rested.

The election was a rout for the incumbent.

Sedro levered the fencing over the tailgate of his pickup and rolled it into the box. He strolled back my way. "What are you going to do with the things that don't sell?"

"It's all going," I said. "What doesn't sell, I'll give. I don't want anything left of the place."

"It will look odd standing here empty."

"Thinking of burning it. I don't want the contractors to have all the fun."

"Hasn't there been talk about turning it into a hamburger stand or something to service the tourists?"

"First I've heard of it," I said. "And until I see a piece of paper telling me the store stays, I figure I have a right to drop the bitch."

"Surely you signed something that mentioned the building. Even if they just want the land, any edifices would be included in the sale."

"Didn't read it too close."

Sedro scratched the stubble of his new beard. "Let me get to work on it."

"Eh?"

"Never mind, never mind," he said. He rooted through his pockets and came up with his truck keys. "I'll be gone a few hours."

"Where are you off to?"

I was cut off by a bony upraised finger. He slammed and pinned the tailgate and drove away.

I had spent the night before in the storeroom. First thing in the morning I stripped the room of my books, the TV, the overflow stock. I would leave the daybed. Somehow it belonged there. How many nights had I crashed fully clothed on it after an evening of hilarity or a night of meditation? Patsy Jillian had slept there, had gripped the edge of it our first night together. I didn't know what was up with Patsy. Just when I thought I was completely free of her, my mind's eye would dredge up her image and make me phone. I could never reach her, and she never returned the messages. Inside I knew she wasn't what I wanted. Patsy represented a wonderful interval in my life, but an interval nonetheless. I thought about her less often now, and when I did it was with the nostalgia I felt for the passing of the hardware store. The only thing that bothered me was the irritation I felt at having been unable to analyze the situation myself. Resolution has a hollowness about it when you've had no hand in the answers.

They had made the formal announcement two weeks ago: a tunnel from the mainland to Royal Island and from there a bridge to Salish Spit. It began a period of delightfully rancid pigshit on the television. Everything was accomplished with great pomp and circumstance, public relations oozing from every mouth and armpit. Political swine beamed and corporate muscle gleamed. Audrey Weeks was on the tube for a few days, fairly trembling with triumph, proclaiming a new era of economic resurgence.

Utterly fascinating in its degradation was the sponsorship campaign. Corporate backers would be contributing funds to the project, in return for which their logos would be plastered on the bridge and at the entranceways to the tunnel. It would not look like a bridge so much as a Finnish hockey jersey. "Bert's Barrel of Bosoms and Beer Emporium — Official Table Dancers of the Tunnel."

The other side behaved much the same. The lunatic fringe protested enthusiastically but raggedly. They had a worthy goal but no rational means of achieving it, with the usual result that they helped scuttle their credibility.

Certainly from both sides came the voice of reason — from behind a hand or around a corner, or anywhere a camera and a reporter were not. Not much patience for measured commentary when a project of this magnitude is involved.

Since then the town had been in stasis, waiting and watching and waiting some more. Sort of a precoital depression. For months I had been fuzzy of head and unaware. But with the confirmation of the project came a reaffirmation of my old nerve. I was back in the books, studying and brushing up on scientific developments, initiating fresh hobbies in the lab at the house. Two nights ago I got stirred up at the Square Rigger and sang a few songs. When I broke a string on my guitar I burned the thing in the fireplace just to get a laugh. A good sign, I think, of my return to vibrant mental health.

But back to the big closeout sale.

I watched Sedro's pickup vanish round the corner. The oil drum halves were lined up for the barbecue. The doors from the store were off their hinges and propped on sawhorses to serve as tables. A collection of the more unwieldy items — a couple lawnmowers, a bandsaw, wheelbarrows, folding cots and the like — was arranged for easy access on the grass. The horseshoe pits were raked. The beer kegs were tapped and waiting in the shade of a makeshift canopy extending from the eave of the tool shed. The stage for Island Madness, a bluegrass band from Campbell River, was set up. The amps and microphones were covered by an orange tarpaulin to keep off the morning dew.

A pair of bald eagles soared over the site and, apparently satisfied with the preparations, banked and reversed direction, back to the shore and their roosts high in the cliffside snags.

I poured a beer from the first keg, got mostly foam, adjusted the tap and threw the foam in the grass. Poured another and sipped and wiped the frothy mustache from my lip with my bare forearm. I raised my face to the sky, reveling in that last trace of bite you get in the fall as the sun struggles to retain its strength before another dreary winter sets in.

Robert drove up and parked. Bargains pulled him like Huskies a sled. He waved and darted into the store. Don arrived with Snuffy and they almost ran over Robert as he hustled out clutching various exotic items the purpose of which even I had forgotten.

The shock still showed on Snuffy's face. We were used to him wandering off on strolls, and they had always been therapeutic. But since Eagle's return Snuffy's periods of absence had grown longer and more unsettling. Deep inner torment was grappling with his constitutionally good nature. He began poking around the scattered goods.

"This is not a wake," Don said. He stopped in front of me and gazed around at the picnic area. Hands in pockets. He had dressed for the occasion, a suit jacket shiny with age, belly straining at the buttons, all three of which were fastened.

"Nope," he said. "No death here. You've had the store for a good piece of time. Just retiring, is all. Funny how since we heard the news everyone is calmer than ever. Are we accepting the inevitable, Jack? Or giving up? Or looking forward to the change, good or bad? Maybe we need shaking up. Maybe we've lost touch with things, being squirreled away here in the Valley so long."

"Hard to tell," I said.

"Yeah."

"I heard Snuffy's been staying with you and Donna."

"He can't stand being alone these days."

We followed our friend's progress across the grass. Snuffy had spied the horseshoe pits and it awakened something in

him. With a lopsided grin, he picked up all four shoes and stood
fondling them like a favorite pair of work gloves. Dark volcanic
sand clung to them and he brushed it off with care. He dropped
the silver shoes to the ground and took his position to the right
of the far pit. His left hand held a gold shoe. His right grasped
the other in the middle. On a day like today he needed no
preparation. He bent once at the knees, drew back the shoe,
swung and released and painted a glittering arc. Endoverend-
overendoverend the shoe came toward us then hit the sand with
a thunk, its steely arms corralling the post.

Ringer!

"Oh jeez," Snuffy said. "Oh jeez."

He crept up on the pit. He circled it. He took a step nearer
and jumped back, afraid to break the spell. He reached out a
hand and jerked it away as if from a flame. He stood up straight
and looked our way.

"Oh jeez," he said. "Oh jeez."

He danced a bit in one place then bolted for the store in
his awkward shuffle. As he rounded the corner he ran smack
into Robert, who was staggering under the bulk of six rolls of
oilcloth. Robert slammed to the ground, the rolls sprang free
and Snuffy ricocheted off the wall of the store.

"Oh jeez," Snuffy said. He raced inside and we could hear
formless thrashing.

Robert was stooped over collecting his oilcloth when Snuffy

hit him from the rear and drove him face first back into the gravel.

"Jack!" Snuffy screamed. "Chalk! I need chalk! I got to put a line through the other ones! I got five and a batch and now I got to put a sideways line through the up and down lines to show the batch. I got it!"

I broke into a jog.

"Oh jeez," Snuffy said and beat me into the store.

By the time I got there Snuffy had pried the lid off a can of latex. I stood in the doorway and watched him dip a finger in the paint and swab a bold stroke through the chalk marks on the blackboard. He stepped back to absorb better the magnificence of his creation. He radiated pride. Then I had to scurry out of the way as he flew past me and out the door.

"I could sue him," Robert said. He picked grit from his nose. "I was a lawyer, a good one, and I know."

I rejoined Don and we watched Snuffy play by himself. Nobody wanted to break the spell. He had all four shoes in his hands. He dipped and swung and released and almost fluked another ringer. The shoe landed far short but bounced off the grass and clanged against the post, leaning. So close.

"Oh jeez," Snuffy said.

The next shoe landed on the grass again but refused to bounce and lay there sadly. Snuffy was bang on with number three, but the horseshoe struck the very top of the post and caromed sideways into the picnic tables, wiping out the paper plates and dispersing eight pounds of potato salad, which hit Robert in the chest like spud shrapnel.

Snuffy still had one shoe left. He took his time, dipping and swinging, rocking and aiming. Everyone watched till he finally let it go. It arced high over the pit, glanced off the far barbecue and imbedded itself into the corrugated tin of the storage shed. I went to pour some beers as Snuffy wrenched crazily at the shoe. Robert snorted, wiped off the chunkier bits of the potato salad, and headed back into the store in search of more plunder. Keeping a wary eye on Snuffy, Don moved the tables back twenty feet.

There was not much left to do except blow the foam off the beer and sip and watch the Snuffs. He was still pitching half an hour later when a symphony of horns drew us to the parking lot in time to greet a parade of vehicles turning off the main road. It looked as if every resident of the town had arrived in one stinking, belching herd.

Dale James, in his Honda Civic, was in the lead. He was still going about thirty knots when he hit the parking lot, causing him to skid sideways as he jammed on the brakes to avoid hitting Robert, who was overladen with a gigantic pile of curtain rods. Dale's father, Jason, high in the cab of his Peterbilt, never had a chance to avoid the collision. The big rig climbed the back of the Honda like a camel mounting a housecat, bending the car in two so severely that it raised the front wheels off the ground. The side loading doors of the truck's trailer flew open and out charged Island Madness, the bluegrass band, screaming and swearing at the maltreatment of both their instruments and their persons. It was just the first of the rear-enders. It had all happened too quickly — and the vehicles had arrived too closely — for anyone to stop short, and the funnel-shaped driveway added to the effect. The accidents spread back like a shockwave right out onto the highway, where tourists and their ilk hammered into the cars trying to force their way into the hardware store grounds. Doors flew open and as the principles set to badmouthing and face-slapping and gauntlet dropping, I made a beeline for the beer kegs.

I had caught a fleeting glimpse of Elizabeth as she emerged from Bernice and James's car. She had insisted on overseeing the sale, only too aware of my cavalier attitude toward money. Half the day's profits would be hers.

I had wanted her to have it all. After my unilateral decision to sell the store and pay off the hospital, I was expecting Elizabeth to tear me to shreds — through the courts, physically, any way that came to mind. But I misjudged her, as I suppose I have been doing for a long time. She was gracious and generous about the whole thing, and it clearly pained her that I had assumed she would behave otherwise. We had talked about it long into the night, bringing us closer to the point where we could again share our lives, but something left us short of the commitment. The infidelities still hurt too much, or represented too much. I gained a new respect for my wife, and had I been paying closer atten‑ tion I would have remembered that Elizabeth had always been a princess in a pinch.

As I drank my beer under the tree I felt that tingle of excite‑ ment I used to get while waiting for her to arrive home.

By now the store was busting a gut with people. So was the parking lot. Indignant survivors of the monster wreck were threatening lawsuits while Robert bounced from group to group, advising them on their legal rights and being rudely brushed off. Gradually the acrimony gave way to grudging understanding — the news of free beer and food out back had a large part to play in that — and the folks spilled onto the grass and into the store.

Audrey Weeks had arrived without my seeing her. She was standing near the back of the property, surrounded by her town council. Since the announcement they had taken to traveling together in a pack, like the Stanley Cup champs making the rounds, waiting for the victory parade. They were surveying the site, pointing here and there, mentally erecting the bridge, already knee-deep in its promises of revitalization. I didn't care. Give them their glory.

Spying me by the kegs, Audrey detached herself from the group and came over. Her toadies were lost without her, and a couple of them started to follow, until they were strung out in a line, the brave adventurers out front glancing back for support. Audrey and I silently toasted each other. She was in a good mood, and we talked of the Valley and the Spit and the Island. Isn't it strange how those in opposition all their lives can yet have the same dreams and desires, and through all the crap I felt in tune with her. We talked of Eagle and of her concern for him, which spilled from her eyes, and now and again when someone would sidle up and try to badmouth her I would give him a look, and damned if I didn't find myself standing there protecting Audrey Weeks — protecting her!

By midafternoon there wasn't much left inside the store. Ravaged yet serene, smoke and carnage and litter yet eerily calm. Outside, battle was still being joined.

In the middle of a ragged circle of people by the picnic tables stood an ugly blind giant. Tangled in his fist were several loops of binder twine. On the far end of the makeshift leash was a vile, shit-brindle dog with the snout of a possum. Mange had left it patchy and torn. It was Eagle's version of a seeing eye dog, though it was completely untrained for the task and in fact was barely house trained. It was constantly being tugged and flung in short arcs as its master stabbed the air with his fist to emphasize points in his story.

Yanked to and fro, the animal bided its time. The second it felt some slack it would scuttle across the surface of the picnic table and bury its snout in a bowl of taco salad. More punctuation would jerk it back, eyes bulging, head liberally coated with guacamole and salsa, bits of clinging parsley and jalapeño peppers giving it a festive appearance. A leprous piñata. It would snarl and fart and snap at the other food before feeling the binder twine go slack and making another dash for the Mexican fare.

No one was inclined to interfere.

Eagle was having a tough time being heard above the clamor of the bluegrass band — pathetic amateurs, it turned out — and his face was flushed with the exertion. He yanked the mutt back one last time and the beast landed with a thud on the grass. It struggled to gain its feet, narrowly dodging one of Snuffy's errant horseshoes. It coughed and spit up an unchewed wad of taco salad, or something. Then it started eating the grass.

On the other end of the leash Eagle groped around on the picnic table, latched onto an enormous ham and heaved it in the direction of the stage. The banjo player's strings snapped like parting tugboat cables as the joint of meat slammed into the head of the instrument. The man catapulted backward into the fiddle player and the two of them went to the boards, crushing a guitar case, a paper bag full of homegrown and the mandolin player's ulna.

Eagle resumed his story.

Around four-thirty the hydro boys came by to disconnect the power and I followed them into the store. Elizabeth was still there, tallying up the day's profits. We waited till the power box was removed from the wall and the hydro boys went out to the barbecue area.

The dim light in the store painted Elizabeth with a weak wash of color.

"Let me see if I can scrounge up a Coleman lantern," I said. I went to the counter and idly tapped the weigh scales. "Give you a little light to write by."

She looked up from the stacks of money and chewed on the end of her pen. "I'm pretty much done."

"Anything left in here you want?" I waved at the remnants. She already had dibs on the weigh scales, and the rest of the stuff was broken or useless. Even the old cash register had been pulled up. The store no longer was one.

"I don't think so," she said.

"You going to stay for the barbecue?"

"I … I doubt it."

"Suit yourself."

"Still with the attitude."

"Don't start on me."

She returned her attention to the paper and tapped it with the pen. "We made a fair amount," she said. "Not as much as we should have, all things considered."

"All things considered," I said. "That means for all your sound fiscal sense and tough talk about driving a bargain you did exactly what I would have done with all that junk."

"That's the thing," she said. "It really is junk now that the store is gone. And I couldn't … It's just that if someone can use it and we can help … "

"Yeah."

She wound each bundle with an elastic band and dropped the money into a gym bag at her feet. "I'll go deposit this and come back. I may as well visit for a while."

"If you're going to the bank you'll have to walk," I said. "There are vehicles jammed together every inch of the way to the road. You'll never get out."

"What should I do with it?"

"Stick it under the daybed," I said. "It's the only place out of sight around here."

When Elizabeth returned from the storeroom I was sitting on the counter, smoking a cigarette.

"Are you ever going to quit that filthy habit?" she said.

"I tried to go cold turkey," I said. "But I was going through two loaves of bread a day — burning them in the toaster then deep-breathing in the kitchen. You get that Russian rye bread smoldering and it's as good as a pack of Camels."

She smiled and strolled around the store. When she turned back to me her jaw was set. "I'm thinking of coming home."

"Why?" I said. Two months ago, two weeks ago, two days, minutes, I would have pinched myself and said hell yes! "Why?" is what I said.

"You can't even take care of yourself," she said.

"I do fine."

"I suppose you've been cooking well-balanced meals and cutting down on your drinking?"

"I told you hanging around with Bernice and James would turn you into a lunatic. Taking care of me is a monstrously asinine reason to want to come back. Besides, you never cooked a meal in your life. No, no — however well intentioned, I don't need your help. When I get hungry I can plug in the curling iron you left behind and stick it into a can of spaghetti."

"I love you," she said.

"I love you," I said. "Yes, I do. But I don't know if that's enough anymore."

"I thought you'd jump at the chance to have me back," she said. "What made you change your mind since the last time we talked?"

"Things," I said. "Events. All this around us. Everything has to be right for me or you'll just be another part of the problem."

"When did this happen?"

I slid off the counter and shoved my jeans back down over my boots. "Just now, I think." I looked out through the greasy window. "Yeah, just now."

"Are you feeling too weak to reaffirm our commitment?"

"Too strong," I said. "I feel very powerful these days, and I want our relationship to nurture that strength, not whittle it down."

"Are you saying it's over for good?"

"Not saying anything of the kind. Just figuring, is all." I knew she wanted to talk longer, to share, but I couldn't. Victims of bad timing. I walked outside and around back.

The women had the paint brushes and Eagle was giving directions.

"Remember to paint in each brick," he said. "Don't cheat on a blind man."

Two of the local women were opening cans of paint while others were painting an enormous fireplace on the back wall of the store. One was busy dabbing away at the hearth, trying to draw a set of fireplace implements. Another was painting knick-knacks on the mantle. A pair were working on the logs, swabbing on red and orange flames.

"Work, you bitches!" Eagle screamed. "Work or I'll send you to the mines!"

Everyone was laughing and singing.

Years back in Seattle, Eagle and I started this traditional toast. Late at night we crashed a gentlemen's club cocktail party and it wasn't long till they figured us out. Before the local cops could arrive to carry out the actual bouncing, Eagle and I drew a fireplace in chalk on the mahogany paneling, toasted the Queen, the President and I believe Joe Pepitone, then dashed our glasses to bits against the wall, whereupon Eagle put his pants back on and we departed, absconding with four decanters of port and a serving girl from the kitchen.

"Isn't it done yet?" Eagle asked. He waved his arms around, slopping rum and Coke out of his beer mug and sending the wicked creature on the end of the leash into spasms of choking. "Jack, you around? Get them women on the job."

"It's done," I said. "It's good enough."

"Good enough doesn't pay the butcher," Eagle said.

It was a solemn occasion.

"The Store," I said, raising my glass.

"The Store," came the response from the people sober enough to pay attention.

There were three or four satisfying smashes against the fireplace from the real glasses, but mostly just a clatter from the plastic cups hitting the wet paint and forming a pile of rubble on the ground.

Eagle heaved his mug with all he could put into it, but in his enthusiasm forgot to shift the leash to his left hand. The dog flew through the air right behind the beer mug. When the animal reached the end of its tether the binder twine broke and put a smart bit of English on the beast, sending it cartwheeling off into the paint cans. The patchwork thing scrambled to its feet and raced for the woods while the good folks set to screaming about the freshly splattered designs on their clothing. Several of them had paint all the way up to their faces.

When they turned on Eagle he deadpanned, "It's none of it permanent, you dildos."

So it continued and the barbecues were flashed up and the salmon steaks, marinated in teriyaki sauce, were spread over the grills, and the burgers and hot dogs were flattened and rolled and set to hissing and spitting on the iron, and the band played on, and dancing broke out, and the usual spats flared, and kids got tired and wanted to go home, and people drifted, drifted, drifted off, somehow untangling the clot of vehicles in the parking lot. They made no big production out of leaving, just drifted and percolated away.

Quieter now, the band packing up and grousing about the destroyed gear and the broken arm. But they got paid, which seemed to astonish them, and they went away happy.

So by the time Snuffy lost it there weren't many people left. He was pitching shoes, had been all day. Dip, swing and release. He hadn't come close to another ringer, but it was his deal, his part in the festivities. Nod and smile and say hi to everyone as they stopped by to compliment him or tease him a little.

It was Eagle, I guess. He wasn't acting any differently than he had in the old days. In fact his infirmity he used as an excuse to behave as he liked with impunity. If it was too much trouble to make his way inside or to the tree line when his bladder was full, then he just pissed there on the spot and approach at your peril, boys and girls. But the unavoidable fact was that the man could not see. So he stumbled. He banged into people and barged into objects. He grew testy with frustration at the inconvenience, the unfairness, the indignity.

And Snuffy pitched his shoes, just pitched. Dip, swing and release and watch Eagle. Pitch and watch Eagle. And let it simmer and bubble, bubble like a lava pit. And then he broke. A wrenching, mewling, incomprehensible sob or moan or howl. He was on his knees in the horseshoe pit, slamming his face into the coarse volcanic sand, rubbing, driving, pounding his face, scraping, abrading, eroding, bleeding. He moaned once more, an inhuman wail, and ran from us, ran with a terrific need to escape, ran bleeding and sightlessly into the barbecue drums. Then screaming as the coals leaped free of the ash and sprang onto him as if they were parasites, feasting on him and burning his clothes and his skin.

We sprinted over to him but he was up and gone. His awkward shuffle carried him into the trees, and for all our fear and passion we could not catch him, and when the sun went down we could not find him. We went back to the store.

Eagle was waiting for us. Donna had gone home to wait for Snuffy to show up there — he had always fetched up at their house after his solitary treks. He would do so again. Please.

Sedro drove up as Don was leaving. I poured the old man a rye and Eagle and I beers from the last keg and we sat down at the picnic tables. Sedro was not as sanguine as we were about Snuffy's safety, but there was nothing we could do until we heard from Don. As we waited I asked Sedro where he had been all day.

"Dynamite," he said and inclined his head toward the pickup.
"What?"

"You wanted to level the store so I thought I'd provide you with the means."

"Where you get the shit from, Da Vinci?" Eagle asked.

"Old friend of mine runs the mine on Royal Island. Ferry broke down on the way back or I would have been here long ago."

"I don't think this is the best idea you've ever had," I said.

"Hold on, young Jack," he said. He chuckled and took a pull at his rye. "I know we can't very well go blowing up a building right on the edge of town. I don't know what got into me. Used to be the way we'd do it in the old days. Just a wild hair left from my youth, I imagine. I thought it would be a big joke but when I actually put the box in the truck I realized I was off base. I'm getting on, boys. Forgive an old crock his aberrations."

I forget sometimes that Sedro's old days are a hell of a lot farther down the road than ours. If he could put up with the changes I suppose we had nothing to bitch about. We laughed and drank some more and Don came back and told us Snuffy was safe. The relief gave fresh impetus to our partying and we decided that if we couldn't blow the store up we could at least torch it. Two of the volunteer firemen were passed out under the canopy over the kegs, so I rousted them and sent them off. An hour later they were back with a small pumper.

Elizabeth and I stood together, watching the store go up. I

looked around at the firemen and the few stragglers who had stayed for the show.

Up in the windless night sky. Sparks and stars, stars and sparks, twinkle twinkle. The roof was punched through by flames and the walls came tumbling down and the hoses were played on the blaze to keep it controlled and we watched the last of it go, burning and burning long into the night until it was gone. Just gone. I simply stood staring at the glowing charcoal remnants of a part of my life.

Wastage and resupply.

We stacked the empty beer kegs in the back of Sedro's truck and put the tables and sundry other items in mine. Sedro called Elizabeth and she jumped in with him for a ride back to Bernice's nunnery. Eagle got in with me. He was bitching about the loss of the dog. We yelled our goodbyes and waved and tooled off after I let Sedro and Elizabeth get a head start. Eagle and I had our windows rolled down, glorying in the play of cool night air after the singe of the fire.

"Pretty good day, when you think of her," Eagle said.

"Pretty good day."

We were at the spot on the road home where Dave McCauley hit the deer with his motorcycle last year when I remembered the gym bag full of money under the daybed. I had to stop the truck, I was laughing so hard.

Eagle wondered what was so funny, so I told him.

T W E N T Y - F O U R

There were two important pieces of news the next day. The first had to do with Snuffy. He was gone again. As it turned out his burns were superficial, so after dressing them and taking care of the scrapes and cuts, Donna and Don put him to bed in the basement suite they had fixed up for him. In the morning he was gone, and they were worried enough to call the police, who were out there looking for him. Don phoned me at home and together we checked out all his usual haunts but we came up empty handed. We'd have to hope the cops tracked him down, the poor bugger.

The second item was that they officially started the tunnel. It was impossible to arrange the infrastructure for a project of that magnitude in such a short time, so it was clear that right from the start it had been a foregone conclusion it was going to be built. All the platitudes about consulting the electorate had been just that. Audrey Weeks even phoned to apologize and absolve herself of any ties to the chicanery.

The fuckers had done it again.

Objectively, the project was interesting in its ambition. They will bore from the mainland under the Strait of Georgia and surface at Royal Island. As well, a pilot and service tunnel will accompany the main mole hole along its route. The tunnels will be lined to contain and support the exposed earth and to provide an internal surface on which to attach lights, power lines and the like. I wouldn't mind getting a peek at the tunnel-boring machine, a big toothed monster of the same sort used for the Chunnel.

Popping up on Royal Island, our motorist will enjoy a scenic three-mile drive to the foot of the bridge that will connect Royal to Vancouver Island right at the site of the old hardware store that served the Salish Spit community so faithfully, if haphazardly, for so many years.

Two days later, Sunday, there was still no word about Snuffy. We prayed he was safe, off somewhere locked in his titanic internal struggle. That was the day I also had Sedro to pray for, though it looked as though he would be all right.

Sedro was in the hospital. It had happened at the Salish Spit Open Fastball Tournament, our annual clash of recreational athletes still pining for the days when we were young enough to think we all had a shot at the majors.

Our team, sponsored by the Square Rigger, was facing the perennial favorites, the Salish Hotel Mountaineers, in the final. Bottom of the tenth. I was standing on third, jockeying the pitcher, when the umpire called my name.

"Jack!" the ump yelled when his first call failed to register. "We need a batter up here. You got to send someone to the plate."

Bemused, I called time and went to the bench. I hadn't seen Sedro because he was shielded by Eagle's back, cradled in the man's arms.

"I'm okay," he said when I arrived.

The team clustered around.

"I'm okay. I mean it."

Eagle slowly released him and he sat down. "He fell right at my goddamn feet," Eagle said.

"It's the excitement," Sedro said. "Too old for this, the running around, the … I haven't for years … "

"Jack," Elizabeth said, grabbing me by the elbow. "Get him to the truck. I'll take him to the hospital."

"No, I'll go," I said. "You stay here and —"

"It's nothing," Sedro said. "Rest it off and I'll be fine. Really, come and see me to the truck and I'll lay down a bit."

"You're going to the hospital," Elizabeth said.

Sedro was pale and shaky but was growing stronger by the minute. He insisted on making his way to my truck. I bundled him in the cab and gave Elizabeth the keys and off they went.

We all wandered back to the field. It was as if someone had dropped me on my head.

I love him, was all I could think. Over and over.

There was nothing I could do for the man for the moment, so after a quick conference with the ump and Bert Bevin, the Mountaineers' captain, we decided to continue. Bases loaded, tie score in the bottom of the tenth. But Sedro had been our last player and we had no one to replace him. Faced with a forfeit, we stalled, trying to come up with an idea.

"Well," came Bevin's voice through the crowd that had formed at home plate, "you know what I think? I do believe we win the trophy. Nothing against Sedro — good man — but you guys should have picked up some reserves. Trophy's ours if the show can't go on."

"The show will go on, you fuckboat!" Eagle screamed. "Gimme a bat, Jack. Who cares? Gimme a bat and let's do her."

Everyone swapped glances.

"Why not?" Bevin said. "I've always believed a handicap shouldn't stop a man from doing what he wants."

"Of course *you* agree, Bevin," I said. I turned to the ump. "How about you?"

He shrugged. "Beats anything I've ever seen. But go ahead, if you want."

It was all over quickly.

With some help from the ump, Eagle got himself positioned

in the box. The Mountaineers' pitcher, a skinny redhead with a terrific fastball, let fly right down the middle.

Waving his bat to make it look like a swing, Eagle deliberately stuck his entire torso out over the dish. The pitch hit him square in the melon, rebreaking his nose. It took him about five minutes to follow the hollered directions and touch first base, but touch it he did, blood streaming down past his big grin and into his beard.

While Bevin and his teammates surrounded the ump, screaming and threatening various types of vengeance, I guided Eagle to Sedro's truck and we lit out for the hospital.

Not without a wink from the ump.

While Eagle beat his fist on the dash, savoring his heroics and already developing a storyline on which to build a legend, I thought again of Sedro's age. Even the fact that his keys were above the visor bespoke of days past. It really wasn't that long ago, was it, that you could do that?

Sedro was all right. It was his heart, but the attack was so minor the doctor referred to it as a skirmish. By the time Elizabeth got him to the hospital he was clamoring to return to the ball game. But how minor can anything be when you hit seventy?

Eagle and I visited awhile and when Sedro dropped off to sleep we left. They wanted him to overnight in the hospital. Elizabeth had left Bernice's car at the ballpark so I told her to take the truck. I'd hold on to Sedro's till the next day when I picked him up and took him home. Eagle and I went back to the house and in the morning I let Eagle sleep in while I returned to the hospital.

Sedro was looking good. We hit his place by nine o'clock. When we entered Sedro started cleaning up. I told him to sit down and relax but he was having none of it. He was moving slowly but with determination, shuffling around the cottage and brushing off my attempts to help. He did the dishes and stacked them on the sideboard. Twenty minutes later he had swept the kitchen floor and made his bed.

I went out to the porch.

It can be strange down by the shore at Sedro's place. With the cliffs backing his property and the water out front and the arms of the bay embracing it all, it becomes quieter as the wind gets stronger. There is a blanking out of all sounds that don't belong, and even during a howling winter storm, when you have to holler to be heard, the particular sounds of the gale echo true to the ear. The wind was picking up as I stood there waiting for Sedro to finish his chores. Pines and firs on the cliffs waving and sighing and snapping, occasionally pattering the roof with small branches and cones. Waves cresting and gobbling up sand and proffering bits of bark and kelp and sand dollar shell and broken mussels, then the hiss as the wave subsides and drags it all back seaward. All of it spinning an insular cocoon around the cabin, the isolation enhanced by the low stratus ceiling.

I heard Sedro sit down on the couch so I went inside and parked across the room in the deck chair.

"Elizabeth said you can pick up the truck any time," he said.

"When were you talking to her?"

"She came by the hospital first thing this morning. Left just before you got there."

"Oh."

"She's a good woman."

"Yes, she is."

"She wants you back. She wants to come back. Young Jack, you'll have to decide what to do about her. And I mean soon. You're being selfish and irresponsible about this and you're spreading the misery around."

"I don't know what to decide. I'm not sure I want to be with anyone. Throughout my life whenever I've been paired up I turn complacent. Inertia sets in and I lose the fire that drives me. That makes me turn on the woman I'm with. Alone I drink too much, get in shit, but somehow learn more. I grow, I progress."

"Sounds to me like you've convinced yourself that being alone is the only way you progress. Perhaps you haven't met the right person with whom to grow alongside. You can be in love, desperately in love, with the wrong one."

"But when I feel the love I have to act on it," I said. "If it turns out I'm with the wrong woman, someone gets hurt. I don't like hurting people."

"You're hurting yourself," he said. "Besides, Elizabeth is the right one."

"Yeah."

A car geared down for the steep hill behind the cabin. Winding and braking for the descent, then fading off and rounding the corner at the bottom and crunching over the scattered pine cones on the road and the gravel on the driveway. The back door swung inward and Sedro leaned forward on the couch to see who it was.

Don stood in the archway between the kitchen and the main room. He had on his worn suede bomber jacket and a button-down tweed hat pushed back to reveal his receding hairline. His hands looked burdensome so he folded his arms across his chest in a manner that provided solace. "They found Snuffy," he said. His tone squelched any relief I felt.

"Where?" I asked and looked at Sedro.

"They have him," he said. "He's in Vancouver. They got him right in the hallway."

"Brace up," Sedro said. "And tell us what happened. Brace up, man."

"He killed Manny Parsons," Don said. "It was on the news. Donna phoned Vancouver and told them Snuffy had been living with us but they wouldn't release the details. But by all accounts on the radio and TV he was waiting for Parsons as he came out of court. Stabbed him in the chest with a kitchen knife and Parsons was dead before they got him out of the building."

I looked over at Sedro again but couldn't capture his eyes. He was looking at his hands, silent and slack, boneless. He curled in on himself and I thought it might be his heart again, but he made no further move, just stared at his hands, resting his elbows on his knees, just stared at his hands.

"The poor simple bastard," Don said. "The poor, poor child."

We didn't know what to do but the situation plainly called for communion. So we sat and tried to figure it all out, but it was pretty plain why he had done it. We made some phone calls but learned nothing.

When tragedy strikes, the fraternity men share dictates a recap of the victim's life — harking back to the golden times detoxifies the present reality. Sadly, we soon realized we didn't really know much about Snuffy. We had no comedic stories in which Snuffy came out on top; there were no tales of ribald foolishness; he had no grand accomplishments we could parade for approval. He was just a man who had never really caught a break, and for whom we had done the best we could, but perhaps had stopped short of truly inviting him into our lives.

I left about three in the afternoon. Eagle would be wondering where I was. I walked the shoreline and when I got home and told him about Snuffy he cried. Then for hours he poured out the guilt he felt for Snuffy's need to avenge him and the anguish of the blindness itself. He even went back to the pain of his childhood, the agonies I had always assumed he had pounded to bits through sheer force of will.

By the time he was finished, so was I.

At that point we started laughing about something and in the midst of the general hilarity I poured us each a drink and excused myself to the bedroom. I had a new broom and it was time to break it in good and proper.

I had made a fool of myself with Patsy. I should never have started in with her. Or I should have treated the whole thing as an instance of weakness and quickly chucked it from my emotional backpack. But now I was rid of it all. Finally.

I dialed Patsy's number and got past her stupid butler. I started in and told her it was no good. I told her I was sorry for being such a pain in the ass. I agreed with her evaluation of the entire episode, even overdoing it, to the point where she broke in and tried to absolve me of any blame. But I was having none of it. If I can consider myself a hell of a guy when I prevail, then necessarily I must own up to being a bum when I fuck up. It wasn't as difficult as I had expected it to be. I even managed to tell her that I loved my wife, and how much I loved her at that. Strange, but I began to feel as if I were talking to a friend, someone with whom I'd never been intimate. It was good and it was true and it made me feel alive.

I hung up the phone and went back out into the living room.

"You did the right thing," Eagle said.

"Was I talking that loud?"

"Loud enough for me to hear over the receiver."

"You were listening in on the other phone?"

"Sure."

"Where the hell do you get off —"

"Easy, big fella. Just making sure you didn't piss in the fruit jar again. Weird as it seems, you're on some kind of roll these days and the more bullshit you cut back on the stronger and longer the roll will be."

"Eavesdropper."

"Ouch! Now that hurt. That hurt bad. I been called a lot of things in my life, but nobody's ever called me such a lowdown, filthy cocksucking thing as an eavesdropper."

I couldn't help laughing. "As if you're in a position to lecture me about the women in my life."

"Jean's just taking care of a few things back east. We talk every day. Don't you worry about me, partner. Get your own sorry ass out of the sling first."

"Yeah, yeah."

"That Patsy did look good, though. Now that you and her have called it quits, do you mind if I fantasize about her when I get under the covers and spank the student?"

"Jesus," I said and reached for the bottle.

There was some hurt, but I felt guilty at my lack of guilt. The feelings don't wither simply because a decision was made, but the relief outweighed the sorrow. Guess I was learning. I felt atavistic, animalistic. Tactile and highly charged. It carried through the night, cheating me of sleep.

I was up at six and off for the glacier. I was wearing a new pair of hiking boots — nylon uppers reinforced with leather, vibram sole with a stiff shank. It had been raining, so there would be mud the whole way up. Nylon gaiters would keep the sludge out of the boots. Jeans, T-shirt, rugby jersey and a Gore-Tex jacket. The pack was perfect. It was a black monstrosity, fine for open-trail hiking, but I had cut the pockets down and resewn them so they were almost flush with the pack rather than leaving them to protrude and snag on branches and deadfall on the way through the bush. For the same reason I had stripped the pack from its aluminum frame and reinforced it with straps. It was now formfitted to my body and though I couldn't comfortably hump as large a load without the frame, it made for more streamlined progress through the rainforest.

I was moving fast then hit the deadfall near the creek. It slowed me down. Climb under the angled trunks and your back aches and the pack, for all its innovations, catches and snatches your feet out from under you. Climb over instead and the rotting bark gives way and introduces your ass to the stream bed.

The stream is the most direct route to the glacier but naturally it has the most deadfall.

Heady aroma and labored breathing and scrapes and such. Needn't have brought the pack, for I hit the terminal moraine so charged with adrenalin and gut-lightning that I didn't stop to eat or drink or rest. I turned and plunged back down, taking the fastest way, climbing and sliding and charging through the bush, along the bed, over the rocks and around the trees, violently, heedlessly. Branchwhipped across the face — don't care 'cause now I'm racing. Ragged breathing and hacking up wads of brown shit — got to quit those bloody cigarettes but can't think about it now — thinking of nothing but humping through the last line of bush and onto level ground.

Clear! Three miles from home. Breaking into a jog, pack jostling and chafing, boots not made for running, all the way down to the beach then cut left and a real test through the sand, knees trembling and the taste of fried scallops in my mouth, coppery and raw.

I flop on the dog run. Pack and jacket are soaked and steaming. No blisters, but a couple hot spots, so I dry my feet and dust them with powder. Under four hours. Not bad, not bad. Used to be able to do it that quickly without treating it as a competition. Have to cheat lately, run on flat ground, take unnecessary risks coming down. Of course that's what age and experience do for you: teach you the most efficacious way to nibble at the rules.

It was raining again. A great gray horseblanket lay overhead, slashing the tops off the mountains. I felt good and breathed deeply of the sodden air. It felt like the inside of an orchid greenhouse, but softer and cooler, and arranged solely for my benefit.

Eagle had been cooking and the kitchen was a shambles. A huge pot of chili was simmering on the stove. There must have been ten gallons of the stuff. I stirred it with the wooden spoon and automatically added more crushed peppers. I burned my mouth tasting it but gloried in the warmth that spread from my stomach all the way out to my skin. I stripped off my work socks and tossed them in the hamper.

The bathroom door was open and Eagle came striding through it. He dropped on the couch and I started laughing for no good reason. It was just the thing to do — like the first time I put my hand on a dolphin in the wild and laughed till I cried because no other response was appropriate.

The chili was hot and good and we slathered the buns with butter and washed the lot down with cold milk. It was Tuesday and it was noon and I had the rest of my life to grab hold of and run with.

T W E N T Y - F I V E

We hit the Square Rigger at five. Most of the regulars were there and we swapped what little information we had on Snuffy. Bert Bevin was over at the pool table and I slapped my quarters on the rail to challenge the winner. Besides being the captain of the Salish Hotel Mountaineers, Bevin was the foreman of the steel fabrication shop at the north end of town. He wasn't a bad guy when we were growing up, but he went goofy a few years back after his wife and daughter ran off with a father-son pair on vacation from Oregon. Bevin was still looking beat-up from the last game of the ball tournament, and while we were shooting he'd periodically stop, stare into space and softly curse. Even at that his concentration on the game was greater than mine.

I hit the cue ball a firm stroke, driving the eight ball into the corner pocket but following it in. I laughed, peeled off a deuce and fluttered it onto the table. Bevin snatched it up.

"That's right," he said. "It's a different game when there's no umpire on your side. Just you and me. You and me, one on one, straight up, head to head."

"Thanks," I said and headed back to the bar.

Don slid a pint my way and Robert shoved his stool over. Eagle was in his usual position. He had taken to standing by the new computer cash system Don had installed. That way he could run his mouth in all directions but retain his orientation by keeping one big mitt on the machine.

"Win or lose?" he asked.

"Scratched on the eight ball."

"That's disgusting," Eagle said. "You're pitiful, Thorpe. No reason to lose to Bevin in anything. Hell, I beat his team single-handed myself. What was that, a double or a triple I hit? Bevin! How many bases did I get on that last —"

"Eat my shorts!" Bevin screamed. The tournament loss had affected him as nothing had in his life. "You were hit by a pitch, and you know it! The rules say that if a batter makes no attempt to avoid a pitch, he can't take his base. You did it intentionally. You stuck your fat head right out over the plate. That goddamn ump made an error in judgment."

"You're an error," Eagle said. "You're a big fucking disaster, Bevin. You let a blind man beat you on a standup triple in the biggest game of the year. We got a hunchback in the minors right now, gonna call him up next year and he'll throw a perfect game against you losers. My old man's been dead ten years and he'll go four-for-four. You're dogshit, Bevin!"

I was laughing when I heard the crack. Don had rapped Eagle's hand with the ruler he had started keeping behind the bar for that very purpose. The problem with Eagle's using the cash computer as a reference point was that he had a tendency to tear the thing free when excited. So Don had to judge things correctly. Let Eagle get too fired up and the computer ends up dangling by the cord; smack his hand clear when he's drunk and Eagle loses spatial orientation and careers through the crowd, leaving the door open for more serious damage. Good timing today — Eagle stuck his fingers in his mouth, sucked at the knuckles and replaced his hand with care.

It was dusk when we heard the explosion.

Because we were inside, and perhaps due to a muffling effect from the rain and low cloud ceiling, it was hard to tell its direction. At first I thought it might be a sonic boom, that one of the fighters from the Air Force base had slipped supersonic over the Island. The windows shook and the whole pub quivered. The building emptied and we all stood around aimlessly in the parking lot, milling and babbling until somebody called our attention to the smoky hump of particles rising above the tree line over by the bridge site.

That was it. By the time we crammed into the handiest

vehicles and arrived — breathlessly, like kids at a house fire — the shore was crowded with cops and volunteer firemen and civilians. The dust and debris had settled. The cops were pushing people back from the wreckage.

We picked our way to the shore. Eagle had a length of driftwood and was pressing it into service as a cane, swinging it back and forth at knee height, cracking people in the shins as he cleared us a path.

The bridge had barely been started. Some pilings were sunk and a few girders were in place, but the thing extended no more than twenty yards out over the chuck. Or had, for the explosives had severed the outermost pilings and dropped the bridge into the sea, where it lay partly visible, twisted.

The cops saw us standing there and Kelly Clark came over, singling me out.

"Kelly," I said.

"At least he had the decency to pick a time when the crew was off," he said.

"Probably an accident," I said, staring at the dead steel beast out in the water. "Bet some welder got his torch too close to a can of hairspray. You should be down in the water looking for evidence, Kelly. Maybe find the black box, that flight recorder thingme. If he was a local boy, you let me know. Even if he was working for the enemy, the least we can do is hold a benefit for his family."

"Cut it out, Jack. This is serious."

"I know. Disgusting, isn't it? Couldn't have been an accident."

"Exactly."

"I thought they were dedicated to peaceful opposition."

"Eh?"

"BAT GUANO," I said. "Apparently they've upped the ante."

"They have nothing to do with this and you know it," Kelly said.

I gestured back at the charred foundation of my old hardware store. "They're feeling their oats, Kelly. Started off by torching my store out of pure spite. Or maybe they were just practicing for the real thing. Either way, I suggest you start rounding up the usual suspects. Protest is healthy, a cornerstone of democracy, but when it gets out of hand and the mob turns ugly, there's no telling where it will stop. Look into it carefully. Won't be surprised if you find a few kidnappings and airplane bombings you can lay at their door."

"Jack —"

"My store, Kelly!" I stared up the slight grade. I pulled at my hair with the anguish of a cartoon character. "My fucking store! It's all I had left in the world!"

"It's okay, buddy," Eagle said. I dropped to my knees and Eagle stood over me, sympathetically rubbing my head. "We'll take care of you. And I'll get those pricks if I have to track them to the ends of the earth. Like Inspector Clouseau did to that Jean Valjean guy."

"Thanks," I whispered. "Thank you." I buried my face in the folds of his jacket.

"If you two assholes are done," Kelly said.

I got to my feet.

"Where is he?"

"No idea."

"Aiding and abetting a felon is a felony itself."

"Jack's not a betting man," Eagle said.

"Shut up!"

Eagle pulled a beer out of an inside pocket, took a swallow and handed it to me.

"I mean it," Kelly said. "I can't cover this up. It isn't some little misdemeanor they'll leave us to handle."

"I really have no clue," I said. "I presume you'll check his cabin, but you know as well as I do that he won't be there."

"I don't know him at all. That's why I need your help."

"He's gone," I said. It was only then that it dawned on me that Sedro really was out of my life again. "He won't be back. Whatever the reasons he had for returning, in his mind they're resolved. If he's not complete, he's at least finished."

I looked over at Eagle, hoping he'd have something to add, anything at all to show his agreement or his support. He was nodding slowly and sniffing, catching the scent of the shoreline and the lingering remnants of cordite.

"Let's get out of here," he said.

He brought his knobby cane into the attack mode again and we headed back through the crowd. When we reached the vehicles Eagle leaned on the first one he whacked with his stick.

"Didn't know Da Vinci felt that strong about the whole thing," he said. "Not that I don't approve."

"He didn't," I said.

"Then what gives?"

"That?" I said, waving at the wreckage Eagle couldn't see. "That's just his signature piece."

It wasn't an answer to satisfy him, but Eagle sighed and stood upright. We had both run out of questions. We were just glad to stow all of it away.

TWENTY-SIX

Sedro was gone and the swallows were back. The scrabbling of their feet greeted me as I stepped up onto the porch after my approach along the shore. Two of them poked their beaks out of the hole above the door, then strafed my head and shot out toward the beach. They dipped in unison, pulled a sharp ninety-degree left to parallel the trees, then disappeared into the foliage. The door wouldn't budge. I punched the glass out of the window, nicking my hand, and opened up.

I had a good look around. Had I been wishing before? Was this all part of some grand self-deception? There was no affirmation of life here. Where it had been an alchemist's den, it was now a wastepile. The hope in the air had given way to a weak mustiness.

I couldn't clear my mind of the thought that Sedro was dead. There was nothing to support the belief but it underlay all my perceptions. The kitchen was neat and orderly and I picked up and drank from the bottle of Plainsman Rye sitting on the counter.

I roamed the rest of the place and finally accepted that this had been a way station for the man. He had spent the better part of his life in Salish Spit but in his mind he had just been passing through. He had culled the mildewed books from the shelves in the period since his return, but had neither replaced them nor added to their number. There were no collections of anything, no leaves or beetles or sea life. There was nothing tossed around, bits of shell or bark or a plant cutting or a newspaper. I was inside an empty chambered nautilus, going around and around with nothing of substance to indicate sentient existence.

Sedro had built a sort of empire here in Salish Spit. But when he captured the crown he realized he held nothing, or that it held no power to galvanize and sustain him.

Personally I think the lecture that his prime was a leisurely glissade down from the peak held no water. That was not his style, and I doubt if in his heart he ever had a peak in the first place. He had led himself on a selfish, willful charge through life. Here was a man steeped in the scientific method, devoted to the rational. Yet when confronted with anything that threatened a deviation, he had reacted with an aberrant viciousness: blow it up, cut it off, tear it down. A simplistic, vengeful approach.

The cottage held nothing for me except for the letter. I saw it on the coffee table when I walked in but had been ignoring it. My name was on the envelope. I picked it up and slipped it into the inside pocket of my leather jacket and walked out the door without closing it behind me and hit the beach.

I have done nothing more than glimpse the place since, and have neither need nor desire to do so.

I didn't open the letter until I was on the ferry, strolling the railing, trying to keep abreast of the seagull that was flying formation on the ship, soaring alongside and occasionally peering my way. I stopped when I reached the forward promenade and read.

When I was finished I let it go over the side and watched the pages sail astern and float into the chuck. Somehow the information didn't affect me as it should have. It might have been the pathetic rationalization, the confessions of a man weaker than his reputation. I felt sorry for him as I read his story, as he tried to explain his acts of passion, his struggles to assert himself, to solve with drama and action what would better have been served by patience.

And that is what set me free. Finally I could love the whole man, the one with frailties and doubts and fears.

Sedro Tuckett became real for me reading that letter.

He had not shot my father.

He had, of course, put a bullet into a man named Thorpe,

a man whose name I bear. The four pages covering Sedro's brief affair with my mother were barely decipherable. They were the ramblings of a man desperate for exoneration. I loved him but did not think I could grant him the total forgiveness he craved.

My father, Sedro Tuckett, was dead. Or alive, living out his life who knows where. Living with the knowledge that having given me so much he had allowed me so little. I could have forgiven him. I would have. But I hadn't been asked until very, very late in the game. And I didn't know if there was enough time left on the clock.

The ship continued its relentless progress to the mainland and I was happy just to go along for the ride.

"All I'm concerned with," I said, "is whether my seeing Snuffy will have an adverse effect on his condition."

The doctor shifted in her seat. She was an attractive woman, early forties, and I liked the way she sat facing me across the low coffee table rather than hiding behind her desk.

"If I thought it would harm him I wouldn't allow it," she said.

"All right," I said. "I'll buy that." I started for the door and stopped. "Tell me — do you think that he is a violent man?"

"He is not a violent man, yet he committed the ultimate act of violence. What does that tell you?"

"That his problems are deeper than the learning disability he's always had. Fine, then. Fine. But will he ever be released? Will he have to spend the rest of his life here?"

"That's conjecture at this point. The primary goal is to help your friend get well. Nothing else matters for the moment."

"Lead on," I said and swept my hand across my body.

As she passed she paused and rested her fingers on my shoulder. "Don't expect too much," she said.

"Lady," I said, so weary of it all, "I don't expect one goddamn thing."

Snuffy had his own room. Although the windows were barred, it had more the feel of a hospital room than a cell. That was good. By all accounts he was perfectly calm after the stabbing, offering no resistance, and in fact had been so lucid the defense was briefly afraid he would be declared free to stand trial. But here he was staring up at the TV the boys had kicked in to get him.

He seemed like the Snuffs of old, looked like him. And he locked onto my eyes as I entered and greeted him. But he locked on without recognition, stared, then turned back to the TV. Calm but empty. The doctor stayed in the room. I talked to Snuffy and periodically he would look my way and nod, as if absorbing what I had to say.

But he would just nod and turn back to the TV.

I went to the bed and reached out. I grasped him by the upper arm and gently kneaded it. I had no more to say and very little left to feel. Slowly I returned my hand to my side and smiled a tiny smile at the doctor, who smiled kindly in return. As I walked to the door I heard the bed creak and Snuffy spoke.

"Old goat, he says. You kill me, Jack!"

I gave a cry and whirled. But Snuffy had been talking to the TV.

I left then and tried to think of other things but Snuffy was still on my mind the next day. The Dash-8 banked in the cold northern air, allowing me a glimpse of bleak tundra, then rolled out on final approach for the Davis Flats airport.

Since Yellowknife I had been talking with a woman who was going back to the Flats after a visit with her parents in Hamilton. I asked her why she lived in such a remote location and she shrugged, which was all the answer required. I had been asking too many questions in the past few months, and felt the need to emulate the woman's attitude.

Who cares about why. I just do and that's about the end of her.

I got my old cab driver, Jimmy Crews. It was as if I was being personally welcomed back. We pulled onto the main road. Later I found out one of the motor mounts had broken, so when the engine dropped down on the corner it both revved itself into a frenzy and jammed the transmission in Drive. We slung around a turn, avoided an oncoming Imperial Oil truck and cannonaded down the street. A hard left sprung open the passenger door and it mangled the mailbox in front of the community center.

"Funny," Jimmy Crews said when he finally managed to slam the thing into neutral and wrench out the key. "But every time you been up here somethin' weird happens."

It was still and cold in Davis Flats. A subtle haze of ice fog lent the buildings an undeserved sublimity. Sundogs drew my eye inwards to the sun.

"Only my second time up here," I said. We sat in silence a bit, savoring the calm after the death dance from the airport. The engine ticked as it cooled.

"That's right," Jimmy said. "And a good thing."

"You going to call another cab?" I asked.

"Only one in town." He lit a smoke. "I'm not home soon, the wife'll come lookin' fer me in the truck. Not the first time."

I crossed my arms and waited.

"Yeah," he said. "Remember the first time you were up here spyin'."

"Yeah?"

"Yeah. After I dropped you off at the hotel I went home. Then that night Singin' Joe got all cocktailed up and shot the jar of pickled eggs at the bar with his Browning automatic."

"Disaster follows in my wake."

"Don't get sarcastic. Not sayin' it's your fault deliberately. Just that in the spyin' business weird things are bound to happen. When my brother was a spy we could hardly stand it when he come home to visit, all the weird things. Yup, just tossed each egg in the air, shootin' at 'em before they hit the floor, guys haulin' ass in every direction."

"Your brother?"

"Singin' Joe," he said. "The bartender, Charlie — you don't know him — finally tackled him and called the cops."

"Joe got thrown in jail?"

"My brother," he said. "Talkin' about the time he did the same thing, home on leave from spyin'."

"A real rash of pickled egg shootings."

"Eh?"

"Not often two guys would get it into their heads to shoot a jar of pickled eggs."

"No, no — my brother didn't shoot no pickled eggs."

"But you said —"

"What he done was he run a pool cue through the glass on the beer fridge."

"Right."

"Spies!" He spat out the window.

Jimmy's wife arrived with the truck and dumped me at Sedro's place. The old man wasn't around, not that I had expected him to be. Whatever internal foe Sedro Tuckett was trying to vanquish obviously was of the kind that drove the man to isolation. So be it.

For now Salish Spit and the Valley and the Island and Sedro were behind me.

The first day in town I bundled up and walked to the hotel. The restaurant was gorgeous in its tackiness. I shucked my coat and settled into a chair. Curious nods from the other patrons. A gold ceramic owl stared down with rhinestone eyes at my table. Grecian columns were fabricated around the steel poles supporting the roof. In the corner a fiberglass pond allowed water to trickle down stepped terraces, though at present no water flowed — a rusted pipe gaped dry-mouthed from near the top. The brown carpeting looked flayed from the back of a very old elk. Wallpaper, once gold and blue, peeled off and curled up and clung to the walls only because of the layers of tar and nicotine that had been deposited by smokers ever since the invention of dirt.

The coffee was good.

I ate and said howdy to the locals, then went back to Sedro's place. I struggled with the balky latch on the door and entered and hustled to start a fire. I poured a glass of rye and took it to the couch. It suited me fine, this place. I would think of Elizabeth and Patsy and Snuffy and Eagle and from time to time of Sedro. Whatever. No need for immediate decisions. I'd wait till spring. Yeah. Spring is always a good time of year for me.

So the winter came, a harsh piece of work that limited my activities to reading and slinging draft at the hotel pub to pick up some spending money. Surprisingly, I didn't stick out up here. In a company town like Davis Flats, most men are up to make a whack of money working as many hours as they can on the rigs. But the town also supported people much like myself, who through a variety of circumstances found themselves at the end of the earth without really knowing how they got there.

I spent Christmas alone and went back to Salish Spit in January. I approached the trip warily, not sure if it was the prelude to a return or just a visit.

How did I know it was time to go home? I just knew.

"Don't be stupid," Eagle said. He was sitting on the bed while I stuffed his clothes into the suitcase and two garment bags on the floor. "I know you, and you ain't staying up there forever. You're going to start missing Elizabeth again and end up back here with her."

"Probably," I said.

Elizabeth was living in the house now, but I had just arrived in town and hadn't yet talked to her.

"We been roommates since you left," Eagle said. "And she ain't so bad."

"I'm glad the affair is progressing nicely."

"Pound sand up your ass," he said.

"When does Jean get here?"

"Five o'clock. Funny, but how could I know the only woman I really had it for would decide to come back, to show up in my life again from halfway across the country?"

"I told you when you sent Jean back to her husband it wouldn't work. She loved you. So she pined and moped and pissed around till she eventually left him anyhow. So tell me, did playing the martyr back then help at all? Or did it just give you all those years apart, years you're kicking yourself for missing? Ah, shit. Here you are happy as a wino with a warm place to whizz and I'm putting you down for it."

"That's what I've been doing to myself. Somehow with everything that's happened it don't seem right to be so happy."

"Dumb as it sounds, I agree. But that's the way it works. Sometimes the resupply overlaps the wastage and the glacier's on the move again."

"Eh?"

"Never mind."

"Listen, say everything had been different. Say I had stuck with Jean back then and that was it. We might have moved, we could have ... What I'm saying is do you think —?"

"No," I said. "I don't think you'd be sitting here with two good eyes."

"That's not what I was gonna ask."

"Yes, it is."

"Arright, arright."

I handed Eagle the suitcase and tucked the two garment bags under my arms, trailing their nylon tails on the floor as I struggled with them across the dog run.

"We'll have plenty of time to fix your place up before Jean arrives. You don't want to spoil her."

"Maybe I do."

I snorted and grinned. "Come on," I said. "Straight ahead. Let's go home."

He tasted the word. "Home."

By the time I got Eagle squared away Elizabeth would be off work. We couldn't go to a restaurant or a bar or even the beach for this meeting. So we'd talk at home.

I was almost all the way back.